AVALICE HOUSE

AVARICE HOUSE

* * * * * * * * * * * * * * *

AVARICE HOUSE

BY

JULIAN GREEN

TRANSLATED FROM THE FRENCH BY

MARSHALL A. BEST

Published by HARPER & BROTHERS
NEW YORK *and* LONDON

AVARICE HOUSE BY JULIAN GREEN
COPYRIGHT, 1927, BY HARPER & BROTHERS
PRINTED IN U.S.A.
A-C

AVARICE HOUSE

* * * * * * * * * * * * * * *

CHAPTER ONE

* * * * * * * * * * * * * * * *

EMILY WAS SILENT. SHE HAD
moved her rocking-chair to a place in front
of the window, and from time to time she tapped the
floor with her heel to increase its motion, contract-
ing her forehead in a sudden frown so that she
seemed to be giving way to an impulse of annoyance and stamping her foot from ill-humour.

She was a girl of about fifteen and rather small.
She sat with her arms clasped close about her neck
and rumpling the white kerchief, her only ornament,
which covered her shoulders above her sombre dress.
Her face wore an expression of unrest which aged
it; the nose was prominent and without grace of
line, the nostrils too distended; the thin lips seemed
glued to the teeth and dark shadows marked the line
of the cheeks, accentuating the heavy and wilful jaw.
The eyes, which usually lighten ugly features and
lend them a sort of poetic tenderness, seemed in her
to emphasize all the unattractive traits, and the
sharp glance of their black pupils held the look of
an animal at bay.

In another part of the room her mother sat
hunched over her sewing. Mrs. Fletcher was hardly
taller than her daughter, but she was heavier—to the

point of being a trifle short of breath. She lifted
her head now and then to speak a few words in a
voice that was soft and low. In her somewhat flabby
face, deep wrinkles had already taken seat, though
she could not have been far beyond forty. Her hair,
done up at the back of her head, left bare an expansive neck; her arms, in fact her whole body,
generously filled the clothes she wore, which she had
made from the same drab stuff as Emily's. She
drew her needle in and out with careful attention,
and seemed to be absorbed by this single effort.
Whenever she broke the silence with some remark to
her daughter, her words gave the impression of
springing from deep meditation. Almost always she
began with a "We must" or some equivalent phrase
of obligation.

Emily did not answer. She sat looking out of
the window with her back to her mother. It had been
raining for hours, and a dubious light revealed only
the dim outline of trees at the foot of the lawn
and a grey mass of hills with their tops shading off
into a grey sky; the rain-freshened grass alone gave
a note of colour and life. The girl's eyes searched
out this scene with the sort of attention one gives
to examining a painting, her glance moving insistently from one point to another. One guessed
that this was one of the small diversions in a life
devoid of greater business, and that she probably
indulged in it often. Each time she heard her mother
speak, Emily's hand caught at the corner of the table

beside her and brought the rocking-chair to a halt, while her face assumed an expression of patience and she uttered a little sigh. When the silence was resumed, she pushed against the table with a bend of the wrist as if she were trying to shove the table away from her; then, withdrawing her hand suddenly, she folded her arms again and let herself sway with the motion of the chair.

This little procedure went unnoticed by Mrs. Fletcher, who seemed accustomed to her daughter's ways and expected no reply. Her low voice made a melancholy sound, and an effort of ear was needed to catch the trailing ends of her sentences.

After a while Mrs. Fletcher looked up and set her work aside. Her black eyes blinked when she looked toward the light of the window. She sat listening a moment to the dull sound of the rocker on the floor, then called to her daughter. Emily grasped the edge of the table and looked round sharply.

"I want to talk to you," Mrs. Fletcher said. "Come over nearer to me."

Emily went and sat down on a sofa, saying nothing.

"You must finish this sewing for me," her mother said to her, handing her a white petticoat; "my eyes are tired. Keep your stitches close together."

The girl took the petticoat and examined the sewing.

"I've been thinking about several changes I want

to make in our household arrangements," Mrs. Fletcher went on, folding her hands in her lap. "You must help me, Emily. . . . Put away your sewing." She saw that the girl was not giving her the attention that she wanted. "I have been figuring up last month's expenses. We shall have to cut down even more."

She breathed a little heavily and seemed troubled by the hard frigidity of her daughter, who watched her without opening her lips.

"There are three of us in the house. One servant ought to be enough. We must get rid of the chambermaid, Emily. We can get along very well without her, and it will mean a saving of thirty dollars a year. What does she do, anyway? Waits on the table, helps make the beds and clean the rooms. It's not worth the money; we can do it ourselves. We are poor, Emily. You know that."

"Yes, Mamma." Emily's voice was short and sharp, in contrast to her mother's.

"She must leave at the end of the week. She's young and strong; she can easily find a place in town, and your mother will have that much less to worry about."

"Is that all, Mamma?" Emily got up.

Mrs. Fletcher took her hand and smiled; she did not answer immediately.

"I have something to ask of you," she said at last. "I want *you* to tell the girl that we can't keep her."

"Me?" There was astonishment in Emily's voice. "Why, Mamma?"

"I ask you to, my dear," Mrs. Fletcher said plaintively. "You know I can't bear to talk to that girl."

"But why?" Emily drew her hand away from her mother's.

"Oh, I don't know!" Mrs. Fletcher's voice and gesture spoke impatience. "Your mother is made that way, child. I have my faults and you must put up with them. Just go and speak nicely to her. She has done her work well enough, and we must remember that she knew your father. Tell her that the next time we go through Glencoe we will give her a reference at the parsonage."

Emily frowned and said nothing. She had returned to her chair and unfolded her work, hunting for her needle to go on with her sewing. Her hands trembled a little; she set to work with enforced application.

Meanwhile her mother continued in a quieter tone:

"As long as the dining room connects with the kitchen, it's a positive extravagance to pay some one to serve the meals. We can wait on ourselves."

She stopped for thought and looked over at her daughter, who went on sewing in silence.

"In the morning you can make your own bed. It amounts to nothing. I had a much harder time of it when I was young. At your age I was working all day, and I thank my stars for it now; it's a very good thing to make a few sacrifices—and, anyway, we would have been driven to it sooner or later; we might as well begin now."

She stopped again and took breath, shaking her head.

"Haven't you anything to say?" she began again, annoyance in her voice. "Aren't you interested at all? Don't you know that our money has been eaten into until I don't know what's going to become of us five years from now? We simply must plan some real economies; otherwise I'm not going to answer for the outcome. You don't want us to have to sell Ashley House, do you?"

At these words Emily looked up and glanced furtively toward her mother.

"No, Mamma."

She was sewing badly, the stitches uneven and errant. Too many thoughts crowded through her mind. Her mother's words did not ring true; she had so often heard her talk of selling Ashley House that she was no longer frightened by that threat, but her nervous nature could never hear these words without a keen and painful distress. They troubled her so profoundly that she felt oppressed with physical pain; only by bending double and biting her lips could she resist a strange desire to cry or scream.

She turned a little more toward the window, struggling against a frantic impulse to jump up and throw her work at her mother's feet. Her hands clenched over the cloth, and again and again she snapped the thread with the violence of her stitches.

The room where they sat was high and gloomy. Dark plush hangings half hid the two tall windows, and the daylight came through sparely. Chairs upholstered in faded cloth formed a semicircle about the fireplace as if arranged for a meeting. Mrs. Fletcher was sitting in one of these. A large oval table indicated that this was dining room as well as parlour. Over the doorway an inscription, in red-and-black Gothic script, reminded those within that God is everywhere and that He hearkens to all the words of our lips.

Mrs. Fletcher had stopped talking. She relaxed her head upon the back of her chair and allowed her glance to wander from side to side in the room. She sat in a negligent pose with her legs stretched out, feet crossed, and now and then she tapped her lips with her fingers to suppress a yawn. Or she would raise her head and take a breath as if on the point of speaking, but would reconsider at once and sink back into contemplation. Finally she resumed her monologue.

"Tell her that she must leave on Saturday morning. That will make an even month to pay her for. Of course I ought to have thought of getting along without her before this; but the damage is done now."

She glanced over to her daughter, who appeared not to be listening.

"We must stop up the hole in the dike," her soft

voice went on; "we must find new ways to economize."

"I don't see how we could economize any more than this," Emily said after a moment's thought, "unless we sell our beds and sleep on the floor."

"Whatever do you mean?" Mrs. Fletcher exclaimed in astonishment. "Why, we are living like rich people, and we are poor, poor," and she pounded her fist on the arm of her chair for emphasis. "We have hired help; we keep up a house big enough for a family of six. And look at this room we are sitting in, look right around you—pictures, rugs, curtains. Is this a poor folks' house?"

Emily lifted her eyes and rested them on her mother. They were glowing now, and a tight little pucker appeared at the corners of her mouth. She pretended to resume her work, and said in an altered voice:

"I should like to know what kind of economizing you want to do. If you mean selling the few things we have left . . ."

She stopped as if the words choked her.

Mrs. Fletcher sat up. "Well, I am only doing what I can to find ways and means. It's for your sake as well as mine."

"You had better not touch anything my father left us," the girl exclaimed. "When he was here, you would never have dared to help yourself to his belongings."

Mrs. Fletcher answered with a look of anger.

"Be still! What I sell is my own."

"Your own? Didn't you sell the silver candlesticks from the parlour? They used to be in his room. And the little placques from the wall each side of that mirror? He brought those back from Europe with him."

"They were mine"—Mrs. Fletcher's face changed colour;—"he had given them to me. You have no right . . ."

Emily jumped up from her chair without heeding what her mother was saying, and crossing to the other end of the room she opened a large oaken chest that stood on a table. The lid bore a copper plate on which the name Stephen Fletcher was engraved in ornamental letters. The chest was empty now, but the inside of it, lined with green cloth and divided into compartments, appeared to be intended for silverware. Emily stood beside the table for a moment, her hand resting on the open lid; she was on the point of speaking when her mother suddenly rose and crossed the room. A quick flush mounted Mrs. Fletcher's face; she began to shout in a voice that grated with emotion:

"Don't say another word! It's none of your business! You have no right . . ."

"No right! You know these things were mine as much as yours. What's in the family should stay there, Mamma. You have enough money, anyway, without disturbing the things that belonged to Father."

"I have no money at all. Everything in this house belongs to me and I shall do as I please with it. If your father heard you now, he would turn you out and make you shift for yourself."

"That's not true!" Emily cried. "If my father were here, we would not be living like poor folks and I'd be a little happier."

"Stop!" Mrs. Fletcher was leaning back against a chair, shaking with anger. She gathered up the sewing that her daughter had thrown down and inspected it hurriedly, frowning at the uneven line of stitches. "This is how you work, and you expect the Lord to take care of you, and you reproach your mother for sacrificing her own belongings when she deprives herself in order to keep you alive! Oh! . . . " And she threw the garment on the floor and strode toward her daughter with arm upraised.

"You are not going to touch me!" said Emily, with hate in her eyes, and she dropped the lid of the chest and ran from the room.

"You're a laughingstock," she called from the hall. "Everybody makes fun of your crazy goings-on. You call yourself a saint because you read the Bible every night—but torment me all you want, you're no better than I am!"

CHAPTER TWO

* * * * * * * * * * * * * * *

S CENES OF THIS SORT WERE NOT
infrequent at Ashley House. Mrs. Fletcher's
outward composure masked a disposition that was
restless and easily irritated. No sign of ill temper could
be read in her face and it was easy to misjudge her
in this respect. In spite of what her daughter said,
she was by no means a laughingstock; in fact, there
were many who never spoke of her except as "good
Mrs. Fletcher." This she knew, and it was a secret
satisfaction to her, all the more so because she prided
herself on her virtues. In talking she ordinarily
held her hands clasped and spoke in a hesitant voice.
Her eyes seemed ready to close, as if the light hurt
them or the lids were too heavy to support; they
looked at one sadly and timidly and fixed themselves
on nothing. In profile, the bulk and coarseness of
her nose gave a masculine effect that was not apparent in front view. She wore her hair in broad grey-
ing bands that covered her forehead and temples
and were gathered up behind in a large flat knot.
She held herself so badly that she might have been
taken for a hunchback, and this dwarfish arch of her
figure confirmed the impression of candour and humility that her first appearance conveyed.

But one had only to prick her egotism or her pride in order to transform all the benevolence of her features. It seemed at such times as if she had received a lash across the face. Her small body became erect; her eyes opened wide and a yellow spark which glowed in the depths of the pupils gave them an amazing vivacity. She was no longer the same woman; she lost all restraint and let herself go in the most violent language, not stopping short of threatening the offender with blows. It was only in such moments as these that there seemed any resemblance between mother and daughter.

She had been a widow for eight years. A mediocre portrait hung above the mantel in the parlour as a daily reminder of a husband whom she had never missed. The artist had painted him against a sombre landscape of dark mountains towering in a cloud-strewn blue sky, a grotesquely romantic setting for the poor little man of timorous mien who had sat for the portrait. His shoulders were rounded and gave him an appearance of feebleness which was not altogether false. His hair was painstakingly brushed down to cover a bare forehead; he wore a brown suit, and a white silk cravat encircled his neck, while his fine black eyes were fixed with apparent absorption on a flint which lay in the palm of his right hand.

He had been one of those reserved and taciturn men of whom no one has anything to say after they die, and who seem to have travelled along between

good and evil as between the hedges of a broad high-
road. He had met his wife at Savannah, where he
was secretary of an export house, and they had lived
for some time there. But the tropical rigours
of Savannah's climate had been too much for his
health; a year after their marriage he resigned and
retired to a place not far south of Washington, on
an estate inherited from his father, to which some
ancestor had given the name of Ashley House.

The house was built on the pattern of the simplest
dwellings of its period, boxlike in shape, with a col-
onnaded veranda commanding almost the entire
front. It was a low-standing building pierced with
many small windows, and had only one story above
the veranda. The walls were painted light grey and
the gentle slope of the roof was tiled in brown. No
decoration relieved the simple façade; only a slight
red line underscored the flat modelling of the columns
and gave a solitary note of colour to the general
monotone. Giant trees planted at random in front
of the house succeeded in lending it almost an impos-
ing air, standing up above the roof with their great
lower branches caressing the walls.

The view from the veranda was fine and open.
The little plateau where Ashley House stood was
set off with a rim of rocks, a natural wall at the end
of the long garden. Far away the horizon was
marked by an unbroken line of high hills, blue in the
distance, with darker splotches barely visible at
times to indicate the masses of woods which spread

halfway up their slopes. But by going to the foot of the extensive lawn, one discovered another landscape, unsuggested from above, which rose up suddenly as one approached the rough dark ridges of rocks; a deep and fertile valley stretched away to the hills; sweeping tracts of cultivated land unfolded northward and southward to the limits of vision, corn and wheat and cotton fields deploying their colours upon the duller background of the meadows. Long roads reached out over the countryside and strung together big and little villages embowered in trees. Here and there a patch of bare earth showed vividly in dark, framing the stacks of harvested grain left out to dry in the wind. Behind, on the hill, stood Ashley House, half hidden by oaks and pines, but showing between their trunks the grey of its walls and the small square windows strangely prisonlike in effect.

Here Stephen Fletcher had chosen to establish himself, committing to this place the remainder of his days. Something of the melancholy of his birthplace had crept into himself and become a part of his nature. He loved to stroll placidly beneath the Ashley trees, his eyes cast down as if he were hunting for something lost. Sometimes he stopped to examine a stone at his feet; if it proved unworthy of interest he would give it a little kick with the toe of his boot and continue on his way, but if it was odd or unfamiliar he would stoop down and gather it up with a gesture almost of tenderness, studying it slowly;

then he would drop it into a pocket of his suit and go on with his solitary walk.

When anyone spoke to him he replied gently and politely but with a tone of enforced patience which was a little troubling; consequently people avoided speaking to him except from necessity. On rainy days and in the evenings he occupied himself in his own room with scientific works and books of religion. Time went on without bringing visible changes to his way of life. He saw his daughter born and watched her grow up without displaying the slightest interest. His life was somewhere apart and remained unknown to all. At forty-five he was attacked by the malady from which he was to die, but at first not a soul observed that he was ill. He continued his strolls beneath the trees, stopping to ponder over the stones that his foot disturbed; but sometimes now he was seen to clutch at his chest with his hands, while his usually pale and waxen face took on a purple flush; then he would lift a large white silk handkerchief to his face and cough behind it. Watching his shoulders then, one might have thought him convulsed with merriment.

Mrs. Fletcher failed to find true cause for affliction in her husband's death. Poor, and brought up in poverty, she had married him under pressure from a family who wanted to get her off their hands, or, as they said, provide a future for her. She was then twenty-five, and, although not beautiful, was conceded a certain charm. Her figure was heavy but well proportioned; she had fine eyes and hair, and a skin that was then in all the freshness and texture of youth. Such as she was, Stephen Fletcher looked upon Kate Elliot and found her fair. Later he revised these sentiments and took pains to avoid her company. He had married her because he was bored with his own solitude, and he returned to the love of that solitude as soon as conjugal life had taught him to understand its merits. With the aid of time, he ended by regarding his wife as an enemy—a point of view which she herself soon shared—and in the ensuing struggle it was he who carried off the victory, because he knew how to say nothing and she did not. She was young and opinionated, with a decided taste for debate, but to all her vehemence Stephen Fletcher returned a bored detachment and left her insults unanswered. There is no way to attack a man whose weapon is silence; one must flee from him or submit to the letter of his law. After a number of futile scenes, this truth at last broke through into Mrs. Fletcher's brain; she swallowed as best she could the humiliation of finding herself shelved by a man she had never even loved; and peace returned to Ashley House.

When she succeeded in convincing herself that she was less unhappy than she had thought, Mrs. Fletcher became reconciled to the pleasure of an easy and tranquil life. Except for two rooms where her husband worked and a hall where he liked to walk, she was mistress of a large house, an immense garden, several carriages, and a staff of servants. She could stay at home or she could call the carriage and go visiting among her neighbours, returning when she liked, not returning if she chose to stay away. Greater freedom was unimaginable; and just because it was so great, Mrs. Fletcher never dreamed of exerting it fully. She knew that she could live as she desired, and in the knowledge she was content.

Like everyone who had spent only a short while at Ashley House, she concluded at once that it would be impossible to stay there long. The nearest town was fully an hour away; it was insufferable to be so cut off from the world. The house itself was dismal and without a single room that was well lighted or inviting. During the early part of her married life she never dared to broach this to her husband, but later she was less reserved and reproached him personally with all the deficiencies of the house. She even went to the extent of assuring him that she would perish of gloom there—if she didn't lose her mind or go crazy first. These words were whistled to the wind like so many others—and Mrs. Fletcher herself had already altered her opinion of Ashley House and believed only half of what she said. One becomes habituated to any place in the world and learns to find some reason for putting up with it.

Mrs. Fletcher's whole outlook changed when she accepted that discovery. Her restlessness gave way to resignation; her egotism was undisturbed, and she became aware of the sort of pleasure that comes from the avoidance of all emotions, either painful or agreeable. She went in and out and up and down in the house, wandering from room to room and telling herself that it all belonged to her, rubbing her hands in the pleasure of possession. After all, what if the house was a little gloomy? . . . No one could call it really ugly, and it did have a fine situation.

When the first clashes occurred between her and her husband, she no longer had any real desire to leave Ashley House; and as Stephen Fletcher little by little ceased to take his meals with her or even to see her at all, day in and day out, she persuaded herself that the enemy was falling back and proceeded to enjoy the ground she had gained. Now at last she gave rein to a tendency which she had held in restraint so long that it had almost been deflected. Kate Fletcher had been raised by a mother who had known wealth and then at a stroke had lost everything in the Civil War. Kate's childhood had been a childhood of poverty, and the word she most frequently heard throughout those days was "economy." In the name of economy she was deprived of toys and obliged to wear the same dresses year after year, eking them out by letting down hems and carefully patching the worn spots; in the name of economy she was not sent to school and had to learn her a b c's as best she could out of grimy books bought secondhand. Later, and again in the name of economy, she moved to the country with her mother and spent her time in sewing. It goes without saying that she never danced, never went out, and dressed in clothes picked up at rummage sales and made over by herself— altogether a sort of charity-child existence. When she met Stephen Fletcher she was a grown girl devoid of gayety or hope, who seemed indifferent to everything and who expected nothing from the world or from herself. Her black eyes mirrored the boredom of a spirit incurious and resigned, readily giving way to the will of others. It is not too hard to understand how she could have been pleasing to Stephen Fletcher. A sober-minded man of his orderly nature, valuing his time and his privacy, would be attracted by just such negative qualities as hers: her air of timidity, her hesitant speech, and her self-effacing manner with the world.

Marriage almost transformed her. Overnight she found herself rich and freed from all her old restraints. Anyone who observed her then would quickly have concluded that the sudden change had gone to her head and that she often acted without knowing quite what she was doing. She would chatter along as never before, and give way to excesses of joy which bewildered her husband and left her a moment later in self-conscious blushes. Her feelings sometimes excited her to the point of tears. It took weeks for her to cease wondering at all she saw about her.

Amazed at finding herself rich, she suffered a revulsion at the mere thought of economy. She wanted to spend for the sheer joy of spending, but she made out very badly at that game. Prodigality is not so easy to practice as it appears unless one has been trained to it; Kate Fletcher discovered this soon after her marriage.

She plunged at once into a series of indiscriminate purchases and indulged her craving to the limit. Two months passed in a fever of spending, until the day when she discovered that not one of her purchases could be classed as an extravagance. They all bore the same stamp: they were useful articles, and they were good bargains. Her first impulse to congratulate herself soon changed colour, and thereupon she resolved to buy nothing but luxuries. The word had something seductive and at the same time malignant about it, and she determined to explore its meaning. In the shops which are distinguished chiefly for the vacuity of the customers and their passion for surrounding themselves with beautiful things, she wandered up and down, but never felt at ease. In spite of herself she assumed an air of guilt, kept her eyes cast down, moved quickly away from the counter when a clerk approached her, and eventually went out with flushed face and empty hands. She admired with all her heart the jewels and silks and velvets, but an instinct more compelling than her will would draw her away from the spell of their charms like a hand laid upon her shoulder.

In any other store, however, she would finger things carefully and with enjoyment, thumbing them over to discover the best bargain. She would linger by the counter talking to the salespeople, and argue them into exasperation when she thought she could knock off a little on the price of what she wanted. Her early training clung to her so firmly that her new condition of life had no effect; she was a niggard even in prosperity. She soon recognized this warp in her nature and refrained from doing it violence; even without superior intelligence, she was able to feel what was hurtful and what was helpful to her natural happiness. Being powerless to master her old habits, she resolved to return to them and to carry on her life in the channel which seemed to suit her best.

Few people came to Ashley House. Stephen Fletcher had no taste for conversation and no need of confiding in anyone. His wife, too, found silence and solitude a natural enough condition; but she believed that one ought to have visitors, and during the first month of her marriage she often invited friends to come and spend the day with her. But she was aware of how little pleasure they could have in these visits—for she was a maladroit hostess and never knew how to talk to them—and, beyond that, she disliked their looks of surprise on entering her parlour. Evidently they found fault with the furnishings and her manner of arranging them; they were hardly to be called in style. She often caught in their faces a look of amusement which cut her to the quick. At such times as these she detected the yawning gaps in her education and learned to hate all the principles of economy which her mother had instilled in her. She would dream of an immediate trip to Washington to buy fine things, such as new cloth for upholstering the furniture; then, by a natural impulse, she would touch the plush of the chair on which she sat and say to herself: "But this is still very good." Little by little, her relations with outsiders all fell away.

She lived after her own taste, and saw her husband so rarely that she had no trouble in convincing herself that she was sole master of Ashley House. Now that she had returned to her natural path after a brief digression, she thought of nothing but ways and means of economizing; this was the most imperative need of her nature. Her inclination would have been to close off a large part of Ashley House and dismiss the servants, instinct directing her back toward the conditions in which she had lived before her marriage; but she lacked the hardihood for so large a gesture, and she knew, too, that her husband, in all his patience and abstraction, would never consent to changes on that scale. Instead, she was compelled to satisfy her craving as best she could.

She first took pains to reduce the expense of her wardrobe. Recalling the useful lessons learned from her mother, she designed her own dress patterns and sewed the dresses by hand. The materials she used were all alike, black or some other sober shade, a little coarse but substantial. She possessed to perfection the knack of buying the material; she would rub the samples between thumb and finger, stare at them, sniff them, and she would never determine on a purchase until after laborious discussion with the salespeople. When it came to bargaining, she generally won out, thanks to her persistence and a kind of guile which took the place of intellect in her make-up. Above all, she showed consummate skill in applying the difficult snip of the shears which decides the form of the dress. After laying out the cloth on a large table-top, she studied it lengthily and with absorption, and attacked it with the greatest precautions; but once she began to cut, she proceeded faster and faster and snipped out generous pieces with assurance. She made three dresses for herself in this way: one for summer, another for winter, and a third reserved for very special occasions. Out of doors she always appeared with an Indian shawl over her shoulders—none other than the table cover from her bedroom. Her economies went farther than her mother's had ever gone.

Her dominant passion sometimes came in conflict with other instincts which contradicted it and which it always overruled; for she was a woman in arms against herself, and there was an almost ascetic quality to her determined renunciation. In most respects her senses were not acute, but she had a certain predilection for good food, and it was distasteful to her, for example, to drink her tea without sugar. She did so, nevertheless. Two or three months after her marriage, when she was already living practically apart from her husband, she succeeded in conquering her natural terror of the dark and formed the habit of undressing without lighting the lamp. For those who know the horror of night fears, and the comfort of a single ray of light, this apparently simple act acquires a special mark of resolution and courage. It is in this way that many human passions gain such ascendancy that they are effective for good and ill alike.

CHAPTER THREE

* * * * * * * * * * * * * * * * *

EMILY WAS BORN AT THE BEGIN-
ning of 1872. Already such a distance sepa-
rated Stephen and his wife that they looked on the
child as the token of a period past recovery and felt
in it a sense of mockery and embarrassment. Stephen
Fletcher kept to his library or went out only for
his solitary walks about the house; he concerned
himself not at all with the child, and it was understood that she should not be spoken of. Mrs.
Fletcher felt little more affection for her baby than
for her husband; she began taking care of it as soon
as she could in order to save the expense of a nurse;
but she did so without pleasure and with the bitter sense of caring for a creature whose birth she
had never for a moment desired.

And Emily required a large measure of attention.
She appeared so fragile and so tiny that the servants, when they were summoned to look at her in
her cradle, found nothing to say about her; but
one could read in their faces all that they dared
not put in words—the pity and fear of seeing the
little thing die before the month was out. She
lived, but her pallor lingered. She never cried, and
she created astonishment with her circumspect little

glances; she seemed to have a sort of grown-up manner, which made people say: "Oh, look! Wouldn't you think she was surely going to say something?"

She spent her childhood quite alone. Every mark of affection was denied her; she grew up silent and self-contained. Often she would crouch down in a corner and amuse herself with the simple objects that her hand could reach—the feet of the furniture, the fringe of a curtain; or she would patiently trace the cracks in the floor with her finger nail, trying to pick out the pins or needles or other small things that sometimes fall there.

She slept little and lightly. In the morning her mother would sometimes find her sitting up in bed with her hands clasped over her knees, staring into space as if at some absorbing scene. "Why, what are you looking at?" her mother would ask. The child would look up without replying, and brush back the locks of hair that hung across her forehead. The expression of mystery which she wore at such moments made Mrs. Fletcher impatient. "Did you sleep well? Are you all right?" she would ask, while the little girl sat on the edge of the bed and put on her slippers; these were not words of affection, and they were spoken in monotone untouched with kindliness. Emily replied with an invariable "Yes" and said no more.

Now and then, in a hall or on the lawn in front of the house, Emily met her father. Stephen Fletcher

had no love for her. He would fix his dark eyes
upon her and contemplate her without a word, shaping his lips as if about to speak; then he would
abruptly turn away with an unintelligible mutter
of words. Between these two appeared a certain resemblance which the years accentuated. Like her
father's, Emily's shoulders were slightly rounded,
but she held her head erect and thrust forward in
a listening attitude. Like him again, she had black
and very mobile eyes, high fleshless cheek bones,
features that were restless to the extent of seeming
discontented and moody.

Toward the end of his life, Stephen Fletcher
avoided all sight of his daughter. He might have
had some unavowed reason for fearing to meet her.
If he saw her from a distance in his walks, he looked
the other way, and when possible retraced his steps
and withdrew under the trees. When he happened
to come out of his room just as she was passing
in the hall, he would promptly retire inside the door,
with a nod of his head that combined timidity and
anger.

His death came in 1879. Emily was only seven,
but one would have hesitated to call her that, either
because her serious manners were unnatural in so
young a child, or because her face had a grey and
careworn quality that gave her a look of age. Her
mother kept her briefly informed of her father's
progress: "Your father did not sleep last night. He
is not doing so well as yesterday." One morning

she came to Emily's room and with a theatrical
gesture quite unlike her took the girl's head in her
arms and pressed it against her bosom; then she
clasped her by the hand and led her to the door
of the room where Stephen Fletcher's life had just
ended.

Mother and daughter went in. Emily had never
gone inside this room before. The windows were
hung with brown curtains; on the table lay an open
book, stones of various colours, a magnifying glass;
and near it an armchair had been pushed a little
aside as if some one had just risen from it. A large
four-poster bed, hung with brown velvet like the window curtains, stood in the corner of the room. Emily
turned her eyes in this direction; suddenly she shivered and gasped and raised her hand to her mouth.
Her father lay in the bed; his body was bent double and his face was toward the wall. The blanket
had been thrown off and hung beside the bed; the
sheets seemed clasped between his legs and wound
about his body. There was something hideous in
his immobility, which was not the repose of sleep.

Emily stood for a moment transfixed by this scene
for which she had been totally unprepared. She
opened her mouth and made the motion of putting
her fist in it as if to smother the groan that rose
from her throat. Drops of perspiration beaded
along the roots of her hair, and she turned away
suddenly as though giddy. She buried her face
in her mother's skirt, and Mrs. Fletcher put her

arms around her and kissed her again. "This is what death is, Emily," she said firmly, when they were out on the stairway. "You must not forget your father, and you must honour his memory."

No doubt the mother acted with the best intentions in giving this turn to the scene. Her husband's death hardly touched her feelings, and it left her perplexed. She felt the uneasiness common to those somewhat elementary souls who are fearful of making a mistake when circumstances call for a display of emotion which they know themselves incapable of feeling. She questioned herself as to how she ought to take her husband's death, what would be the correct attitude to assume; and with that lack of naturalness which seems somehow natural for the self-contained, she resolved to carry it off with a touch of theatricality.

For a sensitive disposition like Emily's, the test was severe. Leaving the death room, she shivered and clung to her mother's arm. She had never before been placed in the presence of death. The word itself had only the vaguest meaning in her mind, and what she had just seen seemed hideous and incomprehensible.

Her thoughts lingered there for days on end. Its macabre fascination held her mind and refused her any escape. She recalled many details which had struck her on first entering her father's room and which she had subsequently forgotten—such as the soundless motion of a curtain hem that fluttered

on the floor in a little draught. Her mind called
up the picture of an ugly hole in the dead man's
nightshirt, from neck to shoulder, uncovering a skin
of unbearable pallor; she guessed that her father
might have torn it in the convulsive effort which
he must have made in turning toward the wall, his
arms rigid at his sides. Sometimes, abandoning
her thoughts completely to this morbid course, she
wondered what had been the expression on that face
which she had not seen; and since she now could
never know, her imagination supplied the deficiency.
Then she would fall to her knees and hide her face,
as if to evade the unspeakable sight she had conjured up.

Little by little she grew more composed, but the
impression she had received was never to disappear. She avoided the society of her mother, who
inspired her now with a sort of dread, for she
could never think of her without thinking also of
her father. Her life became more and more solitary; no one bothered about her, and for this she
was grateful. She loved above all to shut herself up
in her room and sit by the window, watching hour
after hour the landscape of rocks and hills unfolded before her. By a natural bent she often gave
way to musing. She talked to herself in a low
and colourless voice, glancing from side to side uneasily. And now and then she would have an access
of sudden terror that roused her from her chair
and sent her running out of the room.

CHAPTER FOUR

* * * * * * * * * * * * * * *

EMILY WAS EIGHT YEARS OLD when a new event altered the course of her life. In 1880, Mrs. Fletcher's brother died of the fever at Savannah, and as Mrs. Elliot, the mother, had no one left but Kate, it was decided that she should come and live at Ashley House. The negotiations which followed this plan may be passed over. There was no true bond of affection between mother and daughter, and it is easy to surmise that they exchanged numerous letters before arriving at an agreement on a number of capital points, notably on the figure which Mrs. Elliot would concede as the price of her board and keep.

The death of Stephen Fletcher left his wife in utter freedom to do as she pleased, and she pleased above all to make some important economies. With her dreams on the verge of realization, she was not anxious in the least to burden herself with some one who in a sense would take the place her husband had left vacant, and—being certainly less discreet than he—would try to meddle continually in household affairs and volunteer advice on all that had to be done. "It's all up!" she ejaculated when she read the letter claiming her hospitality; and she replied

posthaste to explain that her husband had left her
nothing but debts and that her mother must not
dream for an instant of coming to live at Ashley
House—in fact, she intended to sell the estate within
the following year.   But Mrs. Elliot was not to be
put off; she met lie with lie and asserted that she
could pay out a considerable sum the very day of
her arrival.   "As long as I am alive," she added,
"you are not going to sell Ashley House."

She arrived a few days after Christmas.   At a
little over fifty, she was heavy and gross like her
daughter, but she carried her head almost arrogantly
and with a touch of nobility that Mrs. Fletcher
had never had.   Her black eyes suggested Emily's,
except that their expression was placid and a little
sly, with none of the unrest of her granddaughter's.
Her long nose, her thin lips stretched in a half smile,
gave her an air of complacency, and it was impossible to look at her without fearing that she would
let fly some mean or mocking remark.   When she
swallowed, the rolls of flesh along her jaw produced
a sort of turkey-gobbler look of disdain, and emphasized the effect of disgruntled haughtiness that
always impressed people on first sight of her.   She
wore a black dress with very full skirt and close-
fitting waist, trimmed with linen collar and cuffs.
When she arrived she had on an enormous bonnet
covered with black tulle and plum-coloured silk
ribbons which she had tied beneath her chin.   Two

compact masses of glistening curly hair showed out at the level of her temples.

She spoke softly, but her words carried a note of authority and she still knew how to make her daughter fear her. When she stepped out of the carriage she looked about her inquisitively and mounted the steps of the porch with a tread that echoed. Mrs. Fletcher hastened forward to meet her with an air of eagerness and embraced her effusively; then they both went indoors, followed by a negro servant who carried a small black wooden trunk covered over with thick plush.

"Is that all you have with you, Mamma?" Mrs. Fletcher asked, eyeing this object uneasily.

Mrs. Elliot burst out laughing and said merrily:

"Right you are, Kate. You didn't think I was rich, by any chance? There's not a poorer soul than I am south of the Mason and Dixon line, and that's saying a good deal."

"But what do you mean?" Mrs. Fletcher queried, suspicion in her voice. "You wrote me . . ."

"Don't worry your head about that, my child," her mother replied more soberly. "There's some proverb or other . . . You know your Bible so well, help me out. 'The Lord will provide.' That's it!"

She laughed again, and added:

"Make that your motto. It will bring you luck. . . . But I don't see your daughter. Where is she?"

Emily was sent for and was found in her own

room. She came into the parlour timidly and stood
as far as possible from Mrs. Elliot, large-eyed, her
hands behind her back; and when her mother pushed
her she took two or three steps in the direction
of the armchair where the newcomer sat.

"Come nearer!" Mrs. Elliot commanded sharply.
The little girl obeyed.

"Now curtsy!" her grandmother continued, pressing her flabby hand on the girl's angular shoulder. Emily flushed, not understanding what was
wanted of her; on a chance she bowed her head.

"Stupid little brat!" Mrs. Elliot exclaimed as she
embraced her. "I can see right away that you're
not good for a thing." She kissed her on the mouth
and pushed her away with a laugh. "Kate, you
don't know how to bring up a girl. I'm the one
to look after her from now on."

Emily went to a chair and sat down. She watched
her grandmother with a mingling of fear and surprise, yet something or other in this portly woman
had immediately drawn her, and she foresaw that
she was of a make-up quite different from her
mother's. To be sure, Mrs. Elliot was more than
a little awesome, but her very bluffness inspired a
queer sort of confidence, where the chilling mildness
of her mother only turned the girl away. She
began to listen to the conversation.

It was decided that Mrs. Elliot should take the
room that had been Stephen Fletcher's. Mrs.
Fletcher called it the nicest and most comfortably

furnished in Ashley House; of course it was rather shut off from the rest of the house, but that made it all the quieter.

"And what are *you* up to?" Mrs. Elliot suddenly asked, turning toward her granddaughter. "Stand up and let me look at you."

Emily stood up and took a few steps forward.

"Let's see. Who do you look like? No one in my family, anyway. Turn around. Look how bad her posture is, Kate! She's almost humpbacked, that daughter of yours. Stand up straight, you little goose. You're just like your father. Remains to be seen if you're like him in other ways, too."

She leaned toward her daughter and muttered: "Let's hope not. If she's as crazy and sickly as that . . ." She completed her thought with a motion that seemed to mean "might as well drop her in the river with a millstone round her neck."

Mrs. Fletcher bit her lips; Emily flushed deeply.

"Oh! So the truth can't be mentioned around here!" Mrs. Elliot exclaimed in feigned astonishment. "Well, let's go and look at that room. I'll lean on your shoulder, Emily. I'm a little tired."

They went upstairs. Mrs. Fletcher went first, digging for a key in the pocket of her black serge apron. She had said nothing for some time, and appeared vexed and preoccupied.

The room was in order and scrupulously clean, and Emily saw at a glance that it had not changed since the last time she had entered it—the day she saw her father lying dead upon the bed. The memory of that day struck her with such force that she could not suppress a start of terror. The book still lay on the round table, but it was closed now, and the cross which was stamped on its black leather cover revealed that it was a Bible. The coloured stones had been arranged in a small glass cabinet hanging between the two windows. The curtains of the bed were open far enough to show a blue-and-yellow counterpane. With a distressing sense of looking at forbidden things, the child hung back and stood behind the others.

Mrs. Elliot examined the room rather lengthily; one almost expected her to ask the price, as if she were in a hotel. She drew aside the window curtains and frowned at the landscape. She moved the toe of her shoe across the rug as if to test its thickness; she tried out one after another the three chairs upholstered in red plush, and poked at the mattress with her fists. Finally she declared herself satisfied.

Mrs. Fletcher said not a word throughout this whole procedure. She stood in the middle of the room with her hands clasped, trailing her mother with her eyes from point to point. Now and then Mrs. Elliot cast a sly smile in her direction, as if amused by her bad humour, and made malicious little comments to Emily. Emily laughed at them in spite of her constraint, but they touched Mrs. Fletcher where she was most sensitive.

"Look," said Emily's grandmother, stroking the

worn and faded plush of a chair back. "What fine velvet this is, and what a lovely colour!" She arched her eyebrows elaborately and cast a hypocritical look toward Mrs. Fletcher, who stood unmoved. Or she teetered a chair which had a castor missing. "And this upholstered armchair must be Hayes's presidential chair itself." She cocked her head with exaggerated comedy.

In spite of her sarcastic pleasantries, she evidently liked the room, and she promptly moved into it; but she ventured to suggest a few small improvements in the furnishings. The rug was old; there were spots where it had grown so thin that it was already fraying. The seats of the chairs badly needed being done over. The severe tone of reproach in which she mentioned these things was exasperating to her daughter, and Mrs. Fletcher could no longer restrain herself. "But, Mamma," she cried, "think of the expense all this is going to mean. In your house do you . . ."

"In my house," Mrs. Elliot broke in, "everything is plain but nothing is shabby. This is shabby, my dear; and this, and this." And she pointed to holes and worn places, and went on in a tone of finality, "We'll have to fix all that."

Mrs. Fletcher did not reply. But in the course of the following weeks, Mrs. Elliot's desires were carried out and the chamber was completely renovated.

In contrast to Mrs. Fletcher, who economized by

preference and exactly as one follows the whim of
a passion, her mother had always economized by
necessity and against her inclination. She had never
forgotten her days of affluence; their loss was still a
bitter reality to her, and such fastidious economies
as her daughter's seemed as ridiculous as they were
unnecessary. Consequently she had no scruples whatever about putting her to all the expense that seemed
desirable.

Confronted with Mrs. Elliot's formidable will,
Kate Fletcher felt like a small child, and trembled
with chagrin that she had ever let her establish herself at Ashley House. Surely she should have known
her well enough. Had a few years' separation been
enough to let her forget that hypocritical and domi-
neering nature, her greediness, her insufferable temper if she were not deferred to in everything? And
how could she ever have believed that Mrs. Elliot
would pay her own expenses? What a fool she was,
she thought, weeping with rage at herself.

Full of her grievances and the sense of her own
shortsightedness, she watched her mother parade
about the house criticizing its appointments, and she
said nothing more. She swallowed her wrath as
best she could and resigned herself to what she was
unable to prevent. Little by little, Mrs. Elliot developed her small habits and imposed them on Ashley House. She required that no one should go
through the parlour between two and four because
she took her daily nap there on the couch; she re-

served for herself the most comfortable armchair
and had it moved over to the window. She also
had the dining-room table turned so that she would
not have the light in her eyes at meal time and
could still keep her place at the head of the table,
which she thought the most desirable. To these
small exactions she added others considerably more
important. She wanted to have the woodwork
painted, the walls repapered, the furniture done over,
exactly as if she had been in her own house. Every
time her daughter saw her looking at a chair or
fingering a curtain, she began to tremble and thought
with pitiful anger, "I'm in for it now!"

She made up for it as best she might. Fortu-
nately, Mrs. Elliot had no special taste for food and
ate as little as possible for fear of becoming stout—
which enabled Mrs. Fletcher to cut down the grocery
bills. The two vegetables were replaced by rice alone;
then the dessert was cut out; finally the helpings
were reduced and the meals became more and more
abbreviated. Each new expense by Mrs. Elliot en-
tailed a new economy by Mrs. Fletcher, who hesitated at no sacrifice whatever. It was Emily who
suffered most in this strange duel. Her sheets were
taken away; she had to wear her linen twice as long
as before. Her shoes were in such a state that the
gravel hurt her feet and the dampness of the ground
came through, and since her mother forbade her to
take them to the shoemaker's, she stayed in the house

or went out only on the veranda. To be sure, Mrs. Fletcher inflicted similar penance on herself; but in contrast to her daughter, who fretted under these hardships, she had the encouragement of her faith and suffered them all in silence.

CHAPTER FIVE

* * * * * * * * * * * * * * *

IT FINALLY BEGAN TO SEEM AS though Mrs. Fletcher had a supernatural ally. One February afternoon in the parlour, looking at some chairs that the upholsterer had just brought back, her mother suddenly became faint. She leaned against a table and put her hand to her head; her face grew purple and she scowled sharply with pain. Emily, who was alone with her, looked on with fright.

"What's the matter, Grandma?" she called out, seeing her shiver and drop her head to her shoulder.

"Nothing. Go get your mother," Mrs. Elliot muttered. She pulled off her bonnet, letting her hair fall in confusion. At the same time she took a step toward a chair, but her knees bent under her and she faltered. Her eyes had a vacant stare and seemed unable to focus. She reached out her hands in an effort to grasp a curtain that hung in the doorway, and suddenly she crumpled in a heap on the floor in front of Emily, who ran crying from the room.

Mrs. Elliot recovered quickly enough from this attack, and in the course of a few days felt quite

well again, except that she was often tired for no
apparent reason and took to falling asleep in her
chair. She determined on a week or two in bed
so as to get entirely rested. She talked freely of
her attack and never tired of describing the sensa-
tions that accompanied it; she attributed it to the
long trip she had just made and the excitement of
seeing her daughter again after a six years' separation, and she repeated this to everyone who came
to see her—Mrs. Fletcher, Emily, and the servants
who brought up her meals.

She seemed somehow altered, but it was difficult
to discover in what way. Physically she remained
unchanged; one barely noticed that her eyes appeared less hard, her glance less sharp. There was
something in addition. Was it only that she talked
more, and less bluntly? Mrs. Fletcher gave her ver-
sion of the matter when she told her daughter, in
a surprisingly expansive moment, "It seems as if
the Lord had softened grandma's heart." No doubt
she meant that Mrs. Elliot had a better side to
her nature than one would have supposed, and that
it needed the shock of violent pain to reveal it, as
sometimes happens; or perhaps her pious expression
merely hid a little glow of triumph that had to be re-
leased in words.

Two weeks went by and Mrs. Elliot expressed
no desire to get up. It was apparent that the invalid's life had begun to appeal to her. Emily visited
her several times a day, and a real intimacy sprang

up between them. The little girl had forgotten her
earlier fears, and the painful memories which her
father's room revived in her gradually gave way
under the new impressions she was receiving there
now.

Her grandmother carried on conversations with
her that sometimes lasted for hours; and Emily, by
nature so timid and unresponsive, entered into them
with all manner of observations and confidences.
What she loved above all in these dialogues was
that her grandmother treated her exactly like a
grown-up and never made her feel that she was only
an ignorant little girl who didn't even know her
a b c's. Encouraged by that, she gave way ardently
to the unfamiliar pleasure of expressing some of
the thoughts that had occupied her lonely childhood.

Mrs. Elliot listened with attention, lying with her
hands folded benignantly on the counterpane. She
reclined comfortably against three or four pillows
piled up behind her, and nodded her head and smiled
from time to time. Occasionally, when she began
to talk, she would hesitate in the middle of a sentence, hunting for a word, and it sometimes happened that her tongue would become twisted and
she would not succeed in saying what she meant.
Emily would see her flush and stammer, while a
curious shadow passed across her eyes. "What's the
matter with her?" the girl would wonder, uneasy at
this trouble which she failed to understand.

Mrs. Elliot was no longer the same person. She

had lost the spirit of her first days at Ashley House,
and with it the glint of mockery which used to lend
special meaning to her phrases. Still, when she
found herself blocked in the midst of a sentence, one
could see a flash of irritation in her eyes which
transformed her for a moment and restored the accent of pride which Emily had known in her bearing; but these moments were fleeting, and the somewhat doleful, wandering look of the present returned
at once to her features.

In these hours of confinement she had acquired
a taste for reading, and she called for all the novels
that could be found in the house. There proved to
be a generous supply in the library left by Stephen
Fletcher, who had always prided himself on a taste
for literature. Emily carried the books up to her.
First she asked her mother to read her the titles of
some of them, and said them over to herself going
up the stairs; then she recited them to her grandmother and asked for her choice.

Mrs. Elliot appeared to be profiting from her idle
existence. The colour returned to her cheeks. In
the morning while her bed was being made she
walked back and forth in a small alcove adjoining
her bedroom; she called this taking a little exercise and it seemed to be all she needed. Sometimes
she looked out of the window and noted the passage
of the seasons across the landscape; but she never was
moved by a desire to go down for a breath of real
air, to walk across the grass again, or feel the gravel

or the good soft earth beneath her feet. She shivered and fretted if anyone opened the window without giving her time to cover herself warmly, and when she got up she wrapped herself in a long dark sleeveless woollen garment, which she draped with care about her shoulders, and walked from one end of the alcove to the other at a prudent pace, supporting herself on the furniture. It was noticeable that she held herself less erect than before and neglected her careful coiffure; but she still wore her little tulle bonnets as she had before her illness, though this was more the survival of a habit than any expedient of vanity.

The winter passed and brought no modification to this régime. Little by little, Mrs. Fletcher recovered the ground that she had lost. The day following her mother's attack, she called the carriage—which had not been out since her husband's death—and set off in all haste for Wilmington and Salem to cancel the orders that Mrs. Elliot had put in. She carried on the combat with as much ardour as if it had involved her very existence. The tradesmen who came to make deliveries at Ashley House were turned away. "Mrs. Elliot has changed her mind," her daughter told them; "she no longer wants the things she ordered." So lacking in decision at all other times, she summoned it up abundantly on such occasions as these.

She never paid any of her mother's bills without exacting a reduction. She would go to the stores

with her account book and point out to the proprie-
tors the figures for her purchases of previous years,
marking them off with her large insistent finger. She
always maintained that prices had been raised, and
she cut all discussion short by laying on the counter
the amount she claimed that she owed. If this argument failed, she fell back on a description of what
had been happening at Ashley House. The purchases had not been made by her, but by her mother,
who had not consulted her. Was it fair to make her
pay for things she had never intended to get? And
she emphasized her logic by pounding on the counter
with the palm of her hand. She repeated these
scenes wherever she went and they sometimes yielded
her a slight reduction, for she was a past master
at giving a pathetic turn to her arguments which
ended by making her opponents uncomfortable, no
matter how zealous they might be in their own interests. She willingly played on their personal feelings when that method seemed efficacious. She acted
the beggar, and in her drab clothes she had an air
of poverty that made an impression; she deliberately
wore gloves that were out at the fingers, but when
she was thumbing through her account book she
pretended to show her hands as little as possible, as
if to hide the evidence of her poverty from the trades-
people and so incite them to greater sympathy.

At Ashley House, life was reorganized according
to her wishes. She knew that her mother was more
seriously afflicted than they had thought at first,

and that it would be some time before she could leave her room. It caused her anxiety, because she had a natural horror of illness as of everything that could directly or indirectly remind her of death; but she found genuine satisfaction in the thought that she was free once more to act according to her own designs.

Schemes for economizing spun themselves endlessly in her brain. They kept her wakeful at night, asking herself unwearyingly: "What can I get along without? Where can I cut down? Do we really need this and that?" She dreamed of a hundred new sacrifices and gave herself heart and soul to this pursuit.

But for some time now she had found new worries to torment her. She gave almost no thought to her daughter, considering it sufficient to clothe and feed her; nevertheless, one day when Emily came and asked her to read the titles of some books, she realized the profound state of ignorance in which the girl remained. Not daring to deprive her much longer of the elements of an education, she pondered on how to have her taught without incurring expense. She doubted her own capacity for teaching her to read and write; she felt that she lacked the patience and would not know how to explain anything so simple and yet so complicated. "Everything conspires against me; they want to ruin my life," she complained bitterly. Still, rather than send her daughter to school in Wilmington, she determined to make

the effort herself, and she was already planning a
first lesson when she recalled her mother's words
on the day of her arrival: "You don't know how to
bring up a girl; I'm the one to look after her from
now on."

She went up at once to her mother's room to remind her of her promise. Ordinarily she avoided
the invalid unless compelled to see her. The changes
which she always discovered affected her most dis-
agreeably; the fixed and spiritless face which she
had never known as her mother's, the appearance of
mental decline, the altered gestures, which resembled
the clumsy gestures of a child. Instead, she satisfied her conscience by sending Emily or a servant
three or four times a day to see if anything was
wanted, and she very rarely went into the room herself.

Mrs. Elliot was dozing; her head lolled to one side,
and the book she had been reading when sleep over-
took her had slipped down to the floor. When she
heard her daughter's voice asking if she felt badly,
she started up and denied that she had even closed
her eyes. Mrs. Fletcher plunged at once into her
project for educating Emily.

"I have so much to do," she said quietly; she did
not look at her mother, who sat squinting her eyes
in an effort of concentration. "You have no idea
how much work it is to keep up a place like Ashley
House. It needs twice as many servants as we have.

Besides, there are more of us here now, and you know I am not well off."

She paused in the vague hope that her mother might be prompted to speak about paying her share of expense; when no word was forthcoming, she went on again:

"That's why I am asking you to help me all you possibly can. If you would take charge of Emily, for instance . . . I know you're not well, but it's very little to ask. Just think! She can't even read."

Once more she hunted for words, seized with a sudden timidity such as she had known at Emily's age. In her mother's eyes she read only a vacant and unfriendly stare, and she leaned forward impulsively and clasped the invalid's hands, pleading with a warmth that surprised even herself: "Oh, please, Mamma, do help me. You must! Just think of all the money we can save!"

Mrs. Elliot stared at her for a moment, and answered with an effort that accented every word: "So you would let her grow up without even learning to read and write, just to save a few dollars! I see it is up to me to look out for her."

The blood rushed to Kate Fletcher's cheeks, and she lowered her eyes without replying. She dared not answer the slur for fear her mother would recant on her agreement, but she felt herself choking with anger. How could she ever have believed that her mother had changed for the better? She was as unjust and as spiteful as ever, and for one instant

Kate hated her so that she wanted to strike her across the face. Her eyes lowered, she seemed to be considering deeply; finally she lifted her head and said in a steady voice: "Since you are willing, Mamma, I'll send Emily to you in the morning. I am very grateful."

The lessons were begun the following day. At first they proved rather difficult. The girl had no comprehension of what was meant by study and application, and scarcely understood what her grandmother wanted of her. Besides, her grandmother often neglected to explain things which she herself had always considered easy and self-evident and which her pupil failed to grasp at once. Mrs. Elliot frequently lost patience and threw the book aside, but she always took it up again at once and sailed in on a new tack. She had grown fond of the child and she enjoyed her visits, her naïve talk, and her little forthright ways that resembled her own. Seeing how she differed from her mother, she sometimes thought of Stephen Fletcher and wondered what manner of man he must have been if this daughter took after him as she seemed to, even in her physical appearance. Mrs. Elliot had not known him very well; he had always acted ill at ease in her company, and she could not recall that she had ever had any extended conversation with him. Besides, the memories of that period in her life had become obscure and distorted in her mind, and she discovered that she sometimes confused her son-in-law with other people she knew. As an aid to memory, she studied the portrait of Stephen Fletcher that hung above her bureau and was easily seen from the bed. Its expression was gloomy and sullen, and the gleaming eyes followed the observer hauntingly. This was the room where Stephen Fletcher had lived, the bed where he had fallen asleep at dawn after many a wakeful night, and he seemed to look at it now with a mingling of repulsion and regret.

"What a miserable specimen," thought Mrs. Fletcher, lying and watching him while her granddaughter droned her alphabet, "and how much he looks like Emily." She let her imagination carry her easily onward, and wondered if it did not follow, with such a resemblance of character and features, that the daughter's whole outline of life would reproduce the father's. She envisaged Emily at twenty, Emily at thirty, Emily as an old woman with the melancholy look of Stephen Fletcher, and when the little girl raised her head from her lesson, surprised that her grandmother's voice had ceased to correct her, Mrs. Elliot was startled at the face she saw; for it was not the face of a child, and it wore as if in advance the marks of a troubled and difficult life.

The days at Ashley House now seemed to have acquired their set pattern. Mrs. Elliot never left her room, and the girl's irregular visits were gradually fixed by habit. Mrs. Fletcher divided her time between household duties and long sessions of dress-making, and the lives of these three women grad-ually took on the character of necessity that marks an existence prescribed in even its smallest acts. Forces of change were doubtless at work in the characters of all three, but they proceeded with the slow patience that nature brings to all her motions, and they were of a kind that could pass unnoticed even by those who might most easily have seen them. How her mother's habits of economy had grown into the mania of a miser Emily would have been incapable of saying; and in the same way the indolence of Mrs. Elliot was transformed into a sort of paralysis too easily and naturally to give the girl any surprise. For a long time the old lady talked of getting up; then she talked of it less often, and finally not at all. She took on invalidism as others take on re-ligion—after due consideration. At the present time, no one at Ashley House could any longer have im-agined her wearing a dress and a hat, walking down-stairs, moving about the rooms, or going out in the garden. She was an invalid; no one even considered the possibility of her being anything else.

Emily, too, was imperceptibly changing. She was growing up under their eyes, and the mother and grandmother knew almost nothing about her.

CHAPTER SIX

* * * * * * * * * * * * * * * *

EMILY SLEPT UNEASILY THAT night. Several times she got up and lighted a candle, and opened a book to drive away the thoughts that were keeping her awake; but her attention refused to follow the lines before her and she understood nothing at all of what she was reading. The silence of the whole house frightened her. She sat on the edge of the bed and her hair fell down over her book and covered her face. She was roused at the slightest noise and peered about her anxiously, brushing back the hair from before her eyes. A strong draught came in at the window and made her shiver, but she dared not get up to close it. She huddled herself together in an effort to keep warm, glancing anxiously at the waning candle on the table beside her; and when the wind rattled the sash of the window, she turned about with beating heart and watched the motions of the curtains, which seemed animated with mysterious life.

Her brain was stimulated by the cold and her thoughts came faster and more clearly than usual. Since the clash with her mother, she felt that something had somehow been transformed within her. It was as if one period of her existence had come to an end and another was about to begin. What-

ever she might do, she could never go on living as
she had lived until then, saying and thinking the
same things as before. She puzzled over the reason
for this change that she recognized so clearly in herself, but it baffled her. "Probably it's because I'm
growing up," she thought. And now, in spite of
her timidity and the terror that kept her peering
about her in the shadowy room, she was conscious
of a strange joy pushing up from the depths of her
heart. Summoning her courage, she rose and went
to the window, drawing apart the curtains to look
out. It was a clear and tranquil night; she leaned
forward until she could see the carpet of lawn between the trees. No sound came to her ear except
the uneven whispering of the wind around the house,
and the barely audible crowing of a cock far off
in the valley. After a little while she went back to
bed.

When she awoke in the morning her thoughts of
the night before flashed back into her brain, and
they struck her as childish and unreasonable. Her
mother had just knocked at her door as she did each
day. A dim grey light filtered through the curtains and she saw her room in its character of every
day. In what way could her life have changed if
all this remained unchanged? How could she live
anywhere except at Ashley House—and, living at
Ashley House, she was obliged to obey her mother.
She was absorbed in these gloomy reflections when
Mrs. Fletcher called her again from the room below.

She went downstairs unhurriedly, feeling for the first time a sense of annoyance at having to do the same things day after day without variation; she knew the stairs so well that she could go down with her eyes closed—and she did so, her arms folded, counting the steps in turn. The experiment worked to perfection, and she arrived at the dining room just as her mother opened the door to call her once again. "You take too long getting dressed," she said to her. "It's after half past six and the tea is on the table."

Kneeling by a chair in the dining room, Emily watched her mother as she read the daily prayers. She saw her from behind, her knees on a plush-covered hassock and her hands folded on the table, reading from a diminutive Bible which she had propped against the bread basket. It was still dark, although after half past six. Only the uncertain and niggardly light of a kerosene lamp fell on Mrs. Fletcher's dark hair and rounded shoulders. Emily wondered how much longer she would begin each day like this, coming down from her room to kneel behind her mother and listen while her hesitant voice moved unintelligibly through the prayers. She made mental notes of all the grievances she had against her mother. She despised her for her hypocritical meekness, her timid manners and the guileless, pathetic airs she affected with strangers, hiding under an apparent virtue a heart that was hard and greedy of worldly goods. And why these formulas of piety? Doubtless to tickle her self-esteem with the thought of her own goodness, of which she was safely convinced.

All at once Emily remembered her mother's command that she should dismiss the servant girl. She shook with indignation at the thought of this impending task, and a sudden flush spread itself over her face. A strange desire possessed her to go over to her mother and take her by the hair and shake her until she cried for mercy. The idea struck her as horrible and absurd at the same time, but she painted the scene in her mind with malicious pleasure. She saw herself rising noiselessly, with her hand on the table for help; then she was moving across the room on tiptoe; now she was reaching out her fingers. She saw it all so vividly that she wondered not to find it actual. She closed her eyes and hid her face in her hands as if to force the picture from her mind, and began to cry in silence.

Mrs. Fletcher closed her book and stood up. "Don't forget to speak to the girl," she said, facing round toward her daughter. "She must leave before the first of the month."

"That's it," said Emily to herself. "Don't say anything about the little quarrel we had yesterday, for fear I might get angry and refuse to obey. You're such a coward you don't even dare to talk to the servants."

"What's the matter, child?" Mrs. Fletcher asked,

noticing how her eyes were blinking as if in too strong a light.

"Nothing, Mamma."

"Remember not to let her go without looking through her trunk. I'll check up on the dishes myself."

Emily did not answer, and they sat facing each other in silence. A dismal light began to whiten the windows; from her place at the table the girl could see the heavy branches of the pine trees swaying languidly. She sat motionless for a moment as if absorbed by the trees, familiar as they were to her. Then all at once she made a sort of grimace which resembled a smile, buried her face in her napkin and burst into tears.

"Why, whatever is the matter?" Mrs. Fletcher dropped the bread knife and mechanically arose. She seemed uncertain what to do and stood leaning over the table. Then, as the girl sat convulsed in her place and seemed to be choking with tears, Mrs. Fletcher shoved her chair back violently and called out in a different tone, "Oh, you're not going to be sick, are you?" Then she hurried around to her and helped her over to the sofa, where she made her lie down.

When she tried to put a pillow under the girl's head Emily pushed her away and turned toward the wall, pretending sleep. "Let me alone," she murmured, when she had quieted down.

But Mrs. Fletcher was insistent and plied her with

questions. "Do you feel better? Where does it hurt? Tell me about it," she begged, anxious and irritated at once. "You don't think you're going to be sick?" She watched her uneasily and looked up from time to time in a sort of reproachful despair. Finally she went back to the table and poured out a cup of tea. "Drink this," she directed, taking her daughter by the shoulder to make her sit up. "You'll feel better right away." She succeeded in making her swallow a sip or two before Emily pushed it away with a gesture and sank back on the sofa.

Mrs. Fletcher took the cup away with annoyance and sat down to drink the tea her daughter had not finished. "Did you sleep well? Are you sure you didn't catch cold?" she asked from the table, repeating persistently, "Don't you feel a little better now?" as if she believed that her questions ought to have been an effective remedy.

Without saying a word, Emily stood up and returned to her place at the table; she blinked her eyes and raised a shaky hand to brush back the hair that hung over her damp forehead and cheeks. "See there!" exclaimed Mrs. Fletcher, reassured. "I was sure you would soon be all right." And she sat back in her chair with a glint of victory in her eyes.

"Now," she said, when her daughter had recovered and was drinking her tea, "you can go into the parlour and talk to the girl. I'll stay here and count the china and silver."

Emily had nothing to say. "What's the use?" she

thought. "She'll do as she pleases, anyway. She is my mother, and no matter how hatefully she treats me she's bound to have the best of it."

She folded her napkin and drew it through the ring with a gesture of frustration.

A few minutes later the servant girl passed through the dining room on her way to the parlour, where she had been summoned. She saw Mrs. Fletcher stooping down between the two doors of the china cupboard, and understood at once what was coming. She was a big hulking girl, carelessly dressed and slack of step. She stopped in the middle of the room and tried to find something to say. "Can I help you, ma'am?" she finally blurted. Mrs. Fletcher pretended not to have heard her and went on counting the china. "Don't I give satisfaction, ma'am?" the girl asked again.

"Why, surely, Eliza," Mrs. Fletcher answered mildly, without looking up. She flushed a little and added, "Miss Emily wants to talk to you in the parlour."

Emily, hearing these words from the adjoining room, suffered acute chagrin for her craven mother; she was tempted to open the door and say to Eliza: "Mother doesn't want you any longer. You can see for yourself that she is checking up on the dishes to make sure you have not broken any." But the magnitude of such an act gave her pause and she sat down to wait. Almost at once the maid opened the door and stood submissively before her.

Emily had now regained her composure. "Eliza," she said, "we are well enough satisfied with you, but you must leave at the end of the week. Mother will give you a reference at the parsonage."

She broke off with a sudden desire to say something deliberately intended for Mrs. Fletcher's ear. Raising her voice, she added:

"Anyway, you are not strong enough to keep on with our work. There's enough to keep four or five servants busy at Ashley House, and you can't do it all; so my mother has decided to get along without you rather than ruin your health."

The sound of steps informed her that Mrs. Fletcher had left the dining room. Then, with a surge of anger which she could not repress, she said in a louder tone:

"You haven't had enough to eat here at Ashley House. Watch out that you don't get sick."

She sent the girl back to the kitchen and went out of the parlour. In the hall Mrs. Fletcher came up to her with a smile.

"Well, Emily?" she asked, with her hands folded before her.

"Well, Mamma," replied Emily drily, "she's going Saturday."

Mrs. Fletcher could not check a start of satisfaction.

"Really?" She seemed to find it hard to believe what her daughter had said. She lowered her eyes a little and glanced furtively from side to side, a sign that some thought was labouring in her mind; no doubt she was going to ask more questions, to make her daughter tell the good news over again, but Emily slipped past her and hurried up the stairs. From the landing halfway up she turned and saw her mother go back to the dining room. For a moment her eyes followed the rounded back, the grey head calculating new economies; then she went on upstairs with a little sigh of pent-up anger.

It was now the hour for her visit to her grandmother. When Emily came in, Mrs. Elliot was still dozing. She had changed very little since the early days of her illness, and her face seemed even to have recovered something of its youth. She had gained flesh, and the open collar of her nightdress revealed a massive neck. Her grey hair was half tucked into a soiled muslin cap, which became more rumpled with every motion of her head. A book lay under her folded hands. Hearing Emily enter, she opened her eyes and welcomed her affectionately.

"Sit down," she told her. "Why are you so upset? Has something happened?"

Emily nodded and sat on the edge of the bed beside her grandmother.

"What was it?" Mrs. Elliot turned her head excitedly toward her and took her hands. "Something to do with your mother?"

Emily plunged into a narrative of the preceding day's affair and the trouble she had gone through in the early hours of the morning.

"She makes me so wretched," the girl explained. "I can't look at her without wanting to cry. And I have all sorts of horrid thoughts . . ."

"What do you mean by 'horrid thoughts'?"

Emily pursed her lips, and replied after thinking a moment:

"I just don't love her at all."

There was a silence, and Mrs. Elliot put her arm around the young girl and drew her face up to her own. "Whenever you feel unhappy, just come and see me," she said; and her smile had a suggestion almost of malice.

Emily went on to tell her how she had dismissed the maid, and ended with a toss of her head: "Sooner or later she is sure to think she can get along without the cook. Then she'll sell the furniture the way she sold the silver and the fancy things from the parlour. Why not? She even talks about selling Ashley House, and she's capable of doing it."

"She would never dare," said Mrs. Elliot, clasping her closer.

"Grandma," Emily suddenly asked, "isn't it true that Ashley House will be mine some day?"

Mrs. Elliot looked at her granddaughter quizzically and smiled as she answered: "Why, perhaps —certainly. Why do you ask me that?"

Emily blushed deeply.

"Mamma never looks out for you at all. It's never warm enough in here, for instance—she economizes so on wood . . ." And she lowered her eyes as she added: "I want you to be happy."

"You're a dear child!" the old woman exclaimed, planting a kiss on the girl's lean cheek. "Heaven reward you for your generous thoughts." Emily seized her grandmother's flabby hand in her own bony ones and squeezed it with warmth, her eyes aglow with gratitude. Mrs. Elliot might just have presented her with the house and all that was in it.

"I'm never happy except with you," she said. "I want to stay here and take care of you. Do you want me to read aloud?"

She knew how greatly Mrs. Elliot enjoyed this, and without waiting for an answer she got up and chose a book from the table; she picked a novel of Disraeli's, from which she read a few pages, sitting on the bed with her back against one of the posts. Though she understood very little of its brilliant and artificial prose, she regarded it as the most beautiful thing imaginable. She had read his *Endymion* several times without surrendering to the obscurities of its political and amorous plot, and with no more enlightenment on the human passions than if she had never opened it; but for her the supreme satisfaction lay in reading a grown-up book. Her grandmother must surely find the story fascinating—Emily could conceive of nothing else; but as a matter of fact, Mrs. Elliot was not listening. She stared at the portrait of Stephen Fletcher and lost herself in reflection. All at once she broke in on the reading.

"Listen," she said, beckoning the child to come nearer. "I have been thinking about your future—some very important matters." Emily sat down beside her.

"You are young," she went on, "and it may happen that some day you will need my help. You are going to discover that life is not so easy as it looks to you now, and the advice of your old grandmother may be useful to you. You must promise to keep nothing from me, or I cannot help you at all."

"I'll tell you everything, Grandma," Emily promised, taking her hands.

"Don't keep anything from me, or else don't count on me at all," Mrs. Elliot went on. "I am a prisoner in this room; I can't see a thing for myself, and if I am to guide you I must know about everything that happens."

She spoke with increasing rapidity and clutched at her granddaughter's hand. Emily was surprised at the agitation which showed in her face.

"Don't worry, Grandma," she declared warmly, "I promise to obey you in everything."

CHAPTER SEVEN

* * * * * * * * * * * * * * *

SHE HEARD HER MOTHER CALL-
ing and went out.

In the half-spoken conversation with Mrs. Elliot she knew well enough what was implied. The hostility between her grandmother and her mother was no secret to her; she had inferred it from the tone of reserve with which they spoke of each other, and if it needed confirmation she remembered seeing her mother come out of Mrs. Elliot's room one day, and noticing the pallor and agitation on her face.

"Come with me," Mrs. Fletcher had said when she saw her, and she had led her into the parlour and slammed the door. Then she had told her in a voice that trembled with anger that her grandmother was going to see to her education and that lessons would begin the following day. In spite of her youth at the time, the strangeness of her mother's manner did not escape her; surely it indicated something deeper and more enduring than a simple flare-up of temper. And the ensuing months were to prove that her mother's visits to Mrs. Elliot were ended; she seemed to avoid even mentioning her name, and if she was ever compelled to visit the sick room, she wore an expression of unrelenting severity.

In the times that Emily saw them together, the two
women talked coldly and with constraint, obviously
anxious to cut short a situation distasteful to both.

The years increased this breach. Mrs. Elliot
nursed the smouldering rancour of an invalid, a kind
of bitterness that seems to grow all the more fierce
and persistent because it is unreasoning, and ends
by becoming an essential part of the illness, one of
its symptoms, as surely as fever or pain. Little by
little, abetted by her solitude, she came to believe
that her daughter wished her harm and even hoped
for her death.

On Mrs. Fletcher's part, it had been long since
she had felt the least natural affection for her
mother; to put it as mildly as possible, she simply
did not love her. Still, she would have borne her
presence in the house with some degree of patience
if Mrs. Elliot had not made the mistake of criticizing
her economies and standing in their way. This was
her vulnerable spot, the place where the wound once
made could never heal. The charges Mrs. Elliot
had made about Emily's education could never be
forgiven; she carried them in her heart like a poison
that spread through her whole system.

Emily did not hesitate in her choice between these
two. Mrs. Fletcher spoke to her only to scold or
reprove her or to burden her with disagreeable tasks.
Mrs. Elliot, on the other hand, listened to her confidences, helped her with advice and encouragement;
and it was for her that the girl poured out all her

affection. She went up to visit her each morning
and reported in detail not only her own occupations
of the day before, but her mother's as well, for she
saw how avidly her grandmother drank them in.
As a result, Mrs. Elliot was kept informed of all
the minutiæ that marked her daughter's days, without ever leaving her bed of idleness. She had no
desire to see her on any pretext, but it would have
been hard for her to dispense with Emily's chronicle.

Mrs. Elliot's mind was entirely given over to its
single object, her daughter: what was she doing?
what injury was she plotting against her? would she
prevent the servants from bringing up her firewood?
She listened acutely for the distant sound of steps
in the downstairs rooms where Mrs. Fletcher stayed,
and with the aid of Emily's reports she tried to
guess how her daughter was occupied at any given
moment of the day: now she had finished her breakfast; now she was doing the housework. And when
her granddaughter came in she pursued even farther
her researches after information. She insisted on
knowing what tone Mrs. Fletcher used in speaking
of her—whether she spoke impatiently, or looked annoyed or displeased. Perhaps she frowned a little
when she spoke of the cost of supporting an invalid? Still, Mrs. Elliot avoided asking questions
too pointedly, or in a tone that would confess how
important the answers were to her. Sometimes she
even exercised her guile to the extent of scolding
Emily when the girl, led on by the pleasure of having

an audience, gave rein to her own opinions about her mother or confessed half-spoken secrets that she thought she had discovered; but the old woman never scolded until after her curiosity had been satisfied. If she anticipated a question from Emily which would call for an opinion of Mrs. Fletcher's conduct, she would pretend to be asleep. Being suspicious by nature, she feared that the girl might repeat what she said for her mother's benefit; this would have been the ultimate humiliation and it imposed a precaution from which she herself was the greatest sufferer. She desired above all else that Mrs. Fletcher should believe her indifferent to all that went on beyond her bedroom door, and she made it a point of honour to appear so.

Gradually, however, her reserve gave way a little. She must have understood that deliberate treachery or even a tactless slip was not in Emily's nature; but she waited for years to assure herself completely, and up to Emily's fifteenth birthday, which she had just attained, the girl never heard her grandmother utter a single word that reflected on Mrs. Fletcher.

CHAPTER EIGHT

A SIMPLE TURN OF THE HEAD OR inflection of the voice will sometimes conciliate the most suspicious natures. When Emily clasped her grandmother's hands and promised to confide whatever happened, there was a sincerity and frankness in her face that touched the old woman's heart, and she felt a glow of happiness that she had not known in years. Thenceforward their companionship became more frequent and more open. Not that Mrs. Elliot abandoned all precaution, but simply that she talked to her granddaughter with greater freedom and allowed herself to ask questions which she had withheld until then as too revealing. A lingering doubt still made her ask sometimes, in an almost threatening tone, "I can trust you, can't I?" —as if she feared that she might have embarked too hastily on this new course; but Emily's cool stolidity reassured her at once, and she gave way eagerly to the pleasure of talking about her daughter. She did it with such gusto, one would have fancied that she loved her.

Meanwhile Mrs. Fletcher was so absorbed in her economies that she had no suspicion of the growing *entente* between her mother and her daughter. If

she noticed how frequently Emily visited her grandmother, she simply assigned the everyday reason that
came naturally to mind, "Mamma is looking after
Emily's schooling," and satisfied herself with this
somewhat vague interpretation.

She found her life more tranquil now, and happier. Sometimes, when she allowed herself to think
of what she called her mother's impositions, her spirit
overflowed with indignation; but these moods became
infrequent, and she rarely thought of her at all
except in having her firewood brought in and her
meals sent up.

She developed a similar disregard for Emily.
She had never wanted the child, and had looked
upon her as an intruder who only increased the household expenses; but her early animosity had at length
given way to indifference. Now she spoke to her
seldom, but at least not unkindly, and her ire was
stirred only when the girl touched some deep-seated
vanity or bigotry in her—criticized her efforts at
economy or ridiculed her penny-wise expedients.

She lived on in the loneliness of her small pursuits,
her plans and contrivings—the all-absorbing passion
which redeemed her life from utter boredom. She
was moody and abstracted, out of touch with the
world and oblivious to all that went on beyond the
bounds of Ashley House, and she was equally oblivious to the two lives that shared her dwelling. But
meeting Emily in the hall one day—the day the servant girl was dismissed—she found herself speaking

almost involuntarily and without full consciousness
of the direction her words were taking:

"I know what you have been up to, Emily." She
spoke the sentence with a smile, almost as if she
were joking. Emily flushed and stood speechless,
puzzled by the words and by the strange smile.

"Why, I've just come from grandma's room," she
finally said.

Mrs. Fletcher looked at her curiously.

"Do you sometimes talk about me?"

Emily's face became crimson and she hesitated,
not wishing to lie.

"Yes," she answered.

"Yes?" Mrs. Fletcher repeated reflectively, and
turned away. A moment later she was thinking of
something else.

CHAPTER NINE

* * * * * * * * * * * * * *

EMILY'S ROOM WAS SMALL AND unattractive, but the girl was happier there than anywhere else in the house. She would have spent entire days in it if she could have had a fire, but that, of course, was out of the question. She loved the task of putting her room in order, saying to herself: "This is my very own; all this belongs to me." And she would rest her hand on the back of a chair or on the bureau, repeating with a gesture of authority: "This—and this—and this," as if she feared some invisible antagonist who would dispute it. She attached herself ardently to what she considered her possessions, and she attached herself equally to all, without preference for one or another. From bed to pincushion, everything in the room seemed precious to her and she valued all in the same degree. It was as if the fact of her ownership invested these things with a special quality and an impartial value.

In summer she installed herself in the window seat with her sewing, looking up at intervals to let her eyes caress the lustre of the furniture, which she polished every morning: the massive chest of drawers, the clumsy mahogany bed, and the rocking-chair decked out with its purple antimacassar. This furniture she had grown up with; she remembered it in her room from the remotest moment of childhood, and she cherished it as she had never cherished a fellow human; to deprive her of that, she imagined, would be almost to take away life itself.

The rest of the furniture in the house seemed no less fine to her, and she lingered again and again over each article of it, with a kind of unacknowledged longing; but it was not her own, it gave her no pride of possession, and that was enough to prevent her from becoming attached to it. Sometimes, yielding to an impulse which became commoner and stronger as the years went on, she would say to herself that some day she would be mistress of all this; and she enjoyed going from room to room, examining what they held, until her conscience shamed her with the thoughts that this practice awakened. The secret wish that the time would not be long— what did it imply? She blushed for her cupidity, and at night, awakened by a sense of guilt which the solitude and silence enhanced, she charged herself savagely with having wished for her mother's death.

Still, the wish had its hold on her, and the question haunted her mind with the persistence of an obsession: When would Ashley House be her very own? Would it be soon? She tried to overcome it by asking herself whether the house was not, after all, her own as well as her mother's already. Her mother talked about "our" furniture, "our" house.

But her reason showed her at once the vacancy of these phrases. Never would her mother permit her, for example, to move even a chair from the living room to her bedroom.

These notions possessed her mind for hours together, and she could find no defence from them. She ended by thinking of Mrs. Fletcher only as an obstacle, and this thought defied her will to deny it and gave her great distress. At times she would kneel down beside her bed and try to pray; but she quickly lost all inner peace and only succeeded in disturbing her conscience still further. She found it unforgivable that her mother had sold all the silver and the other little keepsakes of her father, just to cover her month-by-month expenses and save herself from drawing on her capital. The memory of the two little medallions exasperated her particularly. She could see them perfectly, hanging in their places on either side of the mirror in the parlour—Flora in her violet-embroidered robe, Pomona pouring the fruits of the earth from her horn of plenty; she remembered their ebony frames inlaid with filigree, and she said to herself with a bitterness untempered by months: "She had no right to sell them; they were mine as much as hers."

She harboured these grievances for a long time before daring to confess them to her grandmother; but as soon as she became aware of their new understanding, she tried out one or two discreet queries about the future of Ashley House, which Mrs.

Fletcher was threatening to sell at once. "Where would we live, Grandma?" she asked ingenuously; and when Mrs. Elliot had reassured her she went on: "And if we don't sell Ashley House we'll go on living here, won't we?"—hoping that Mrs. Elliot might exclaim: "Why, Emily, Ashley House will be yours some day; you can live here as long as you choose!" This reassurance was not forthcoming, but Emily was convinced that her grandmother could have given it if she had been less circumspect. Sometimes, talking of her mother and reporting some new evidence of miserliness, she caught a look of rancour and cruelty in Mrs. Elliot's eyes that astonished her. It transformed the whole sleepy countenance, like an inner flame that passingly revivified this old and faded face.

As the result of another collision with her mother, Emily finally conquered all Mrs. Elliot's suspicions and drew from her at last an outright word of encouragement and confidence; but it was accompanied by a look of triumph that took her aback and made her suddenly fearful. "This old woman will drive you on to evil"—the thought brushed across her brain. And at the same moment, like a confirmation and a timely warning, she heard her mother calling from the stairs.

CHAPTER TEN

* * * * * * * * * * * * * * *

COMING INTO THE DINING ROOM
one evening, Emily found her mother absorbed
in reading a newspaper, but on hearing her enter
Mrs. Fletcher folded the paper carefully and put
it away in a drawer. They never bought papers at
Ashley House any more, and this was the first that
Emily had seen for a very long time; but she checked
her curiosity and sat down with a book to wait for
dinner. It was clear, however, that Mrs. Fletcher
wanted nothing so much as to be questioned. She
was sitting not far from her daughter and kept
looking at her as if about to speak; she would take
a breath, let her sewing fall in her lap and open her
mouth; then, with a sudden change of mind, she
would shake her head and go on with her sewing
again.

Dinner was served soon afterward, by the light
of a tiny lamp that Mrs. Fletcher almost put out
by continually lowering the wick. Neither of them
said a word—Emily sour and sulky, her mother ill
at ease and timid. Something was troubling her;
it showed in her look of fixity and the deliberateness
of all her motions. Now and then she would sigh
and fold her hands in her lap, or furtively brush

the crumbs on the tablecloth into a little pile near
her glass. Toward the end of the meal she gave way
at last; laying down her napkin, she folded her hands
on the table and said softly:

"Emily, I have been thinking about something . . ."

Emily looked up quickly, with the alert defiance
that always annoyed her mother.

"The cook went to Wilmington to pay a bill this
morning, and she brought back a paper."

She got up and took the newspaper out of the
drawer where she had put it.

"Here it is," she said, sitting down again. She
unfolded it carefully in front of her and pretended
to read it, in an effort to avoid her daughter's
eyes.

"Do you remember what I told you the other
day? You must help me a little. You are old
enough. . . . "

She fumbled for words and went on after a pause:

"I'm thinking about some things that we must
buy. It's nearly the end of October; in another
month winter will be here, and you know we have
hardly any wood left."

"Well?" Emily asked coldly.

"Well, that means more expenses," Mrs. Fletcher
answered. She flushed a little and went on in an
irritated tone: "The firewood is not for me. Heaven
knows I have never burned a splinter of it in my
room."

She stopped as if to collect herself, folding her hands over the newspaper.

"And that's not all. We need blankets. Mine ought to be torn up for rags, they are so old. And this dress I have on is ready to fall to pieces."

She stretched out her arm and bent her wrist to show the part of the sleeve where the cloth was worn through and hung in tatters. Emily leaned over to look at it. "Here, too," Mrs. Fletcher went on, encouraged by this sign of interest, and she stood up and pointed out similar deficiencies around the waist. "See? It's all worn out."

She sat down again and continued: "Now I see by this paper that there is going to be a sale next week."

"A sale!" Emily's voice choked her. "Are you planning to sell something of ours?"

"You don't understand." Mrs. Fletcher became a little red. "I'm not talking about selling, but buying. . . . Why didn't we think of it sooner?" she went on almost volubly. "It's a splendid way to economize. After this we must never go to the stores for anything. You can find all sorts of things at sales, and quite cheap. Listen to this—"

She read with a little quiver of excitement in her voice:

"'Tuesday, the 20th, there will be placed on sale an important collection of furniture, household utensils, clothing . . .'"

"Is it clothes you are planning to buy?" the girl asked sharply.

"Of course. Why not?"

"Why, those are old clothes—dirty old clothes that other people have worn and cast off!" she protested, and her face showed as much revulsion as if a pile of filthy clothing had covered the table before her.

"What are you talking about? We can have them cleaned if they are really dirty. Anyway, this is not the Dark Ages, you know—you don't need to be afraid of catching the plague."

She saw the weakness of this reasoning in her daughter's look of contempt, and she went on to her strongest argument.

"We are poor." She raised her voice and beat on the table with the palm of her hand. "We *must* cut down on our expenses."

Emily's face had grown livid.

"No, Mamma, we are not poor. You make us live like poor folks . . ."

"I do? *I* do?" Mrs. Fletcher gasped.

Emily was on the verge of pouring forth her stored-up wrath against her mother, but the words stuck in her throat. A strange dizziness possessed her and she stared unseeingly at the blurred and distorted outlines of things about her. She would have liked to get up and run away, but was held fixed by an overwhelming lassitude. She sat in speechless confusion while a multitude of chaotic thoughts swept through her mind. Finally she heard her mother's voice, as if from a distance and scarcely distinguishable. "I must have almost fainted," she thought.

Mrs. Fletcher had evidently been talking for some time.

"If we could live any better than this, don't you think we would do so?" she said with restrained vehemence, spluttering a little. "Do you suppose it is any pleasure to me to deprive myself of everything that makes life worth living? Why, unless I struggled constantly to reduce our expenses, there would be times when we might have to cut into the money your father left us; and then what would we have for the future? I still have a little of the money he gave me while he was alive, and with care I can make that hold out, at least for a few years more. But as for his own money . . ."

She took a breath and went on as if talking to herself:

"Father in heaven, grant that I may never touch that money! When I think of my mother's improvidence . . ."

Then she looked up and spoke out loud again:

"Surely the least you can do is to help me. Later you will be thankful enough that your poor mother saved you a house and a little money to live on."

Tears came to her eyes at the touching sentiment of her own words. She folded up the newspaper carefully.

"So I am going to this sale," she recommenced,

lowering her eyes. Then, as if struck by a sudden thought, she clasped her hands emphatically before her and exclaimed: "Good Heavens! now I come to think of it, our carriage is not in fit condition to be used! Whatever shall we do?"

For four months the Fletcher carriage had been in the stable with a broken axle. The last horse, a bony old mare, had been hired out to a tradesman in Wilmington.

Emily looked up to say wearily, "There's always the railroad."

"Never shall I ride on the railroad," Mrs. Fletcher affirmed; she professed a passionate and quite unexplained distaste for that form of locomotion. Could it have been the fear of accident, or an aversion to paying the price of a ticket? Or was it some fine religious scruple that made her regard this modern invention as an instrument of the devil?

Emily shrugged her shoulders.

Reaching out her hand in ostentatious friendliness, Mrs. Fletcher then said: "I had thought of asking the Stevenses to lend us theirs."

"They wouldn't do it," the girl promptly answered. "They are very disagreeable people."

"But how do you know? At least you might ask them—to-morrow afternoon, perhaps."

"I? But I hardly even know them!" The idea of calling on her taciturn neighbors filled Emily with alarm.

"Oh, won't you do a thing to help me?" Mrs.

Fletcher implored. "Do I have to get down on my knees to my daughter to make her obey me?"

In this vein she was going on, but Emily gave up in despair. She said hurriedly: "Very well, Mamma; stop whining. I'll go." And she went out of the room in suppressed fury, leaving her mother overwhelmed and delighted at her easy victory.

CHAPTER ELEVEN

* * * * * * * * * * * * * * *

THE NEXT DAY, FAITHFUL TO her promise to keep nothing from her grandmother, Emily reported this scene in detail. The old woman listened attentively; then she drew her close and said in a low voice, frowning just a little:

"What a clumsy granddaughter! It's lucky for you that you can come to me for help."

A moment later, and without warning, she dropped her bantering tone and moved off to the far corner of the bed; her expression changed from good humour to exasperation, and she glared at Emily with the sternest of frowns and spoke in almost a shout.

"Have you no will at all, you little fool? Will you let that woman go on bullying you until she has you completely under her heel? She does nothing for herself any more. In a week or two she will make you dismiss the cook as she did the chambermaid. Isn't it bad enough to have to do your own house cleaning? Before long she will be using you like a maid of all work while she sits back in her armchair and counts the dollars you have saved for her."

She shook her head with a wrath that made the grey locks dance in her bonnet.

"You'll see," she resumed her harangue; "she will make you her little slavey; she will rob you of your house, reduce your meals to nothing at all, and when she knows you can't defend yourself she will turn you out of doors."

She became tonguetied with excitement, and made a gesture of both hands as if to put something out of sight that offended her eyes. Finally she stammered in an accent of apprehension:

"She will blame it all on me, too—she hates me so."

"Oh, what is the matter?" Emily cried, panicky at her grandmother's hysteria. "I ought never to have told you about it all."

Mrs. Elliot clutched at her hands and clasped them in her own.

"Oh, but you must, certainly!" she said. "You promised to tell me everything. Everything she does . . ."

She interrupted herself with a sudden question.

"What has she been saying about me?"

"Nothing, Grandma."

"Come now, tell me. You know she did." She leaned forward and planted a kiss on Emily's bony hands. "You know I'm only your poor old grandmother who has to depend on you for everything. I'll help you; listen" (she smiled as one does at a child to humour it into a game). "Does she call me a nuisance? Oh, don't be afraid; it won't hurt my feelings."

"She doesn't talk about you at all, Grandma."

"Never? Doesn't she sometimes say I cost her a good deal of money, for instance? She does, doesn't she?" she insisted when Emily stopped to think.

"She has said that your wood fires cost her money."

"The fires in my room?" the old woman groaned. "Why, she must want to kill me! Has she no feelings at all? Me, who nursed her myself when she was a baby, brought her up with all the care in the world —God help me! What else does she say? Go on, like a good girl. The Lord will remember you for being kind to me."

"Nothing else—that's all she has said," Emily answered, growing uneasy under this inquisition.

But Mrs. Elliot was insistent.

"Oh, but I am sure she did. Listen. When she sees you coming out of my room, doesn't she make some remark? Or when my meals are brought up to me, doesn't she say . . ."

"But I tell you she doesn't say a thing," Emily repeated.

"Now, listen to me," Mrs. Elliot returned with signs of annoyance, and she simpered a little in imitation of her daughter: "Something like this: 'What a lot of money we have to spend on your grandmother, Emily . . . '"

Emily stood up hastily and shook her head.

"No," she said with finality.

"Well, my dear," Mrs. Elliot apologized, "I bore

you, I know, but you must be patient and gentle with me. I am an invalid and I have to be humoured. Sit down, dear, and listen. I have my faults and I simply want to know what your mother thinks about them. She might very well think me grouchy, for example; it would not offend me at all. She might also think that I have expensive tastes and that my fire takes too much wood. Does she say I am ungrateful, maybe?"

"No."

"Untidy, then; careless; dirty—something or other; she surely says something or other," Mrs. Elliot exclaimed in despair. "She hates me, I am certain of that." Seeing that the girl made no denial, she sat up suddenly in bed with astonishing energy. The blood rushed into her face, and she called out in an altered voice: "You refuse to tell me anything; you are planning to give me away—you are on her side and against me! So you are going to betray me? Very well, then. Get out of here!"

Her fury had stifled her final words and she made an effort to rise; but her strength departed at once; she fell back in bed and buried her face in the pillow. Emily stood beside her for a moment, rooted with terror and bewilderment at this unaccountable frenzy. She wondered if her grandmother was about to have an attack like her earlier one, and her impulse urged her to call for help; but the old woman's calm and regular breathing somewhat reassured her, and presently she went out.

CHAPTER TWELVE

* * * * * * * * * * * * * * *

FOR A FEW MINUTES SHE WAITED with her ear against the door, torn between remorse at abandoning her grandmother and the fear of exposing herself to a new outburst if she stayed with her. But at length she went to her room to wait for dinner time.

Mrs. Elliot's conduct bewildered and distressed her. She had never seen her in the grip of such a passion; it was beyond her comprehension that this could be the same person who ordinarily treated her with such kindliness. She had received her even to-day with open arms, before suddenly turning about and driving her from the room, and the transformation filled her with misgiving.

She decided, on reflection, that she must act as if the encounter with Mrs. Elliot had never occurred. This decision restored some of her composure, but she had to make an effort to down her growing despondency. All her dreams had vanished at a stroke and her sole support had failed her. She knew now that life was a cold and harsh reality, with no room for illusions; she must accept the maternal halter until fate should choose to release her. What schemes she had been building that very day, and so hopefully! She melted with self-pity at the thought, and, kneeling at the foot of her bed, she burst into violent tears.

Shortly afterward she went down to dinner. Her mother was already at the table, so engrossed in her own meditations that Emily's downcast face and reddened eyes escaped her notice. Without preliminaries, she embarked on a detailed outline of what she wanted said to the Stevenses. Occasionally she would break into her sentences and shake her head, punctuating some unuttered thought running parallel to her speech; then she would pick up the thread again and continue her instructions.

"Tell them that I sent you, and that I did not feel well enough to go out. Besides, it is raining," she put in, to justify her excuse. "Don't forget that we need the carriage early Tuesday morning. Tell them that we'll not fail to return the favour if the opportunity arises."

Emily listened half-heartedly, staring out through the window at the incessant rain. Her spirit was prey to a pervasive melancholy; the futility and meanness of her life disgusted her—this meal she was just finishing, the shawl which warmed her shoulders, all the cares and expedients required to live out a miserable life. "If I can never be happy," she thought, "and each day is only going to bring me new trials, what's the good of living at all?" And she laughed at herself for the day-dreams she had cherished.

All force of will had abandoned her at that moment; she was resigned to anything and would have resigned herself to twenty times as much as anyone asked, if there had been need, without a thought of protest. Her mother sat there facing her, rehearsing in a low and even tone the things she was to do and say, and she found no force to resist her.

Though the rain continued, Emily determined to go without longer delay, in spite of her mother's feeble attempts to restrain her. After pinning her shawl about her and opening an umbrella, she ran across the lawn, and in no time she had passed the gate and was out in the road. Seeing her hurry along, one might have thought she was running away from Ashley House.

The road to Rockley, where the Stevenses lived, was not very long, but it ran steeply downhill and was in bad condition. It was strewn with large rocks around which the mud collected on rainy days, and a pedestrian had to walk in the slippery grass and brambles at the side. This was what Emily ordinarily disliked about the road, but to-day it seemed of no importance; her shoes were full of water, her stockings torn by thorns and prickly grass, and she took a perverse sort of pleasure in this discomfort— the pleasure that comes from abandoning oneself completely to one's fate without a single effort to evade its rigours.

The steep slant of the ground obliged her to run, in spite of the undergrowth which tangled about her feet. Sometimes, unable to check herself, she plunged through the middle of a bush, one hand clasping her shawl, the other clinging to the handle of her umbrella. Long strands of hair clung wetly to her face, and she tried in vain to brush them aside with her forearm. On she went, compelled by her own momentum, like some grotesque and clumsy kind of toy.

When she came in sight of Rockley, she leaned against a tree to regain her breath and consider what she was going to say. Still thinking, she scrutinized the little low house at the end of the road framed among stunted cherry trees. Its tiled roof and grey clapboarded walls wore a dismal and sullen air that made her uneasy. Her mother would go too far with the tasks she imposed on her, she said aloud; then she planted the point of her umbrella in the rain-soaked earth, readjusted her shawl, hesitated a moment, and went forward.

It had been nearly two years since she had seen the Stevenses. Her father had once employed them to farm his land and had sold them the bit of ground on which they lived. Though they sometimes appeared at the fairs or went to the near-by towns to sell their vegetables, they stayed for the most part at home and kept entirely to themselves. There were three of them: the father and son, and the son's wife. During Stephen Fletcher's lifetime the son had worked at Ashley House as a gardener; but after her husband's death Mrs. Fletcher took advantage of a dispute over wages to get rid of the young man. Once or twice thereafter he appeared at Ashley House with fruit and vegetables to sell, but when he found that they bought nothing or next to nothing, he discontinued his visits. Mrs. Fletcher had nothing but ill to say of him and declared that his face was not that of an honest man; but she added that she wanted to keep on good terms with her neighbours and would not hesitate to do them a favour whenever they might ask it; and as if the fact of her saying this to her daughter put the Stevenses under obligations to her, she sometimes went to their house to borrow such things as garden tools or baskets. She forgot her usual timidity to the extent of helping herself to stalks of their rhubarb or ears of corn, for which she offered them such a ridiculous price that they let her have them free, with insolent generosity. Finally there was an exchange of rather sharp words over an unreturned sickle and Mrs. Fletcher decided never to set foot at Rockley again. From then on she never saw the Stevenses; she held the father in special terror, because he had called her an "old miser" and had threatened to "have the law on her" to recover his borrowed sickle.

Emily knew nothing of this controversy, which her mother had been careful not to mention; but she suspected that the Stevenses had no love for Mrs. Fletcher, and judging them on the gossip she had heard from the servants, she guessed that they were jealous of her mother's supposed wealth. Consequently, she had her qualms about approaching Rockley. It was quite probable that the carriage would not be loaned, and she weighed the idea of simply returning to Ashley House and saying that they had refused. But her natural aversion to false-hood soon overcame this temptation.

The gate was open and she crossed the garden without seeing a soul; but when she climbed the steps of the porch an old spaniel trotted up to her and began to bark. A hoarse voice quickly called to the dog from inside the house, and the door opened ab-ruptly. Emily was confronted by an old man in shabby garments, a corncob pipe in his hand. Deep wrinkles marked his face with an extremity of harsh-ness. His small bright grey eyes seemed motionless; his lips had disappeared, and when he talked he opened his mouth as if to take an enormous bite.

"What do you want?" he asked.

There was something so manifestly hostile in his appearance that Emily was annoyed and it restored her self-possession. She was not naturally timid; she closed her umbrella firmly and replied:

"I was sent by my mother, Mrs. Fletcher."

"Mrs. Fletcher?" he repeated, his pipe in his mouth, eyeing the young girl curiously. There was an odd little smile at the corners of his mouth as he told her to come in.

She followed him inside. The room was low and narrow, with two bare windows and a fireplace in which a large log burned half-heartedly on a bed of

embers. A big kitchen table stood against the wall.
From the sooty ceiling to the hard earth floor hung
a blue veil of smoke which poisoned the air with its
acrid odour. The old man took one of the two chairs
in front of the hearth, stretched his feet toward the
fire, and continued his scrutiny of the girl, waiting
for her to explain herself.

"My mother wants to ask a favour of you," she
began, sitting down.

"Does she ever speak of my sickle?" old Stevens
demanded.

Emily did not allow this enigma to break her composure. The face that confronted her was sharp
and stern, the nose filed thin as a beak, the cheeks
heavily scored and sunken in upon powerful, rapa-
cious jaws; his whole expression seemed to say: "Ask
no favours of me. I give nothing and I lend nothing." But the sense of his antagonism stirred her
irresistibly to battle, and she vigorously replied:

"I don't know what you mean. My mother wants
to go to the sale at Wilmington next Tuesday . . ."

Stevens guessed what was coming.

"And so do I," he replied drily.

"My mother hoped that you would lend her your
carriage. Ours is broken down."

"And as for me, I suppose I can go on foot, with
your kind permission."

He chortled between his teeth. Emily did not
flinch, but she felt herself growing red and she nervously brushed back a strand of hair that had fallen

across her forehead. His insolence roused a crazy desire in her to strike him with her umbrella; she wanted to retort, but could not summon her voice.

Stevens watched her in silence with a sardonic grin, and when she got up as if to go he said to her roughly:

"Sit still and get warm. It must be warmer here than it is at Ashley House, I reckon."

"Let me alone!" she exclaimed when he put out a hand to detain her, and she avoided him dexterously and scurried toward the door.

"All right," he called without getting up. "I reckon my boy has told me how you-all live up there. You freeze, that's what!"

She opened the door and closed it behind her with all her force, to escape the mocking laugh that followed her.

Some one was coming up the steps as she went out; it was Frank, the old man's son. Emily stopped abruptly and stared at him a moment; he had changed since she had seen him, but she recognized him at once. He was as tall as his father, with a tiny knob of a head on a giant's neck, and enormous arms that swung at his sides as he walked. A sort of brownish fleece covered his forehead down to his eyebrows and shadowed even more darkly his dark and deep-set eyes. Vigour and health were expressed in his massive nose, full cheeks, and heavily marked red lips, but the shifty look in his eyes was unprepossessing. He wore khaki overalls and an open shirt which rain and perspiration had glued to his skin; he walked noiselessly with a lithe swing of his body, and carried a hoe on his shoulder.

"Good evening," he said.

She tried to pass him and go down the steps, but he guessed from the anger in her eyes that she had had an encounter with his father, and said hurriedly:

"I'm sorry it was my father you saw; I ought to have been here myself. The old man's a little gruff."

She had opened her umbrella, but still did not go. It was raining vigorously and rivulets of water were sluicing down the path.

"Beg pardon if he offended you," he went on.

She stood with her back turned to him and did not answer; finally she heard him open the door.

"You ought to wait here until the rain lets up," he said. Just then the old man called from inside, and when no one answered he came out on the porch. On seeing Emily still there he grinned.

"So it's nicer here, eh?"

His son turned quickly around and glowered at him.

"How's that?" the old man said. "I told her to stay and get warm, but she didn't wish to."

"Let us in," said Frank, and he shouldered him out of the doorway. Emily remained where she stood.

"I was asking your father to lend us your carriage," she said with a quiver in her voice. "Since he does not want to, I'm going."

"No, please don't, Miss Emily," the young man urged; "we can fix it up all right."

She looked around irresolutely, then quickly closed her umbrella and went in, avoiding the two men's eyes. They followed her, first Frank and then his father, who shut the door with a bang. The young man set his hoe in the corner near the fireplace and offered the girl a chair; his courteous manners took her aback and did not altogether please her. She remembered her mother's prejudices and wondered if they were not right.

They sat down facing each other, while old Stevens took up his pipe and installed himself behind them nearer the fire.

"You see," said Frank in a deferential voice at contrast with his somewhat rough appearance, "we use the carriage twice a week—Mondays to go to Wolverton for supplies, and Saturdays to go to market."

"And how about the sale on Tuesday?" put in the old man without removing his pipe.

"You keep quiet," the son answered under his breath. The old man never stirred; his placid face revealed no feeling whatever. He sat in silence, his grey eyes fixed on Emily.

"You see, it's just this Tuesday that we need it," the girl explained.

Frank shrugged his shoulders lightly and looked

away. He did not wish to refuse and he rubbed his hands in embarrassment.

"If Mrs. Fletcher wants it some other day . . ." he finally said.

"No, it was Tuesday," Emily insisted quietly. She pinned up her shawl as if to go.

"Wait," Frank exclaimed. "Mrs. Fletcher and I can go together. Will that do?"

Emily nodded.

By degrees she had grown used to the smoky atmosphere and was almost enjoying the heavy warmth of the room. She listened to the rain's dull pounding on the pane, and noticed that it seemed to be slackening. Furtively looking about her, she discovered little things that surprised and interested her. Everything bore witness to habits of the utmost disorder. Vegetable stalks had been tossed in a heap on the floor near a stack of garden tools. Empty bottles had accumulated in a corner; the wall paper was stained and spotted; and she mentally compared this slovenliness with her mother's rigorous domestic scruples. She thought of the living room at Ashley House, its furniture dusted every day, the floor scrubbed and polished until it glistened. But there was never a fire to sit and read by in that big inhospitable room, and she cast an envious glance at the log that was burning cosily at her feet.

She arose to go, nevertheless. Frank tried to detain her longer, but she had made up her mind. "My clothes are dry now," she said, fingering the fringe of her shawl. The young man stood beside her for a moment, watching her motions out of the corner of his eye and trying unsuccessfully to think of something to say to her. The old man regarded them in silence, his hands clasped over his knees, while he leaned against the fireplace without stirring.

Frank went as far as the porch with Emily and closed the door behind him. "Miss Emily," he said suddenly, as she moved toward the steps, "I am very glad I saw you to-day. I was planning to come up to Ashley House this month, anyway."

The girl stopped.

"I have a favour to ask of Mrs. Fletcher, too," he went on, looking down. "But after two years, it's hard . . ."

"But why?" Emily asked.

"Yes, it is, Miss Emily, on account of that sickle. Mrs. Fletcher didn't like his asking for it that way."

He continued almost at once:

"She can keep it if she wants to."

She still did not understand, and said hastily:

"You can speak to my mother about it yourself when you come on Tuesday."

But he plunged in once again:

"Tell her that my wife is sick, will you?" he asked humbly. "She can't work." And he lowered his voice and added by way of apology, "She's going to have a baby."

The girl looked away; she hardly understood the meaning of his words, but she blushed without knowing quite why—perhaps on account of the look of shame on Frank's face. "A baby?" she repeated, and almost added: "But what is she sick from?"

It was raining less now. There was a moment's silence.

"If you could speak to her about us . . ." Frank ventured timidly.

She fixed her dark eyes upon him, irritated by the servility of his manner, and replied coldly: "You had better explain to her yourself."

Then she raised her umbrella and moved off rapidly. She was already out on the road when she heard Frank call from the porch: "Don't you want me to take you home in the carriage?"

She waved one arm in negation and went on her way toward Ashley House.

At first the road seemed less difficult; it was still raining a little, but she paid no heed; she walked along at a rapid pace and talked to herself in the excitement of her visit. She imagined herself describing the scene to her grandmother, mimicking the manner of old Stevens and imitating his unpleasant way of talking between his teeth; she warmed to the story and involuntarily embroidered on it. She was reporting her talk with Frank in the same grand style when she remembered that Mrs. Elliot was angry with her and would probably not see her, at least for a time. She came to a sudden halt in the middle of the road. Never had she felt so desolate.

CHAPTER THIRTEEN

* * * * * * * * * * * * * *

DISCOURAGED AND UNHAPPY, SHE
returned to Ashley House; her mother's stolid
smugness, when she met her in the hall, irritated her
more than usual. She felt that her life had all at
once changed colour; that from being merely tire-
some it had suddenly grown intolerable. Worry and
weariness combined to dishearten her. Emily knew
no better than anyone else the reason for this quick
and violent repugnance. "Perhaps it's because I am
growing up," she repeated to herself, "and can't be
satisfied any more with this kind of a life." She
wanted to shout a warning at her mother: "Don't
ask me a thing! Not a single question! Leave me
alone."

"Well, Emily"—Mrs. Fletcher rubbed her hands
—"what news?"

"Frank Stevens will come and get you in his carriage on Tuesday," she answered gruffly.

"Good!" Mrs. Fletcher gloated, and planted herself for another question. But Emily went quickly
past her and up the stairs.

"Tuesday?" her mother repeated. "Here at the
house?"

"Yes," Emily threw back as she ran up the stairs.

"Where are you going?" Mrs. Fletcher called, dissatisfied to let her escape so quickly.

"To change my clothes; they are all soaking wet."

She wanted to be alone. If it had been possible she would have run away and never seen her mother again. She felt her heart thumping with a sudden access of rage that terrified even herself. When she reached her room she rushed in headlong, locking the door behind her, and threw herself on the bed. For several minutes she lay there, wrapped in the damp folds of her long shawl, which she had forgotten to take off, and shivering with cold and with emotion. In the agitation of her spirit only one thought came to her, and she repeated it over and over to the wall:

"I'd like to die! Oh, I'd like to die!"

Finally she got up, but her head was whirling with dizziness and she let herself slip to her knees at the foot of the bed. Her ears were filled with a drumming sound; she bent her face to the coverlet, clapping her head in her hands, and struggled to drag herself up from her morbid thoughts by saying her prayers; but her lips recited words that her mind could not follow, and she began to sob in despair:

"I'm a wicked girl. Change me, O Lord, change me!"

When she rose to her feet again the dusk was descending, and she looked about her with the bewilderment of one who has just awakened; she could hardly move her hands, and she knew that she must have slept. Seeing herself in the mirror, she cried

out involuntarily; her ashen face and the long
strands of hair that clung across her forehead transformed her into a wild thing, and her eyes seemed
to grow enormous and glow with a strange dark
lustre.

A shiver passed through her body and she
thought: "I'm going to be sick." She undressed
as quickly as possible and put on a black woollen
nightgown that she wore in winter. Her feet were
icy and she struggled vainly to warm them; she put
on her slippers and rubbed her wet hair with a
towel. The thought of being ill filled her with dread.
She took an old shawl from a drawer and arranged
it like a hood, pinning it over her chest. Then she
lighted the candle and sat down at the table with
her Bible open before her.

She read from some of the Psalms. Every sentence seemed written especially for her; they warmed
her heart and brought her a melancholy solace,
teaching her that resignation to an existing order is
almost always better than rebellion, and that an act
of wrath is never an agent of good. After a while
her eyes became clouded and tears coursed over her
cheeks. She toyed mechanically with the things
around her, fluttered the leaves of the Bible, took a
match and tried to stop the wax that dripped from
the candle—intent on these small distractions to re-
lieve her consuming wretchedness.

A little later she heard her mother calling and
went down. Dinner was served, but no effort of will

could make her swallow a mouthful. She shivered incessantly. Mrs. Fletcher watched her with a distress that contained more than an element of irritation, and asked her impatiently:

"What's the matter now? You're not going to be sick, are you?"

She tried to force upon her a plateful of soup; the tragedy of seeing the dinner wasted gave her a determination quite foreign to her usual timorous tone. "Eat it!" she repeated. "I tell you you must!" But Emily obstinately shook her head.

She had to go up to bed before the dinner was over. Her mother dared not force her to wait; she even offered to help her, alarmed by her shivering. "You will be well to-morrow," she said as she went upstairs with her. "Won't you, now?"

Emily went directly to bed. She spread her clothing on top of the covers to help her keep warm and quickly fell asleep, but bad dreams startled her into wakefulness many times before morning. One in particular, more terrifying than the rest, made her groan aloud in fright. She was sitting at Rockley all alone in the room where she had been received that afternoon. A violent rain was beating on the panes. She looked about her in the gloomy half light and recognized the hearth, the chairs, the hoe leaning against the wall; and suddenly she saw her mother lying stretched at her feet, face downward, her small fat hands half closed in the gesture of grasping. For a moment Emily stared at her with-

out daring to stir. Then, slowly and difficultly, like
the memory of some remote event, it came back to
her that she had killed her with the sickle. Deliri-
ously she rushed about the room, hunting for something with which she could cover the body. At last,
on the wall behind the door, she discovered an old
brown overcoat which she tore down and threw hastily over the corpse. Somebody knocked; she barely
had time to sit down and call "Come in" when the
door opened wide as if the wind and the rain had
burst it in, and young Stevens appeared on the
threshold. Little rills of water coursed in the folds
of his clothing. He seemed embarrassed and stared
down at his shoes, but almost at once he stepped
forward and said: "I wanted to speak to Mrs.
Fletcher. It was about that sickle, miss."

Emily made no answer; she struggled to keep her
eyes off the brown overcoat, and failed; she could
hear the hoarse rasp of her breathing and it seemed
as if hours were passing. Finally the young man
walked over to the corpse and snatched away the
coat. With a shriek of terror Emily fled out through
the door, raced across the garden in full flight, and
found herself stumbling along the road in horrible
mud like quicksand. People were coming behind her,
running like herself and faster than she, and in a
moment they would overtake her—how many of them
she did not know. One of them shouted something
but the wind drowned out the words; he shouted
again and his voice was like a long wail—perhaps

not the voice of a man at all. The girl made an ultimate effort, climbed to the roadside, and began to
run her fastest, but the voice pursued her and she
shuddered with terror; it was the voice of her
mother, crying: "The sickle! the sickle!"

She awoke in a bath of perspiration. She
stretched out a trembling hand to find the candle and
matches, and was able to calm herself only when the
light was burning on the table. She sat up in bed,
motionless, her face pressed to her knees, rehearsing
the dreadful details of her nightmare. Not until
daylight would she put out the candle and go back to
sleep.

CHAPTER FOURTEEN

* * * * * * * * * * * * * * *

IT REQUIRED AN EFFORT TO MAKE
herself get up next morning. It pained her so
sharply to move her limbs that she cried at every
motion. A continual shivering shook her whole frame
and made her teeth chatter; her cheeks were aflame
with fever and her eyes glowed with an unnatural
brilliance. She went downstairs, nevertheless.

Her mother had counted on finding her recovered,
and could hardly conceal her anxiety. "What's the
matter with you?" she asked, in a voice that shook
with annoyance. "Are you going to be sick, to add
to my troubles?" Emily answered only that she was
cold, and her mother made her put on another shawl
on top of the one she was wearing, and on top of
that a man's big cape that had once been Stephen
Fletcher's. Then she was struck with what seemed
like a splendid idea: "Go up to your grandmother's
room, where there's a fire. You will be better off
there than here."

Emily acquiesced with pleasure. Of her own accord she would not have gone to her grandmother's
room, for fear of a hostile reception, but she was
happy to have the excuse of obedience and went up
without delay. Still, she hesitated at the door a mo-

ment, and called out timidly; receiving no answer, she went in.

As she sat down at the head of the bed, her grandmother awoke from a light doze and smiled cordially.

"That's a good girl," she said, and clasped Emily's hands affectionately. "You are generous to forget an unkindness so promptly. I thought about you yesterday afternoon—I missed you. Weren't you afraid I would still be cross? Never mind—it's only because I am sick, you know. I have a bad temper, but I am very fond of you, Emily."

She suddenly asked, "You didn't tell your mother?"

Emily shook her head.

"Why, what's the matter?" Mrs. Elliot exclaimed when she noticed how the girl was shivering. She fingered a corner of the cape, which she had noticed only now, and asked, "What are you wearing this for?"

The girl proceeded to tell of her visit to Rockley and her compulsory outing in the pouring rain. She added briefly that she had not been able to sleep and that whenever she closed her eyes she was haunted by nightmares. Mrs. Elliot's face became purple with indignation as the tale went on; she condemned her daughter roundly for exposing Emily to the indignities of old Stevens, and charged her with a lack of all self-respect. When Emily described her return to Ashley House on the muddy road, she cried out in wrath: "And now you are sick! and all on account of that woman and her awful stinginess. She could perfectly well have taken the train; but, oh no! that would have meant spending money"— and she mimicked her daughter's grave and worried look in matters of money. "Look at the fire she gives me—me, an invalid, and her own mother. It's not good enough for paupers, a couple of smoky sticks on a pile of cinders."

Emily leaned over and saw that the fire was actually no more than her grandmother said. The charred faggots were gradually burning out, and gave off nothing more than a sooty smoke.

"She would rather be drawn and quartered than put a single extra chip in that fireplace," Mrs. Elliot went on. "And God only knows how many cords of it she has in her cellar. Emily, my dear, there is no heart so hard as the heart of a miser. Affection counts for nothing with your mother any more."

She stopped for a moment and then said abruptly:

"Did you know that she came in here yesterday afternoon?"

"In this room?" Emily asked in surprise.

"Yes, actually into my room." She smiled expansively. "After you left for Rockley I felt sick and had to call, and she came herself."

"Why, what was the matter, Grandma?"

"Nothing, Emily, only a bad headache; but I had to call and your mother came in. Do you know it is nearly a year since she last came into my room? I can see how she has changed."

She looked at Emily and shook her head.

"Yes," she went on, "she has wrinkles around her mouth that were not there before"—she illustrated with her finger—"the wrinkles of a miserly old woman. And her complexion is dreadful. You never told me how yellow she had grown."

"She never goes out at all," Emily said.

"Oh, and how she has aged!" Mrs. Elliot pursued with a kind of vehemence, "and how ugly it makes her look! Have you noticed how she stares at you? She hardly spoke to me at all, but I could feel how spiteful and bitter she was. What a lot of things she must keep shut up inside her! Does she talk to you very much?"

"No, Grandma."

"Does she never talk about me?"

"No."

"She thinks about me just the same; that's certain. If you could have seen the expression on her face when I said I was cold and had to have more wood on the fire . . . ! Father in heaven—do you know something, Emily . . . ?"

She lowered her voice and whispered mysteriously:

"I should hate to have her fix my medicine, if I had to take any."

Emily trembled and stared at her grandmother incredulously.

"What do you mean by that, Grandma?"

Mrs. Elliot shook her head again; grey strands of

hair escaped from her bonnet and fluttered over her cheeks.

"I only say what I think, my dear," she replied with a sorrowful smile; and almost at once she continued, "I forgot to tell you that she talked about you."

She watched the girl as she said this, but Emily sat unmoved and did not utter a word. No doubt Mrs. Elliot's excited tone made her fear that yesterday's scene was going to be repeated.

"She said," Mrs. Elliot went eagerly on—"she said that increased expenses were going to force her to dismiss the cook and depend on you to do all the housework with her."

She stopped a moment to appraise the effect of her words. A flush of pink was mounting Emily's cheeks.

"I heard her, absolutely," Mrs. Elliot said, a little louder. "She was stooping down in front of the fireplace putting the wood on, and she muttered it between her teeth. If she had said it to my face, I don't think I would have hated her so for it; but do you suppose she would dare?—she is such a coward . . ."

She sat up suddenly in bed and shook her fist at the door, crying with bitter stress: "You contemptible creature! God's punishment be on you!"

Her forehead and cheeks grew purple. She seized the hand of the terrified Emily and shook it violently while she said: "She wants to get rid of me.   She says I eat up all her money."

She became breathless with emotion, and she watched her granddaughter with eyes full of anger and anguish; tears quivered on the lids, and she opened her lips but could not form a word.

"But she never even speaks of you, Grandma," Emily protested.   "She's not going to touch you; I promise you."

"It's no use," Mrs. Elliot moaned in a stifled voice. "She has made up her mind to poison me."

Roughly dropping the hand to which she was clinging, she hid her face in the covers and burst into sobs.

CHAPTER FIFTEEN

* * * * * * * * * * * * * *

MRS. FLETCHER KNEW NOTHING of these conferences between her mother and her daughter, and was far from suspecting that she played so important a rôle in them. Sometimes, to be sure, she wondered what Emily and Mrs. Elliot could find to beguile the time, but her curiosity was not very active and she satisfied herself by saying: "She probably teaches her her catechism or makes her read the Bible." She left entirely to Mrs. Elliot the responsibility for teaching the girl, and gave herself no concern to find out just what might constitute her educational program. "She will teach her what she taught me," she sometimes thought, "and that's enough."

This left her completely master of her time, and she abandoned herself to the thousand and one petty matters of which her days consisted. She was up before daybreak and went herself to wake the cook, an old negress who had belonged to the Fletchers as a child and had not chosen to leave them when the war set her nominally free. During his lifetime Stephen Fletcher had never paid her any wages, but he always spoke to her in a tone of friendliness that he accorded to no one else, and treated her with the greatest degree of kindness. As for Mrs. Fletcher, she deemed it sufficient to give her her meals and allow her to sleep on an old straw mattress in a garret; she rarely spoke a word to her that was not a command, and always in a voice that her timidity made curt and disobliging.

By half past five the two women were already at work, the negress doing her baking and Mrs. Fletcher sweeping the rooms and dusting the furniture. This took until half past six. A little later Emily came down and found the dining room in order and breakfast on the table, her only task each day being to clean her own room and carry out the program of sewing that her mother assigned each morning.

The rest of the day moved rapidly for Mrs. Fletcher. In addition to the tasks of the chambermaid whom she had dismissed, she set herself unending little duties that almost always kept her active until evening. She never neglected to examine all the rooms in the house to be sure that nothing was missing and nothing broken; she counted and recounted the miscellaneous knicknacks that Stephen Fletcher had brought back with him from his travels —she had allotted to each a specified place from which it was not to be budged. For the last few years the most elaborate suspicions had haunted her. She readily attributed covetous designs to anyone and everyone who came near Ashley House, including those who lived there. She went up to the garret surreptitiously almost every day and carefully examined the cook's wretched mattress, inspired by a fear that the old negress would tuck away some little object or other between the ticking; and she felt the mattress up and down and back and forth. She even went so far as to look through the old cook's personal belongings to see if she had hidden coins or bills. From similar motives of precaution she scribbled the names of her most treasured possessions on little scraps of paper; this clumsy inventory she slipped between the leaves of her Bible, and checked it jealously several times a week. She had no regard for any qualities in the objects themselves, but only for the contingency of some day finding it convenient to get a little money for them.

For her naturally morbid leanings made her anticipate a future of the direst misery, so that she lived in constant dread of the years to come. Nothing would ease this doleful apprehensiveness, and there were times when her fears unaccountably multiplied and assumed a precise objective. She would live in agony for a while and talk of nothing but selling Ashley House or discovering new economies to eke out her waning funds. Her mind was a prey to more and more suspicions, which kept her uneasy by day and sleepless at night. She would get up in the darkest hours and go downstairs to assure herself again that all the doors and windows were securely fastened; and timid as she was she roamed about the house with her lighted candle to hunt out any burglars who might be hiding.

For a long period she was tormented with one particular fear. She would jump out of bed, when everyone else was asleep, and tiptoe to the door of the cook's little room, where she would stand and listen to her regular breathing. She accused her mentally of planning to run off with the silverware in her pockets; a theft of that sort would be so easy, and she often said to herself, "If I thought of it myself, why mightn't she?" And she never went back to bed until she had gone down to the dining room and hastily counted the spoons and forks, which she kept tied up in packages of tens to facilitate her reckoning. They were always locked away in the cabinet, and she carried the key about her neck, but her precautions only magnified her mistrust and made her say to herself: "Since I take such care of them, there must be some danger; my instinct would not deceive me." And in the silence of the night she lay recalling just how the cook had acted throughout the day. She would find, for example, that she had been more sullen than usual; that she had twice come into the parlour to speak to her, contrary to all precedent. Her inflamed imagination pictured her forcing the door of the cabinet and speeding away from Ashley House with the silver in her apron, while she herself, its rightful owner, turned and tossed in her bed and wondered whether or not to go down once more and see. "I must!" she would say at the end of a half hour's torment; and quickly as possible she would slip down again.

One winter she decided that she could endure it no longer. She remembered how she had once sold some gold and silver pins that her husband had given her in the early days of their marriage, and she determined to do likewise with the tableware. To avoid possible friction with her daughter, she took refuge in a ruse. She announced that the silver was not to be used except when company came—something that had not happened at Ashley House since Stephen Fletcher's death—and then she packed it away and replaced it with plated ware. A few months' habit confirmed the substitution, and Emily would have forgotten the real silver entirely if it had not come to her mind one day when she was reckoning up the things that were to be hers. She went to the dining room and stooped down in front of the cabinet. By a miracle the key was in the lock. She opened the door, pulled out the oaken chest with the copper plaque on its lid, and looked inside. But her hand groped in vain in its green-velvet-lined depths—the chest was empty.

Mrs. Fletcher had carried out her scheme with the utmost secrecy, not untempered with misgivings which haunted her for a long time. But excuses easily manufactured themselves, and she ended by being persuaded that she had acted for the best. She regained some of her peace of mind, but still lacked the requisite courage to tell Emily. Nevertheless, she wanted Emily to know that she had sold it, and wanted her to understand and approve. She debated about how to circumvent her anger. First she removed the key from around her neck and returned it to the lock; then she took pains to speak of the silver from time to time, saying how useless it was to them, how much it was worth in money, and how badly the money was needed to keep up Ashley House without dipping into their capital. Emily listened to her mother abstractedly, but perhaps it was these daily allusions, working unperceived, that finally gave her the impulse to look at the silver.

When she saw that the chest was empty, she immediately thought of thieves; but she was not slow to abandon that notion and guess the truth. She hated her mother for it and wept with chagrin in her own room; but she mastered her anger and constrained herself to be still. Nothing could have irritated Mrs. Fletcher more. Unable to discover whether her daughter knew the fate of the silver or not, she felt her misgivings little by little displaced by spite and rancour. It embittered her to think that even in a small degree her peace of mind could depend on a word from Emily, and that Emily would not speak it. But, a week later, when the storm at last broke which she had so desired and dreaded, her initial outburst of anger and indignation made way for a vast relief. Her mind asked only forgetfulness to restore her composure, and she quickly resumed the normal course of her thoughts.

CHAPTER SIXTEEN

* * * * * * * * * * * * * * * *

SHE ALWAYS FELT THAT HER
task had scarcely begun, and that all the economies she had practised until then counted for nothing. This idea returned to her with obstinate insistence, and she repeated over and over, "It is all
still to be done."

Nevertheless, she extracted a singular pleasure
from the cares that harassed her, happy in her un-
happiness—which is the true token of an absorbing
passion. She loved to tell herself that her vigilance
might spare her from a complete catastrophe; but
she never evaded its possibility, and she lingered
over these dismal thoughts with a perverse complacency. Then she would return with renewed zeal
to figuring her accounts and weighing her chances
of finding enough money to tide her over—for the
sum deposited in the bank at Wilmington was not
to be brought into account. In everything she saw
about her, she considered only the market value.
Sometimes in the morning, even before she went to
wake the cook, she would go from room to room
with an appraising eye on each article of furniture
and ornament, or she would sit in her favourite arm-

chair, hands clasped in her lap, absorbed in calculations endlessly recommenced.

She no longer talked to anyone, except to her daughter at meals, and her life became more and more circumscribed. The years increased her natural timidity, which had always been excessive. When she had to give orders to the cook, she sometimes fell into abject stammering, and her annoyance was aggravated when the old negress had to ask her to repeat herself. Mrs. Fletcher was taken off her guard whenever anyone spoke to her unexpectedly; she found herself unable to answer without laborious thought, and suffered so acutely from her mental sluggishness that she avoided even the most commonplace conversations when they threatened to prolong themselves. It was this, above all, that made her avoid her mother; she stood in terror of her taunts and sallies even though the years had greatly dimmed Mrs. Elliot's powers of ridicule.

One day, however, she was sewing in the dining room when she heard a cry from her mother's bedroom. She dropped her work from her hands and listened in trepidation. The house was lapped in silence. For the first time since she had lived at Ashley House, she became aware of the terrors of solitude. The cook was in the village, Emily had gone to the Stevenses to ask for the carriage, and she was alone at Ashley House with a bedridden old invalid. What was there to prevent a tramp from coming in?—and there were always dangerous negroes prowling about. She asked herself what she could do if she were attacked. People at Wilmington were complaining all the time about shiftless rowdies who found stealing the easiest way to make a living—and she thought at once of young Stevens, with his shifty eyes and his enormous fists. Visions of murder and violence surged in her mind, and she suddenly stood up and clapped her hand to her mouth. Perhaps her mother had cried out for help; perhaps she was being murdered at this very moment! Mrs. Fletcher stood where she was, leaning against the back of her armchair. Finally, as she heard nothing more, she went as far as the door into the hall, and waited a moment, listening.

The silence restored her confidence a little; she went upstairs to her mother's room and timidly knocked. There was no answer. Suddenly struck with a new fear, she opened the door hysterically and burst into the room. Mrs. Elliot was stretched supine across the bed; her cap had slipped from her head and her grey hair straggled over her face. The covers were in confusion; everything testified to the violent contortions that had brought her to this position; but at present she lay rigid, breathing in gasps that noisily caught in her throat. Mrs. Fletcher went over to her. Timorously brushing back the strands of hair, she uncovered a face that was haggard and purple and a pair of staring eyes.

As soon as Mrs. Elliot was able to speak, she asked where Emily was. Mrs. Fletcher, bringing in a

basin of water, curtly replied that she had gone out.
No more words were exchanged for several minutes.
Mrs. Elliot's face was calmer, but her features retained a fixity that gave her the look of an imbecile.
Now and again she would move her lips as if to speak,
but her tongue was so dry that she could not form
the sounds she attempted, without an extreme and
painful effort. Nevertheless, in a little while she
called to her daughter, who was putting things away
in the dressing room, and enunciated hoarsely, "I'm
cold."

Mrs. Fletcher came over to the bed and made the
motion of covering her mother's feet with a blanket
which she had tossed aside; but Mrs. Elliot said
"No!" emphatically and pointed to the fireplace,
where the charred remnants of a fire were burning
out.

Mrs. Fletcher did not answer immediately. She
rested her hands on the bedstead and stood there
uneasily; the excitement of the whole scene had left
her slightly tremulous, and she appeared to be shaking her head in refusal.

"Well?" her mother demanded several times over,
tapping on the covers with her fingers like an impatient child.

Mrs. Fletcher looked away and again went into
the dressing room for a moment. She knew she dared
not refuse to bring up more wood, but the demand
exasperated her; ordinarily not more than five logs
were needed for the day in Mrs. Elliot's room, and

when the fire went out about three in the afternoon, it was not rebuilt until the next day. In the dining room, even in the most rigorous cold, no fire was ever lighted. "One fire is enough for a house," Mrs. Fletcher repeated, and let it go at that.

She rearranged some bottles on a shelf, shoved a chair against the wall, made little noises so that her mother would believe her to be busy. She sought in vain for any excuse not to bring up extra wood; she became furious at herself, at her ineffectiveness against Mrs. Elliot. "What am I—a little girl?" she asked herself. "Who is mistress here, anyway?" But for all she could say, she could not muster the courage to hold out against her mother. She finally went back to the bedroom and moved rapidly toward the door, hoping that she might escape before her mother spoke of the fire again, so that she could pretend to have forgotten it. But the old woman was aroused the moment she reappeared and called out with irritation, "Get that wood right away!"

A quarter of an hour later Mrs. Fletcher returned with wood and kindling. Her face was crimson and she was biting her lip. She closed the door behind her with her foot, grumbling in a low voice.

"What did you say?" asked Mrs. Elliot.

Mrs. Fletcher made no answer. Lifting up her skirt, she knelt down before the hearth and arranged the wood on the andirons; then she rose and let down the screen with her foot, making a great clatter. She had set the matches down somewhere in the room,

and in hunting for them she avoided Mrs. Elliot's
eye; her indignation at what she considered her
mother's senile extravagance was so great that she
almost forgot her dread of a dispute and had to
check herself from some provocative remark.

At length she found the matches and lighted the
kindling; then she sat down near the fire, brushing
the stray hair from her forehead, and began to take
notice of this room which she so rarely saw. The
furniture was carefully dusted, the curtains clean
and tidy; Emily's hand was apparent here, and she
congratulated herself that her daughter took after
her in her sense of orderliness. By a habitual trick
of her mind, she commenced to appraise the odds and
ends and bric-à-brac that adorned the mantel and
shelves. Gradually she regained her self-possession.

"Tell me what you are saying," insisted Mrs. Elliot, who heard her muttering from time to time.

Mrs. Fletcher started up. "What?" she said. "I
wasn't talking."

The fire had begun to catch and she raised the
screen again vigorously and set about sweeping the
hearth. Her face was deeply flushed. All at once
she put down the hearth brush and quickly left the
room without a word.

Downstairs in the dining room again, she seated
herself near the window. She found it hard to resume her work; she was chagrined and humiliated
that her mother had caught her talking to herself,
and she sat fumbling in her workbasket and mutter-

ing between her teeth. Up to that time she had been able to ignore Mrs. Elliot's presence in the house and had deluded herself with her sense of authority at Ashley House; but during the past hour she had come to understand that her mother was effectively installed there and would depart only when death should summon her. This knowledge filled her with a hideous exasperation. Mrs. Elliot cost money; she had to be fed and her room kept warm, and with it all she was frightfully difficult and exacting. Giving way to her rising wrath, Mrs. Fletcher suddenly exclaimed: "Why is she alive, anyway? What is she good for in the world?"

The brutality of her questions put her to shame, and she turned her thoughts to the articles which her husband had assembled in this room. Mrs. Elliot had had all the chairs done over in plush to harmonize with the green of the rugs and curtains; the resulting effect of affluence did not escape Mrs. Fletcher. If it came to a sale, she thought, she ought to get a good price. Besides, all these furnishings were her own because she had paid the upholsterer's bill out of her own pocket; but even so, how could she think of disposing of them before they had outworn their usefulness? A single contingency could make it possible; she checked herself from wishing it, but the thought was none the less clear. "After she is dead . . ." she said to herself—and left the thought unfinished.

The work of the day was done and she was roaming about the house when Emily returned from Rockley. In the dim light of the hall she failed to notice that the girl was blanched and shivering, but a little later, in the lamplight, she recognized that Emily was really ill and was immediately smitten with painful apprehensions. All through dinner she kept saying to herself with a fearfulness that betrayed itself in her face: "Now she is going to be sick, and that will mean calling a doctor."

She retired early and slept badly. Several times she got out of bed to kneel and pray for Emily's quick recovery. Her imagination played with possible cures; she racked her memory for old prescriptions against coughs and chills. Each time that the thought of actually calling a doctor occurred to her, she put it aside with a sort of violent obstinacy. She held a personal resentment against her daughter for causing her this anxiety, and grew exasperated at the memory of her pallid face and trembling shoulders. The little beast! Couldn't she have waited until it stopped raining before she went out? Wasn't it enough of a cross to have one sick person in the house?

Reviewing the events of the day, she remembered the fire which she knew would now have to be kept from morning until dark in her husband's old room. She was too well acquainted with her mother not to know that she would require it; and what could she do against her? Refuse to give her more than the five logs which had sufficed for so long? Of that she was incapable. Her passion for economy, which otherwise ruled her with so firm a hand, gave way at this point. Plainly, she was afraid of her mother. A little reflection could have shown her that her fears were groundless and that Mrs. Elliot's designs, criminal as they might be, were ineffectual against her. She was little else than a prisoner in her bed. Nevertheless, Mrs. Fletcher did not for an instant admit the possibility of disobeying her, of standing out against her—at any rate openly. It was no devotion to principle that guided her in this, but something more instinctive, like fear of open spaces or fear of the dark.

So she gave way to resignation, and said dolefully to herself again and again in the silence of the night: "It has to be; she must have her fire from morning to night all winter." Whispering these words despondently, she fretted herself to tears, and tossed and turned in her bed until after midnight without being able to sleep. Finally, when her thoughts wandered back to her daughter again, the idea occurred to her of turning this miserable fire to the girl's advantage. Emily needed warmth to restore her to health. Why not let her stay in her grandmother's room entirely until she was quite well again? Thus the doctor would be avoided. The plan appeared excellent; Mrs. Fletcher found comfort in it and fell asleep.

CHAPTER SEVENTEEN

* * * * * * * * * * * * * * * *

THE NEXT MORNING, WHEN SHE saw how haggard and spiritless Emily was, she fell prey to acute apprehensions. After her high hopes of what a warm bed would do for her, she found her worse off than the night before. This disappointment greatly vexed her and she was seized with a sudden desire to abuse the girl for it; but she managed to control herself. She wrapped her up in warm clothing and suggested without preliminaries, as if it had just occurred to her, that the girl should spend the day in Mrs. Elliot's room. She was so well pleased at finding her amenable that for a moment she forgot her fears.

Uneasiness invaded her again, however, as soon as she was alone. She bent to her sewing with a will, but this mechanical labour, instead of fending off thought, seemed rather to stimulate it, and from time to time she would say half aloud, with an energy that betrayed what firm dominion the thought held over her mind: "I don't want any doctors here at Ashley House!"

This time Emily did not forsake her grandmother. She waited until her first access of distress had

passed and consoled her as best she could; this was
not difficult, for Mrs. Elliot possessed an almost
childlike fickleness of temper which age and illness
had exaggerated. Hearing her granddaughter's as-
sertions of loyalty, she wiped her eyes on the coverlet
and soon began to smile.

"I can trust you," she said. "If there was no one
I could trust, how could I ever go on living?"

Two hours later the cook brought up a large tray
laden with plates and dishes, and placed it on a table
which she arranged at Mrs. Elliot's bedside. Josephine was a tall, thin figure, dressed in black of excessive neatness and wearing a white lace cap from
which long ribbons dangled. She was very old, and
the skin of her face had acquired the greyish-yellow
tinge peculiar to unhealthy negroes; little white
wisps of hair curled out all around her forehead.
She wore steel-rimmed spectacles and talked with a
soft Southern drawl.

"Mis' Fletcher want for you-all to eat your luncheon here, Miss Emily," she said; and she added timidly: "You'll be better off here than in the dining
room nohow, missy."

"Josephine," Mrs. Elliot demanded unexpectedly,
"are you happy at Ashley House?"

Josephine hesitated a moment.

"Ah belongs to Mis' Fletcher," she decided at
last.

"That's not true. You are free; you can leave
her if you want to."

"But where would she go?" put in Emily.

"Ah reckon Ah don't want to go nowheres, Mis' Elliot. Ah wants to stay right here," Josephine affirmed.

"Then you must be happy, aren't you?" Mrs. Elliot insisted.

"The Lord God want for me to be . . ."

"Never mind that!" Mrs. Elliot said with a troubled laugh. "Don't blame Heaven for everything. You sound like the beginning of a sermon."

She dismissed her then and began her luncheon with excellent appetite, for she had a fundamental vigour of health which her unnatural mode of life had not succeeded in destroying. Nevertheless, another apoplectic stroke a little more violent than the others would have done for her.

Emily ate little, but she was already feeling the good effects of the heat which prevailed in the room, and she heartily enjoyed the change which had been wrought in her program of existence. She was enchanted merely to escape from eating with her mother. Mrs. Elliot put herself out to display a kindly concern for her and deluged her with questions about how she felt. In an effort to amuse her she marshalled laborious and childish jokes which brought the glimmer of a smile to the girl's wan face, whereupon Mrs. Elliot laughed boisterously and clapped her hands with glee. They renewed their conversation when the meal was finished. Emily gave constant attention to the fire, so that it lent a

mild sort of cheer to this room which was usually
so like the other cheerless rooms at Ashley House,
and encouraged the two women to converse with
greater warmth than usual and without the under-
current of reserve that sometimes tinged their talk
even now. Emily reverted frequently to her dreams
of the future. She talked of them openly to her
grandmother, and often began with such a phrase
as "When I am older . . ." or, without thinking of
its implications, "When Ashley House belongs to
me . . ." Mrs. Elliot seemed to approve of these
locutions, and she gave Emily encouraging glances
and murmured with a smile: "Well, what will you
do?" And when Emily had finished the sketch of
Ashley House under her administration, the old
woman accepted it with an obvious willingness and
added touches of her own which proved that the
thought was not a new one to her.

"How happy we shall be, my dear," she would say.
"I'll be better then—some day I'll even get up. Wait
and see. Then I shall go all through the house and
see just what rooms need doing over. . . . But will
you let me give you advice?"

"Why, Grandma! Of course!"

"Good. The parlour will be opened up again."

"We'll take the chintz covers off all the chairs."

"There will be new wall paper and new curtains
—I am sure that everything is in terrible shape. We
must have four servants, as in your father's time,
and a gardener and a coachman besides. Emily

dear, Ashley House will be completely transformed.
And it will all be your very own."

Emily bubbled over with childish glee as if her
dream were on the point of coming true. She drew
her chair up to the bedside, clasped her hands around
her knees, and stared at her grandmother in a glow
of eagerness. The feverish sparkle of her eyes gave
a sort of wry charm to her pinched face; she began
to talk with unrestrained animation.

"In each room there will be big baskets of firewood," she said, "the way there used to be in the
dining room, and we'll keep the fires burning as long
as we like. You shall have two fine lamps in your
room, and a new rug, too. Perhaps we could have
gas put in."

Hastily but comprehensively she recited the
changes and improvements that she had in mind for
Ashley House. No item in its deterioration since
Stephen Fletcher's death had escaped her attentive
eye, and her memory jealously hoarded up all the
little economies of her mother's régime. It was not
so much that she suffered from the retrenchments
which Mrs. Fletcher deemed necessary—she adjusted
herself readily enough, being naturally simple of
taste; but an imperative instinct drove her on to
oppose her mother's wishes and make every effort to
thwart them.

There was still another motive for her anxiety
—the fear lest Mrs. Fletcher, needing money, might
appropriate pictures or furniture.

"Grandma," she said once, interrupting herself in the middle of a sentence, "you did say that Ashley House would belong to me, didn't you?" Her voice was tremulous and she clenched her hands until the finger tips were bloodless.

"Why, there's no question about it, Emily!"

The girl pondered a while.

"Then how can I keep Mamma from selling off the things in the house? She has already sold the silver, and other things, too. Weren't they partly mine? If I am to inherit the whole of Ashley House some day, doesn't everything here belong to me already, in a way?"

"Certainly!" Mrs. Elliot affirmed. "Nothing could be clearer. Can't you see that that woman is robbing you?"

She lifted herself a little in bed, and propping herself on the pillow, she put an arm around Emily and said to her:

"Did I have to tell you that Ashley House belonged to you? You saw that for yourself, Emily. You have wits—and you must have courage, too. Don't let yourself be taken in. Don't let her cheat you. I am always here to help you with advice, and you will never know her as I do. She's only a weakling, but when her avarice is involved she never gives in."

Her voice suddenly rose and became almost a shout; her face was overcast with violent anger.

"She's like an animal with its prey," she cried; "she and her money, money, money!"

She seemed to imitate the grommelling of a dog over its bone; then she drew her arm away from her granddaughter and lifted her hands to her head with a theatrical gesture.

"How long will you let that woman lord it over you?" she went on. "Every day that you lose is a day gained for her. Before long you won't count for anything; you won't even dare speak to her."

She clutched her granddaughter's wrist and shook her arm.

"Don't you understand? You must resist her, you must be brave, make her know that the house belongs to you. Why, if I were your age, knowing her as I do, knowing that she never had a grain of good in her . . . do you know what I would do?"

She saw the apprehension in Emily's face and stopped.

"Never mind," she said more calmly. "I let myself go and it scared you; but you are only a child."

And she clasped her in a vehement embrace.

CHAPTER EIGHTEEN

* * * * * * * * * * * * * * * *

IT WAS DECIDED THAT EMILY should sleep in her grandmother's room that night, and perhaps the succeeding nights as well, if she had not improved. This was a sort of adventure for her, and she welcomed it as she welcomed any break in her monotonous routine. Josephine helped her to make up her bed on an ottoman, which they then pushed against the wall so that she had to climb over its back to go to bed. This amused her, and she insisted on trying out her bed at once and found it very comfortable.

Toward the end of the afternoon she moved a chair up to the fire and began to read, but in a moment or two the book dropped in her lap; she could not force herself to follow the lines, and her mind, grown suddenly restive, set off on long and tortuous reveries. For several hours no thought had been in her brain except the vexed enigma of her future, and she asked herself over and over this same question, "What is to become of me?" It was like a presentiment, and she grew nervous and uneasy at the thought that perhaps some evil was awaiting her, some great catastrophe, and that she could do nothing to avert or even foresee it. She mentally compared herself to a blind man walking among people who cried out: "Take care! You are too near the top of the cliff!"—and who still continued toward his doom because it was invisible to him. She actually imagined that an inner voice was warning her of a very proximate danger and urging her to save herself. But why were its words not clear?

Her grandmother was asleep and she could hear her regular and strident breathing. Emily recalled the transformation that had been worked in her face and the burning glow in her eyes when she had spoken of Mrs. Fletcher. The memory made her shudder, and for the first time she asked herself, "But why should she hate her so?"

She let the day go by without renewing her conversation with Mrs. Elliot, and they dined together in silence. Mrs. Elliot's waking mood was taciturn, and she made no offer to talk. Soon after dinner she complained of a bad headache and settled herself to sleep; it was not yet nine o'clock.

Emily sat by the dying fire and tried to pursue the reading which she had abandoned before; but she read and reread each page without success, the sentences carried no meaning to her. She closed her eyes and amused herself by listening to the little domestic noises, familiar enough in themselves but new to her at this hour and from this angle. First she heard the sound of dishes, which meant that the cook was cleaning up the pantry; then her mother's footsteps as she went from room to room to see that the doors and windows were safely locked. Finally silence possessed the entire house.

She waited a long time, staring into the fire or toying with the poker to gather up the remnants of the log. These were quickly spent and soon nothing was left but a bed of glowing embers, rapidly paling already. She thought, "I'll stay here until the fire is entirely out." But it was something else, something unavowed, that kept her there in her chair: she was afraid in this room. She heard the wandering voice of the wind and it set her shivering. Superstitious terrors clutched her and she dared not turn round or make the slightest motion.

When she heard the stroke of ten from the dining room clock, she finally got up. The fire had long been out and it had begun to grow cold. While she undressed she recited her prayers to overcome her fear; but a persistent thought dominated her mind in spite of her efforts to down it, "It was in this room that my father died." She lifted off her clothes with quick little nervous motions, and never looked down or shifted her eyes from the door, as if she expected and feared to see it open under a supernatural impulsion.

She opened the window, blew out the lamp, and bounded into her improvised bed. Her heart pounded violently; she turned her face to the wall and drew the covers up above her head. Thus fortified, she felt herself secure, and before she knew it she had fallen asleep.

She awoke convulsively from a restless sleep, haunted with ugly dreams. The darkness was impenetrable. She felt bedewed with perspiration and raised herself in her bed, shivering, brushing away with her hand the strands of hair that clung to her forehead. She heard her grandmother muttering something in her sleep and knew that it must have been this faint sound of words that had wakened her.

Burying herself in the covers, she strove to drive away her beleaguering terror by reciting a psalm she had once learned; but her memory forsook her. She was frantically beginning to say the Lord's Prayer aloud, when a sort of stifled howl suddenly constricted her heart with fright. She guessed that her grandmother was in the throes of a nightmare and she tried to call to her; but her voice stuck in her throat and she tried in vain.

She could only wait and listen to the short and laboured breathing of Mrs. Elliot as she lay there moaning in her sleep. For minutes that seemed interminable Emily remained unmoving, her fingers clutching the back of the ottoman, her legs doubled under her, while she held her breath to hear this painful muttering which froze her with fright. Finally she made out the sound of covers rustled by feverish hands and tossed in a heap on the floor; then almost at once a long hoarse call shivered across her ears. "Kill her!" the old woman shouted in her dream. "She wants to poison me. Kill her, I say!"

Beyond these words the girl heard nothing. She had the sensation of struggling against an oppressive weight; then she sank back suddenly in bed and lost all consciousness of what was happening.

When she came to herself a ribbon of light lay across the rug on the floor between the ottoman and her armchair. Her first thought was that she had just wakened from a hideous nightmare, and she was turning toward the wall to sleep again when she remembered her grandmother's cry. The memory was so sharp and insistent that she could not doubt its evidence, and she shuddered as if she had heard it a second time. She turned her eyes toward the corner of the room where Mrs. Elliot slept, but the bed was only a hulking shape of shadows and she could distinguish nothing. Listening, she heard only the sound of her own breathing. She was struck with an overwhelming fear which stirred her in spite of herself, and she bounded out of the ottoman and ran toward her grandmother's bed.

The old woman lay with her face buried in her pillow. A sheet was tangled about her legs; the blankets were all on the floor. Her shoulders slowly heaved under the effort of difficult breathing.

Emily clung to the bedpost to steady herself. She remembered with a shudder that in this same bed and in this same position she had seen her father for the last time; it seemed as though her grandmother were reënacting, by some grotesque mimicry, the final moments of her father.

Two or three minutes passed before the girl could bring a semblance of order to the thoughts which besieged her. Her eyes sought for the torn place in the shirt, from neck to shoulder, and she was startled not to find it there. For a moment, even though she saw her breathing, she believed that Mrs. Elliot was dead; her mind darkened in confusion. Then she reasserted herself against her fear and repulsion; she gathered up the blankets which lay at her feet, tossed them over her grandmother's legs, and covered up her body.

She waited a little; then she rested her hand on the old woman's forehead in the hope of wakening her; but Mrs. Elliot did not stir. Losing control of herself again, she fell on her knees at the bedside; her anxiety poured forth in tears, and she began to plead with her grandmother for a reply and reassurance; finally she seized her by the shoulder and turned her forcibly over on her back.

She found herself shaking so that she could not go on. Mrs. Elliot lay stretched before her, her face concealed by a tangle of straggling hair. One lock came down across her lips so that each breath she took set it vigorously flying, and the effect was so repulsive, so sordidly ludicrous, that Emily turned away. Automatically she picked up a book which had slipped down between the bed and the wall, and hunted out from under a blanket Mrs. Elliot's be-

draggled cap, from which a ribbon had been ripped,
no doubt in the effort of tearing the cap from her
head.

Though she doubted that her courage could endure it, she drew herself together and advanced her
finger tips to brush back the hair which lay tangled
over Mrs. Elliot's face. The countenance that she
uncovered was so flushed and swollen that it terrified
her and she could scarcely recognize it in the dim
light. She drew back. The motionless body, the
uncertain early-morning twilight, this room—all at
once beset her with a monstrous and tragic ugliness.
Her knees flexed, she thought herself ready to fall,
and, panic-stricken, she rushed to the door.

Outside, by groping along the walls, she found the
top step of the stairway and sat down. It occurred
to her to go to her own room for the rest of the night,
but she hesitated before the thought of traversing
the silent rooms and darkened corridors. On the
other hand, nothing could induce her, she thought, to
reënter her grandmother's room.

It was bitter cold; Emily shivered, rubbing her
bare feet between her hands. Now and then she
heard the branches of the pine trees stirring in the
wind and brushing against the sides of the house
like groping fingers. She said over and over, in an
effort to reassure herself: "I am going to stay right
here until broad daylight. I'm not afraid out here
as I am in the room there."

The minutes went slowly by; the quarter sounded

from the clock in the dining room. Emily huddled against the wall and tried to sleep, but cold and fear of the dark prevented her; there was no window on the stairway and without a lamp it was impossible to see.

Since she had been sitting down, she found herself unable to move, or so much as to lift an arm, without acute pain in the joints. But finally the cold became too much for her and she surrendered; she grasped the stair rail and lifted herself laboriously.

The floor creaked horribly under her feet; the noise frightened her, and she stood for several minutes not daring to take a step. Finally she went down to the dining room. It was nearly half past four, and the daylight was seeping through the slats of the shutters. She opened a window and breathed again. The sky was grey, a few stars still showing among the branches; and she stood there, listening, appeased, while the sound of cockcrow drifted up from the valley.

CHAPTER NINETEEN

* * * * * * * * * * * * * * *

SOME TIME LATER, EMILY SAT BY the fire in her grandmother's room, reading aloud from the Bible. At intervals she would interrupt herself to ask, with a glance toward Mrs. Elliot's bed: "Can you hear me well enough? I'm not reading too fast, am I?" "No, it's all right. Go on," Mrs. Elliot would answer, and the girl would resume her reading. She was wrapped in a coarse grey woollen shawl that covered her shoulders and hung almost to her feet, and she sat bent over the book, which she held on her knees. From her emaciated face she looked out with eyes both lively and thoughtful, in a singular and nunlike attitude. She held the Bible with both hands and looked up frequently at the portrait of her father hanging above the bureau. At such moments she appeared engrossed in difficult inner thoughts; her forehead was scored with creases and something in her eyes suggested a painful inward conflict; but almost at once she would lower her glance and continue with her reading.

After a moment she suddenly said: "Grandma, I've read enough. You must rest now." Without awaiting a reply, she rose and placed the Bible on the table where it ordinarily lay; then she went to the window and looked out, pressing her forehead against the pane. She could see the broad lawn stretching away under the trees and the great grey rocks that circumscribed the garden. Better weather had set in, but the wind still blew with vigour and she could see the tree tops indolently nodding.

"What are you looking at?" Mrs. Elliot asked, drawing her bed curtain aside.

"I wanted to see if it was clearing off."

"The weather is all the same to me," the old woman said, and she let the curtain fall back into place. Her voice was weary and vague, and her words seemed to cost her great effort.

Emily returned to her chair without replying, and sat facing the window so that she could look out. She took a garment from the laundry basket beside her and unfolded it on her lap. She fingered it over carefully to see if it needed mending; finding a torn place, she drew a spool of thread and a needle from the pocket of her apron. Her grandmother, who had been watching her without a word, now said:

"You are very industrious, Emily."

"Yes, Grandma," the girl replied without looking up. She began her sewing in silence, and Mrs. Elliot's next remark was touched with resentment:

"I see you don't care to talk to your old grandmother."

Emily pretended not to have heard and appeared absorbed in her task. She drew the needle attentively in and out, bending over her stitches, and her hair hung down in long strands across her forehead. Mrs. Elliot watched her for a while, then shrugged her shoulders and turned over in bed as if to sleep.

Her breathing became more even, and she seemed to be dozing off, when the sound of carriage wheels in front of the house aroused her, and she excitedly asked, "What's that?"

Emily was standing at the window, looking gravely out.

"It's young Stevens come to fetch Mamma to go to that sale," she said; and she added, leaning a little to one side so as to see better: "It's a very small carriage. . . . . May I open the window a minute?"

"Surely." Mrs. Elliot sat up.

Emily opened it softly and looked out without leaning over the sill. Her grandmother heard the sound of voices from the veranda and recognized her daughter's. "What are they saying?" she asked.

"Oh, nothing," Emily answered, closing the window. "Mamma wanted to know if there would be room for a valise."

"What is young Stevens doing?" Mrs. Elliot pressed, in a tone of keen curiosity. "Describe him to me."

"He is standing by his horse, holding it by the bridle."

"But what does he look like?"

"I described him to you before, Grandma. He is quite tall. To-day he is dressed better than he was last week. He has on a black coat and coarse blue serge trousers."

"What about his face?"

"Why, Grandma, I told you all about him the other day! Besides, he keeps his head down all the time—all I can see is a sort of fur cap."

"Would you call him handsome, Emily?" Mrs. Elliot asked after thinking a moment.

Emily looked around in surprise.

"Handsome?" she repeated. "Oh no!" And she began to laugh. She partly opened the window again and said in a minute or two, as if to herself: "There they go. They'll be very uncomfortable. I wonder what Mamma will bring back."

She closed the window and quietly resumed her work, but from the corner of her eye she could see her grandmother burrowing down in bed to find herself a comfortable place for a nap. After she had gone to sleep, Emily stopped sewing and gave way to thought, staring dreamily before her.

Since the night that she had spent in this room, Emily felt more wretched and tormented than ever. Continually her mind reverted to the notion that her grandmother was going to die and that this was the catastrophe she had foreseen. But this thought, which by all natural laws should have roused her sympathy and affection for the threatened victim, had only the contrary effect: instead of drawing her

to Mrs. Elliot's bedside, it drove her away from it.
Despite her best efforts to overcome a sentiment
which shamed her, she was unable to conquer a sort of
repulsion which she felt for all that concerned Mrs.
Elliot, and especially for this strange malady which
attacked her so persistently without ever killing her
—for Emily was convinced that her grandmother's
nightmare had been followed by one of the ghastly
attacks like that to which the girl had been a terrified witness seven years before. She wondered what
had happened in the room after she had fainted, and
she had no idea how long she had lain unconscious.
She had spoken to no one about it, and Mrs. Elliot,
when she saw her the next morning, had made no
allusion to the events of the night. But the old
woman had appeared depressed and exhausted, and
her face had taken on a most unwholesome tinge—
her forehead especially was as red as if she were in
a rage, though her voice was gentle and she spoke
with faltering weariness.

A scruple of conscience now compelled Emily to
pass the best part of her day in this room. It was a
sinister spot for her, and here, more than anywhere
else, she knew the dread of death. Some one, however, was required to care for Mrs. Elliot, and it
was only natural that the task should fall upon
Emily.

Sometimes, as she watched her lying in bed, she
called up the picture of how this same woman had
looked on her arrival at Ashley House. She remem-

bered her, happy and healthy, getting out of the carriage in her flowing skirts, capped with her fine straw bonnet and its generous bows of black taffeta; and she asked herself with a sort of incredulous shudder if this was indeed the same woman. Mrs. Elliot with her full round face, her freshness of complexion, her heavy curls ranged neatly round her forehead like fat bunches of black and shiny grapes—and Mrs. Elliot now. She saw before her only a poor old invalid, her grey hair straggling in disorder from under a dirty cap.

As if this vision possessed some morbid fascination, she would stifle her repugnance and force herself over to the bed, to bend lingeringly above the slumbering old woman. Even in sleep Mrs. Elliot's face retained its haggardness. The bushy, masculine eyebrows were drawn together in a wrinkle of pain; the discoloured lips, hanging open, showed blue along the gums. A flush spread over the cheeks and across the forehead, a mockery of the flush of health.

Emily would stand breathless, studying this face in which the years had worked such changes. Bloated and hideous, it seemed to hold her enthralled.

To-day, however, she had turned away toward the window to avoid the sight of her grandmother, who lay sleeping on her back, restlessly tossing her hands on the counterpane in her troubled slumber. The girl's imagination ranged over the list of acquisitions that Mrs. Fletcher might bring back from the sale. No doubt she would return with a valiseful of cheap and worn-out clothes; Emily feared above all that there would be some among them intended for herself. It seemed a probability, and she grew angry in anticipation, as if the thing were already a fact.

Thinking of the valise which her mother had taken with her, she met a sudden suspicion which alarmed and distressed her. She remembered how Mrs. Fletcher had tried to get into the carriage with the valise in her hand, but Stevens had quickly reached down for it and had given it back to her when she was installed on the seat. What was the reason? The valise must have been heavy, she argued; and imagining the worst at once, she arose with great apprehension and left the room.

CHAPTER TWENTY

* * * * * * * * * * * * * * *

WITHOUT CONSIDERING ITS IM-
probabilities, Emily jumped at the conclusion that Mrs. Fletcher had carried away a valiseful
of valuables, as a preliminary to new drains on the
family resources, and she asked herself with sinking
heart what her mother could have chosen. She hastened down to the dining room, opened the doors of
the cabinet, counted and recounted the silver cups
and platters ranged there, and discovered nothing
lacking. This first reassurance comforted her somewhat, and she reminded herself that if Mrs. Fletcher
had anything to sell she would certainly not go to
Little Georgetown (where Stevens was to take her),
which was only a village, but to Washington or at
least to the town of Manassas. Nevertheless, her
fears had been too keen to be abandoned so readily,
and she decided to continue her inspection.

It was three o'clock. Figuring that her mother
would not return before half past five, she made a
leisurely round of the downstairs rooms. She bent
particular attention on the little pictures with which
her father had covered the walls. They were sorry
examples of art, but in the eyes of the girl they possessed inestimable value from the fact that they

would some day be her own, and she suspected her mother of wanting to sell them off. A glance was enough to show whether any were missing, for they had been hung according to the most rigorous laws of symmetry; but Emily did not content herself with so hasty an inspection. Mistrusting the uncertain evidence of her memory, she went up to the walls and rubbed her hands over the paper, to see if perhaps a nail had been removed to conceal the theft of some miniature.

She stopped before one of the larger paintings, which hung between the two windows of the room, and regarded it with pride. Forgetting for a moment her mission of inspection, she gave way to the sweet delights which this picture roused in her. She considered it the loveliest thing that was to be seen at Ashley House, and its importance and value were confirmed by the richness of its frame, which was of ebony, ornamented with thick bronze foliage easily recognizable as oak and olive branches intertwined. The subject of the painting was mythological. In a chariot drawn by prancing steeds she saw a woman robed in veils of delicate hue which fluttered and billowed in the breeze. Behind her followed a little band of figures, men and women, joining hands in the pattern of a dance. Each of them wore an expression of lofty serenity which enhanced the singular beauty of their faces. They were garbed in short tunics of rose colour, blue, and orange, bound by loose girdles about the waist, and the visible portions

of their arms and legs bespoke the perfect harmony
of their bodies.

There had been a time when Emily forbade herself
to look at this picture, for it troubled her without
her knowing exactly why, and if her eye accidentally
fell on it she was stricken with remorse and blamed
herself for the slip as if it were a sin; but little by
little her scruples had fallen away and now she regarded it brazenly and with a pleasure and curiosity
that habit did not diminish. She had often sought
the name of the artist at the foot of the canvas, but
it was not to be found; there was only a little copper
plaque set in the foliage of the frame and bearing
the word *Dawn*.

She stood for a long time contemplating it, never
tired of studying the details of costume that the
painter had so cleverly reproduced: the thongs of the
sandals, the garlands of flowers adorning the heads
of the women, the golden buckles which sparkled
with precious stones. Then she turned her eyes to
the faces themselves, and admired with a curious emotion the lively eyes and rosy cheeks of these men and
women. Just at this point she recalled the questions
her grandmother had urged on her about young Stevens, and she could not repress a vehement murmur
of scorn: "Oh no, *he's* not handsome!"

She returned to her inspection, opened the cabi-
nets, examined the trinkets that her father had accumulated. Then she went up to Mrs. Fletcher's
room. It was somewhat removed from the rest of the

house; it contained little furniture, and its white-washed plaster walls gave it a monastic note. A four-poster bed from which the valance and curtains had been removed filled the space between the two windows; the blankets were of the coarse woollen kind that are used in the army, and the pillow was without a case. An ebony desk, a cane-seated chair, and a walnut wardrobe completed its furnishings.

Emily rarely had reason to visit this room, and in fact it was only when her mother was away from home that she dared to enter it. She stared about her with a lively interest, and congratulated herself on the happy idea that had brought her to these regions of the house with which she was not so well acquainted. She hurried to the window to compare its view with the one from her own window; there is nothing that gives a stranger sensation than the sight of a familiar landscape from an unaccustomed point of view, and the girl remained for a long time in the window niche, entranced by the little discoveries that she kept making. The mountains, of which she carried so clear an image in her mind, seemed in some subtle degree to have undergone a change of contour; a forest which was scarcely visible from her room now appeared in its full extent, a new hill showed up, and she discovered a group of houses. For a while she was absorbed in her own inward thoughts; then she started up with sudden vehemence and planted her hand against the wall. "This room is also mine," she said aloud.

She soon discovered that pictures had never been hung on these walls. There was a portrait of General Lee above the desk, but it was only an unframed photograph. When she opened the wardrobe, she found it almost empty. A hat trimmed with crêpe was on the shelf beside two folded blankets; a shawl and a padded sacque hung on a hook; and tucked away in the back she found a bundle wrapped in an old newspaper that dated from the war; it proved to contain something or other made of white muslin. She closed the door and seated herself at the desk. Several of the drawers were locked, and all her efforts to open them were unavailing; she tried in vain to force the locks with little keys of her own, and she even thought of picking them with hairpins, but she gained nothing for her pains but a bad temper, and she pounded on the recalcitrant desk with her fists in exasperation.

She was well enough aware that if her mother had taken anything from this room to sell, it was impossible to find out about it without knowing exactly what had been there before she went, and this Emily did not know. She had the candor to admit it; her only reason for sitting here at the desk was the hope of discovering something about Mrs. Fletcher, something still unknown to her which would throw light on her mother's mysterious projects. Perhaps she would come upon letters or notes; perhaps, even— and her imagination warmed to the thought—she would find receipts, or lists of articles sold or to be sold. But the desk was a loyal guardian of its secrets.

The other drawers were empty or contained only old and uninteresting letters. Emily folded her arms and sat back in her chair. On top of the desk stood a copper candlestick with the candle still intact, and a little Bible bound in limp leather which the girl knew well from having seen it often in her mother's hands. She picked it up mechanically and opened to the flyleaf, where she read this inscription:

For Kate—Here is the most precious possession I have in the world, and I give it to you. GRACE FERGUSON, Athens, Ga., Oct. 12, 1866.

The words had been inscribed with an elaborate attempt at elegance which betrayed itself in a clumsy flourish. Emily scrutinized them closely and a smile broke over her face. "To think that she could ever have been young!" she murmured. She closed the Bible and flexed it in her hand, fluttering the pages with her thumb. A scrap of paper fell out and floated down to her feet; she picked it up and read it eagerly. She promptly recognized her mother's handwriting, but the letters were tiny and crowded together, and she had great difficulty in deciphering them. When she had finally conquered them, she thought a moment, then thumbed through the Bible again more carefully, and found two other papers of the same sort. They were Mrs. Fletcher's inventories.

Emily was not slow to decide what interpretation to give them and what intention had prompted her mother to compile them. Their meaning was all the more clear to her because certain items, which she recognized as more valuable than the rest, had been underscored or marked with a cross in the margin. This discovery overwhelmed her, and she sat there reading and rereading the slips of paper held in trembling hands, powerless to determine what to do. Rage and indignation counselled her to keep the lists and confront Mrs. Fletcher with a demand to explain them, if only for the pleasure of seeing her discomfiture; but she soon abandoned the idea, for she knew it would advance her not at all and would only provoke a scene. Finally, unable to decide on the appropriate procedure, she contented herself with making a hasty copy of the lists and returning the originals to their places, convinced that it would be best to act with discretion.

CHAPTER TWENTY-ONE

* * * * * * * * * * * * * * *

SHE RETURNED TO HER GRAND-
mother's room without a sound and seated herself by the fire. Mrs. Elliot was still slumbering,
flat on her back, her hands spread out on the coverlet, audibly breathing in a monotonous rhythm.
Now and then her lips would shape themselves as for
speech, and inarticulate sounds would issue confusedly from her mouth. Emily could not look at
her without reminding herself that a week ago she
would have turned to her for advice, while now it
was out of the question. This sudden loss of confidence she herself could not have explained, for there
were too many things within her that she wanted to
repress, too many voices that she wanted to silence;
she could never have conceived that a simple sense
of physical revulsion had been able to estrange her
from the only person for whom she felt a little affection. Nevertheless, the picture of her grandmother as she had seen her the night she had gone
to her aid was present to her mind with unendurable
clarity, the hideous face that her timid hand had
uncovered in brushing back the grey hair which had
masked it. At every thought of that night, the same

idea recurred to her mind: "She acted like a crazy woman."

She sat bending before the fire, elbows on knees, hands pressed against her ears to shut out the sound of the old woman's hoarse breathing. The flame fluttered up from the log and opened like a flower in the depths of the fireplace; gradually she grew more calm and her self-possession returned. "I can count only on myself now," she said; "I must defend myself single-handed."

Mrs. Fletcher returned earlier than her daughter had expected. Emily was on the porch when the carriage came in sight of the house. It had rained on the way, and the black leather top had been raised and was covered with large splotches of mud.

"Come and help me!" Mrs. Fletcher called when the carriage had drawn up. She got out with elaborate care, clinging to the seat timorously and groping for the step with her toe, while Frank steadied her by one arm and Emily offered a hand. When she was safely down she stamped her feet as if with satisfaction at being on solid ground again. Stevens passed her the valise, which she took with both hands; then he nodded good-bye, turned the horse about, and set off at a lively trot.

They went inside to the dining room, where Mrs. Fletcher set the valise on the table and unfastened it at once. She seemed elated over her journey and began to talk with an animation that was rare with her; it was apparent that the open air and the small business of the day had stimulated her and put her in a cheerful disposition. Her cheeks were quite pink and she had not even stopped to take off her hat in her haste to examine her purchases. The valise, full to the bursting point, opened almost of its own accord. One after the other, Mrs. Fletcher drew out of it a large grey woollen shawl, a long, drab coat, and a black dress which she unfolded ostentatiously.

"Well," she said with a note of triumph, "wasn't I right? See what fine condition everything is in!"

Emily stood silently beside the table; she looked on without any sign of sharing her mother's enthusiasm.

"Just look at them in broad daylight," she said curtly.

Mrs. Fletcher ignored the comment and tossed the coat about her shoulders, telling Emily how much she had paid for it. "That was giving it away," she declared. "At Washington I would have had to pay twice as much."

"But it's a man's coat!" Emily exclaimed, noticing the big pockets and the lapels with buttonholes. "It hangs straight down like an army coat."

Mrs. Fletcher grew red. "What's that? Well, what of it?" she asked. "It will do very well for winter." Then, disconcerted, she suddenly contradicted: "Anyway, it's not a man's coat at all."

"Oh, but it is," Emily repeated more gently, going over to her mother. She put her finger on one of the big cuffs of the sleeves. "Look," she said. "A woman never wore sleeves like these."

She suddenly bent down over the sleeve and raised her eyebrows. "Oh, Mamma," she laughed, "come nearer to the light! Look!" And she pointed to a spot where the colour of the cloth appeared lighter.

"It looks as if some braid had been ripped off."

"Where?" Mrs. Fletcher was losing her temper.

"Right there, Mamma. You can still see the stitches. It's an old Confederate army coat they have sold you!" She burst out laughing.

"That's not so!" Mrs. Fletcher drew back her arm abruptly and, taking off the coat with annoyance, folded it over the back of a chair.

Not a word was exchanged during dinner. From time to time Emily would cast scornful glances at the pile of clothes which her mother had planted in a corner of the room; and Mrs. Fletcher, feeling her humiliation, took pains to avoid her daughter's eye. They said good night and went to bed a little earlier than usual.

Emily locked her door and lighted a candle, and entered at once on a half-spoken conversation with herself, accompanied by little motions of head and hands as if she were trying to convince some invisible opponent. The blood rushed to her cheeks from this mild exhilaration, and her appearance contrasted oddly with the still and inscrutable front she had presented to her mother just before. Sometimes an attack of coughing would interrupt her in the

midst of a sentence and darken her features with
pain, and she would sit doubled up on the edge of
the bed until the spasm had passed.

After a quarter of an hour she heard her mother's
steps on the stairway and blew out the candle. The
steps continued toward her room and halted at the
door. The minutes went by in silence. Then, "Have
you put out your light?" Mrs. Fletcher's voice in-
quired.

"Yes."

After another pause, in which Emily guessed that
her mother was peering through the keyhole, the
steps moved off. When she could hear nothing more
she closed the shutters without making a sound, drew
the curtains and prudently pinned them, and lighted
the candle again. Then she sat down at the table
and drew out the copied notes which she had made
that afternoon. She examined them with straining
eyes, turned them this way and that in her fingers,
and finally spread them out before her, folding her
hands contemplatively. The light fell upon her
face; sometimes the tremor of the flame made dancing
shadows on her features and marked more decisively
the graceless outline, the long and broken line of the
nose descending to the pinched lips, and the caver-
nous cheeks already seamed with wrinkles. Her hair
hung down in disorder across her forehead and added
to her strangely ageing air.

She sat for a long time motionless, her eyes fastened on the papers, until a new access of coughing

roused her and she got up to prepare for bed. All
at once she was struck with a sudden whim; she
promptly sat down again and took from the drawer
a sheet of paper on which she proceeded to write the
following words: *How I will run my house.*

She stopped, crossed out what she had written,
and recommenced more deliberately: *How I will
live at Ashley House.* But this satisfied her no better
than before and she crumpled up the paper, took a
fresh sheet, and lengthily reconsidered. At last she
wrote with care at the top of the page:

> *To Miss Emily Fletcher,*
> *Ashley House,*
> *Fauquier County, Virginia.*

She reread the address, and below it, with a more
and more hesitant pen, she put a date, January 25,
1888; but she erased the year immediately and sub-
stituted 1892. With more assurance she went on to
the salutation, and dashed off the following letter
without a pause:

MY DEAR EMILY: Yes, indeed, you surely
have cause to be happy. Such a beautiful house,
and so marvellously situated! You can imagine how hard it is not to be envious of you,
my dear—Mistress of Ashley House! Just to
think that when you wake up in the morning
the first things you see are things that you love

and things that are your very own. I can hear
you saying: "These pictures are mine, this bureau, those two chairs, everything in this room;
and not only everything in this room, but everything in the whole house—and the house, too,
and the grounds all around it. . . ."

Just compare your luck with mine. You
know how I am situated, entirely dependent on
my father. There is not a thing in the house
of which I can say: "This belongs to me—this
box, or this book, or this pencil, or this
pin . . ." And if my father wanted to do it,
there is nothing to prevent him from taking
away even the comb that I wear in my hair. I
have nothing, nothing at all. If he took a notion to sell our furniture, or chop it up with an
axe, or set fire to the house, who would dare to
say him nay? He is the sole owner of all this;
he can dispose of it as suits his fancy.

And now to think of you, you lucky girl, sitting in front of a big wood fire in your own living room. Outdoors it is raining or snowing,
and you are sitting back at ease in that comfortable big armchair that I love so when I come
to see you. Perhaps you are reading, or else
you are letting your imagination carry you
along on happy plans for the future, or on
agreeable reminiscences of an unhappy past
that is never to return. Oh, in these hours of

happiness and contentment, please, please think once in a while of your friend . . .

She scribbled some name or other, turned over the sheet, and drafted an answer to her imaginary correspondent.

My Dear Grace: You may be sure that I am conscious of the favours that Heaven has bestowed on me. I am happy; yes, very happy. I am free—actually free! Ashley House belongs to me, and you are right—it is a matchless joy to go from room to room and be able to say: "This is mine, too; this whole enormous house belongs to me alone and no one can deny it." You know I could never say that in my mother's time; I was in a position like your own—and yet what you write does not sound entirely fair. The house you live in belongs to your father, but doesn't it belong to you, too, in a sense? If he set fire to his property, what would become of *you*, I'd like to know? Where would you live? Is he not accountable for your happiness? If he will not take that responsibility, he has no right to have a child. That seems so obvious that you ought not to have any doubt about it; in fact it is the thought that consoled me through long years of struggling. Oh no, Grace dear, there is not a thing in your house of which you cannot say: "This belongs

to us together until the day when I shall be sole
mistress here, like Emily Fletcher at Ashley
House, and then it will all belong to me." Be
strong, be brave; don't let yourself be cheated
of your due, defend your rights, and you will
enjoy them doubly later on.

She signed her name. The letter animated her
with satisfaction and she flushed with pleasure in
writing the final phrases. Then she reread both
sides of the sheet, folded it twice, and slipped it into
her Bible. A few minutes later she was in bed, but
she lay for a long time tense, and the stroke of eleven
sounded before she fell asleep.

CHAPTER TWENTY-TWO

* * * * * * * * * * * * * *

A FEW DAYS AFTERWARD THE
temperature rapidly dropped and a fine light
snow began to fall. Across the Ashley House windows the weighted branches of the pines hung motionless. No sound arose from the silent countryside.

"Winter is here," Mrs. Fletcher announced dolefully. She stood on the porch, dressed in the coat she had bought at the sale, and leaning lightly on a big brush broom.

"Are we going to have a fire in the dining room?" Emily asked from the doorway.

Mrs. Fletcher turned and looked at her.

"If you feel cold, you must go and do your sewing in your grandmother's room," she answered, and she proceeded to sweep away the snow which the wind had drifted up on the veranda during the night.

Emily coughed. "And how about you, Mamma?" she added after a moment.

Mrs. Fletcher continued her sweeping with an air of preoccupation; her colour was heightened by the cold and she breathed with a little effort. "Oh, as for me . . ." She seemed to be hunting for an answer, but contented herself with a shrug of the shoulders. She finished sweeping and shook the

165

snow from her broom. "Go back in the house," she told the girl, who stood watching her. "You will be sick again like last week if you stay here."

Emily went upstairs to Mrs. Elliot's room. She found her sitting up in bed, her head reclining on a pile of pillows. Long strands of hair hung down over her cheeks to the massive column of her neck. As soon as Emily opened the door the old woman began to talk with more than ordinary animation.

"I never slept at all last night," she plunged in. "Who was it who went prowling around? The sound came from your mother's side of the house. Do you know if she got up?"

"I heard nothing," Emily answered briefly. She went to her chair by the fire and took up a book. She had no desire to pursue the subject, but Mrs. Elliot insisted.

"It's not the first time I have heard her. Sometimes she comes to this part of the house well along after eleven o'clock. I hope she never takes it into her head to come in here! Heaven only knows what schemes she has stored up in that crazy brain of hers. But I guess I know how to look out for myself."

The last sentence was uttered in a tone of such signal ferocity that Emily turned with a sudden surge of fear. Looking her grandmother in the eye, she answered severely:

"You give yourself all sorts of false notions about

Mamma. She never has had any idea of harming you."

"Oh, my dear Emily," Mrs. Elliot answered tearfully, "be patient with me, treat me kindly. I am all alone and at the mercy of a daughter who does not love me. I know her better than you do, Emily," she added when the girl made a gesture of impatience. "I brought her up. She is mean and malicious; she harbours a grudge for years. Are you sure you heard no noises at all last night? You would tell me, wouldn't you? Or are you against me, too?"

"Nobody is against you, Grandma."

"Did you hear anyone going downstairs?"

"I heard nothing at all."

"Well, I heard some one stop in front of my door," Mrs. Elliot continued, in a voice that trembled a little. She looked intently at her granddaughter. "It was not either your mother or Josephine?"

"But why should they go prowling around at night?" Emily closed her book impatiently. Taking up the poker, she toyed with the embers under the log. "They're not sleep walkers."

"Very well. Then it was you?" Mrs. Elliot asked in the tone of one seeking assurance.

"Why, of course not!"

"But it must have been one of you three," the old woman burst out, shaking her arms above her head. "If not, I am afraid . . ."

"Of what?" Emily asked, moving quickly to the

foot of the bed. Her face was pallid and her eyes stared wide. Mrs. Elliot folded her hands and answered in a low voice: "I am afraid it may have been some poor soul that death has not set free. This is an old house; it has passed through many hands."

The girl stared round her as if seized with dizziness, and let herself sink to the bed. "Perhaps it was Mamma, after all," she said in a changed voice.

"You must ask her," Mrs. Elliot continued vigorously, "and tell me what she says. Watch her face closely when you question her; she doesn't know how to lie without giving herself away. I shall always believe that she is plotting to harm me, horrible as it sounds. Oh, you did not hear what I heard the day she came in to fix the fire in this room; the way she muttered, you would have been frightened, my dear. Watch her—I say it for your own good. Besides, you know . . ."

She paused to tap her forehead with her finger, then went on in a lower tone and with the liveliest excitement:

"My child, beware of a crazy woman's wiles. In unbalanced minds like that, the last faculty that goes is the faculty to dissimulate, to accomplish the most difficult and most awful purposes by means of patience and obstinacy, masked in a calm and innocent face. Listen to me," she put in when she saw her granddaughter turning away. "Remember that she will never be satisfied until we two are out of her way at Ashley House—until she is complete mis-

tress here and can sell everything in it piece by piece
and never have to draw on her capital. Only a crazy
woman would have such an idea. Do you know that
your father left her enough to live on comfortably
for twenty years? It is in the bank at Wilmington;
but rather than use it she would sell her bed and
sleep on the floor. She has already cut her own expenses down to next to nothing; it is only you and
I who are a burden to her, and without us . . ."

"Good heavens, Grandma!" Emily exclaimed,
struck for the first time with the force of all this.
"How do you know?"

"I am her mother," the old woman said, empha-
sizing each word. "Yes, I know her," she went on
passionately. "Didn't I bring her up? Didn't I
see these instincts developing in her? Listen to me.
During the war, at the time when we lost all our
money, we had to live from hand to mouth. Everyone was in the same fix. We made over our old
clothes, and, as the government requisitioned all the
metal, we got along without any; do you know that
we used thorns for pins?"

"Really?" Emily smiled at these details.

"Yes, indeed; and fruit stones for buttons! Oh,
you should have seen your mother. She was not
quite as old then as you are. How proud she was
to make her shoes and clothing last longer than the
others could! The day that Sherman's troops cap-
tured Atlanta, when everyone was bemoaning the
fact that the war was ending so badly for us, she

came to me with that little timid smile that you must still see in her sometimes, and she said to me . . . guess what."

"I don't know."

"She said to me, showing me her dress which was much too short and all worn out: 'Look, Mamma, this dress will have lasted me through the whole war!' "

She stopped talking a minute and shook her head, watching Emily all the while.

"Later," she went on, "my son, your uncle Harry, recovered a little of our money—a very little, but at any rate we were able to live a little better than during the war. Once in a while I gave Kate a present of a few dollars to buy small things with—jewelry and such—and would you believe it? She had no idea how to spend that money!"

"But what did she do with it?"

Mrs. Elliot opened her palm and closed it again slowly.

"She kept it," she said, "the way she does now. She hid it in her bureau drawer and went about dressed like a beggar, as though she had no pride. I found her crying one day because she was obliged to give up a skirt which she had had for several years and which was worn so thin in places that her petticoat showed through. That was the year she was married, and I had made her buy a new dress. She actually cried, my dear!"

She paused for breath and looked curiously at

Emily, who seemed absorbed in her thoughts; then she went on:

"Well, it has only grown worse since her husband died. It turned her head to find herself mistress of a big house where she was free to act as she pleased. She has only one idea now, which is to get rid of us. And what is there to stop her? She hates me; she wants me to die; she even asks for it in her prayers, I am certain. As for you . . ."

"Grandma!" Emily shouted, motioning her to stop.

"Sh-sh-she hates you!" the old woman stuttered with excitement. "She wants to get you out of the way. You'll see, she will turn you out of the house if you don't stop her."

Emily suddenly arose and returned to her chair by the fire. Mrs. Elliot arranged her pillows and went on in a voice that was hoarse and strident. "Yes, she will! I tell you, you will see. She wishes *you* were dead, too!"

The girl leapt up at these words and returned to the bedside. "That's not true!" she cried. Her face was livid. "She would never dare, never!" And driven on by some irrepressible force, she continued: "You are afraid of her because you are sick; but I'm young and healthy and I'm not afraid of my mother. I shall do as I like here. I shall be mistress of Ashley House before long. Wait and see!"

She shook a little in delivering this pronouncement. Mrs. Elliot watched her without replying and assumed a frightened expression which moved her granddaughter to pity.

"Don't be afraid, Grandma," she said more gently.

Mrs. Elliot lowered her eyes and answered falteringly: "As long as she is in command here, I shall fear for my life."

With a shrug of her shoulders Emily drew up a chair and sat at her grandmother's bedside.

"Remember, Grandma," she said, "you have me here to look out for you."

There was an interval of silence, and Mrs. Elliot's eyes were moist. Brushing away the tears, she said at length:

"Emily, I am afraid of dying."

"Afraid of dying!" Emily exclaimed. "You, a good Christian?"

"Oh, you don't understand," moaned Mrs. Elliot, nervously twisting her hands; her face expressed utter despair. "You don't know what it means to . . . give up life, the . . . joy of living."

Emily remained silent, watching her grandmother with mingled embarrassment and pity, and finding no words she could say to her.

"No, you don't know what it means," the old woman went on. "You are not the kind who enjoys this life. . . . . To think that that woman would cheat me out of the little time I have left on this earth!"

"Oh, it's sinful to talk that way," Emily said earnestly.

Mrs. Elliot did not answer at once; a smile flitted over her face.

"Sinful?" she repeated solemnly. "She wants to kill me—what word have you for that?"

Emily pretended not to see the hand that her grandmother proffered. She arose and replaced the chair, resolved to say no more.

"It makes no difference to you," Mrs. Elliot complained, sinking back on her pillows. "It's no concern of yours, is it? Or at least you think not. And yet if you woke up every night with the fear of never seeing the daylight again, as I do . . .! You have no heart at all, my child; you are just like your mother."

Emily sat down by the fire without a word. She laid another log across the andirons and encouraged the flame with a stroke or two of the bellows; then she opened her book, but listened all the while to what her grandmother was saying. Finally she heard her give vent to a prolonged sigh, as if she despaired of ever touching her granddaughter's heart.

The snow fell ceaselessly outside, reflected within the room in a leaden light. Only the crackling of the wood disturbed the depths of the silence. Emily turned to her reading again, but the sentence to which she casually opened was so remote from her present mood that it struck her as ridiculous; so she put aside her book and sat staring into the flame, her elbows resting on the arms of her chair.

Her grandmother's voice recalled her abruptly from the thoughts which had absorbed her for several minutes.

"Are you still there?" Mrs. Elliot asked.

Emily stood up and went toward the bed. "What do you want?" she said.

"Come nearer," Mrs. Elliot directed softly, and when Emily had complied she looked deep into her eyes.

"You have not given me a kiss for several days," she said, and she took her hand and clasped it between her own.

With a sense of almost insufferable distaste, Emily bent and lightly brushed her forehead with her lips.

CHAPTER TWENTY-THREE

* * * * * * * * * * * * * * * *

ONE AFTERNOON IN NOVEMBER, the sound of steps drew Emily to the window, and she saw a man in a dark-blue frock coat coming up the driveway. He was leaning on a cane and his head was bent.

"What are you looking at?" demanded Mrs. Elliot, who lay tossing and turning in her bed. She slept less easily now, and was always on the alert. The girl described the man in the frock coat and added:

"I can't see his face, but he must be old."

Visitors were rare at Ashley House, and as the weather was bad and the roads worse, only an important errand could have brought him. Mrs. Elliot appeared consumed with curiosity.

"It is some friend of your mother's," she said.

"I don't think so. She hardly knows anyone," Emily answered. "I'll go see who it is."

She left the room and stood at the head of the stairs a moment. Soon she heard a knock at the front door, and her mother promptly emerged from the dining room, her sleeves rolled up, her face expressing something like alarm. When she saw her daughter, she mounted rapidly to where she stood.

"I think it is a call," she whispered, her eyes wide. "I was in the pantry when I saw a man coming. I have no idea who he is." While she talked she rolled down her sleeves and hurriedly fastened the cuffs. "You will have to receive him for me. I'll come and join you in a few minutes."

At this moment Josephine crossed the hall and opened the door, and from where they stood Emily and her mother saw an elderly man come in. He took off his hat and asked for Mrs. Fletcher; then he added something in a lower tone and followed the negress into the parlour.

"It's the minister from Glencoe," Josephine came and told Mrs. Fletcher a moment later.

"The minister!" they both exclaimed.

"What can he want of us?" Mrs. Fletcher asked uneasily. She gave Emily a gentle push and the girl started down the stairs, arranging her hair as she went. "Tell him I am coming right away," her mother added, "but don't keep him if he wants to go on."

Less timid than her mother and much more inquisitive, Emily entered the parlour firmly and went directly up to the visitor, greeting him with her unexpressive voice. She then saw that he was a tall, elderly man with a slightly superior manner. When he nodded his head to return her welcome, long white locks of hair which he wore behind his ears shook down over his shoulders and brushed along his cheeks. His face was long, the forehead prominent, and the features sharp and even; his eyes were light blue of a steely quality. A black silk scarf about his throat accentuated the pallor of his complexion, with its spots of red that the cold had brought out in his cheeks. His clothing was dark blue, of a heavy texture, and he carried a cane of hickory in his hand.

"Madam, I am a stranger to you," he began. "I know your name better than your face, as I have read it in my parish register. I am the minister at Glencoe."

"I believe it is my mother you want to talk to, sir," Emily replied. "She will be here in a moment."

They sat down.

"Then you are Mrs. Fletcher's daughter?" the minister asked, without apparent surprise at his mistake. "I took you for her, but what I said applies equally well to you. You avoid our communion."

"Not intentionally, sir," she replied rather coldly. "We live so far from your church that we can be pardoned for not coming oftener."

"You are lost sheep," said the man of God. "Your excuses cannot save you."

"You judge us very quickly." Emily warmed to the discussion. "I carry out my religious duties at home." She recalled a Biblical phrase and added: "Besides, I say, 'Let no man stand between me and my God.'"

The minister cast her a look of reproach and said, with his eyes fixed upon her: "It is a spirit of revolt that leads you to speak as you do. This comes of a life in which the Christian verities have little share, where the holy days are passed without reverence. Do you read your Bible?"

"Regularly, every day."

She folded her arms beneath her shawl and stared at him unflinchingly; his rough features and brusque manners were not at all displeasing to her, and on reflection her anger subsided. The troubled thought possessed her that she had here before her the only person in the world in whom she could now confide. She had never heard anyone talk as he had talked to her.

"Do you suppose I have come here to argue with you? I know in advance all the answers you can give me."

He straightened himself in his chair and suddenly said:

"I am in need of money for my church. Will you give me some?"

"I have nothing myself," said Emily. "My mother provides for me; she is the only one who can answer you."

"How old are you?" he asked.

"I'll be sixteen in June."

He raised his eyebrows and muttered something that she did not hear very well, and as she got up to go for her mother he called to her:

"Wait; answer me. Have you much work to do? How do you spend your time?"

Emily stopped. "I sew," she said, "and I read. I also take care of my grandmother, who is sick."

"Is that all?"

"Yes."

He took out his watch. "Will you kindly call your mother? My time is limited."

Emily went and found her mother in her room. Mrs. Fletcher was sitting near the window and seemed lost in thought.

"Well, Mamma," the girl exclaimed, "he is waiting for you."

Mrs. Fletcher looked at her appealingly.

"Tell him that I can't come, child. I don't want to see him."

"He is determined not to go without seeing you," Emily insisted. "Why didn't you say that you were not in?"

"You won't help me out at all," Mrs. Fletcher whined. "But it's foolish of me to be expecting favours of you."

She got up and took a comb from the mantelpiece and tried to give some suggestion of order to her ill-kempt hair.

"Then I shall have to go down," she complained as she combed her hair; "and what shall I tell him? Am I a good churchgoer? What did he say to you?"

"Oh, what all the ministers say, Mamma—that we never come to church."

She enjoyed her mother's discomfiture and watched her sardonically.

"What is it to him?" said Mrs. Fletcher. "My spiritual life is nobody's business but my own."

She put down the comb irritably and started toward the door. Suddenly she stopped and repeated emphatically: "No, I don't want to see him! Let him go along. That is final," she added, turning to Emily. "I am not going to see him."

The fear of insulting a stranger gave her a meretricious firmness as she said these words, but she recognized at once the futility of her decision, for if she lacked the courage to talk to him, she lacked even more the courage to send him away without seeing him. She went down protestingly, followed by her daughter, who was finding a lively amusement in this call and would never have missed the conclusion.

They found the minister sitting at the round table, pencil in hand, writing a note which he put into his pocket after they entered. With an energetic bound he sprang to his feet and silently bowed; his keen eyes rested on Mrs. Fletcher with an expression at once superior and curious. She halted several steps away and rested her hand on the back of a chair, as if a sudden faintness had forced her to steady herself. Emily, after closing the door, folded her arms beneath her shawl and silently watched the actors in this scene.

"Will you sit down, sir?" Mrs. Fletcher said at last. He remained standing.

"Thank you, I am quite all right, Mrs. Fletcher, and I have very little time left. You know who I am. My name is Sedgwick and I am the minister at Glencoe. You belong to my parish—nominally, at least, I believe?"

"Yes, sir." Mrs. Fletcher had seated herself, and she sat watching the minister, hands clasped in her lap. For years she had never felt so uncomfortable.

"You are not acquainted with me, I suppose," Sedgwick remarked.

Mrs. Fletcher shook her head. "I knew the Reverend Mr. White, who was here before you," she said lamely.

"You never come to church?"

"No."

"Yet you expect to share in the spiritual rewards of the community? You are Methodists, like myself. You know that in the midst of a little band of men and women gathered together in the name of the Lord, the Lord Himself is present?"

Mrs. Fletcher was too much agitated to follow his words with precision. She nodded an affirmative.

" . . . and that the graces which He dispenses are transmitted to all members of His church, present in spirit if not in the flesh, granted that unsurmountable difficulties keep them away from the meeting place of the faithful?"

"Why, yes," Mrs. Fletcher murmured. Profound

amazement spoke from her face. She cast a glance toward Emily, who sat impassively not far away.

"A charitable view compels me to suppose that you belong to the category to which I have just referred. Have I said anything with which you disagree, Mrs. Fletcher?"

"No, sir."

"Am I to assume, then, that you are an active member of the Methodist Church of Glencoe, of which I have the charge?"

Mrs. Fletcher uttered a little sigh.

"I shall try to go more often, sir," she said.

"Good. To-day I have come to see you somewhat as Esdras visited his brothers in Israel. Our church is under heavy burdens, and you can help us to bear them. The mortgages on the land have not been paid off; we are in debt to the township. In addition, the maintenance of the heating system involves considerable expense. You understand me, Mrs. Fletcher?"

"Yes, sir."

"I take it for granted that you will not refuse your help."

He drew from his pocket a little card which he passed to Mrs. Fletcher.

"Three things to fill in: your name, the address of your bank, and the amount you wish to be turned over to the church. After it is made out, I put it in an envelope without looking at it and pass it on to a reliable agent; he opens the envelope and sends it on to the bank. At the end of the month the sum you have indicated is sent to me without mention of the donor. It is all done confidentially, and of all the people concerned, I am the one who knows the least about it. Do you understand? The war was such a severe tax on the families of the South that one cannot be too discreet."

Mrs. Fletcher had stood up at the first words of this little harangue. Tossing back her head, she looked at Sedgwick with a glance in which astonishment had given way to uneasiness.

"Mr. Sedgwick," she said when he was through, "I never draw on my bank account."

She glanced mistrustfully at the card which the old man extended to her, and refused to take it. The minister stood for a moment dumfounded.

"Come, Mrs. Fletcher," he exclaimed suddenly with anger in his voice. "You cannot betray humanity!"

Mrs. Fletcher leaned against her chair and said with a little flush: "Sir, I am sorry."

The blood rushed to Sedgwick's face and he bit his lip; still he would not give way. "Take the card and consider it more at your leisure," he said, trying to force it into her hand. She made a motion of refusal and drew slightly away.

Thereupon he returned the card to his pocket and took his hat and stick from the table. Under his white hair the skin of his forehead and temples had become quite pink. Mrs. Fletcher, who had sat down again, arose now dazed and abashed. Torn between fright at the thought of a threat on her money, and regret at having offended an old man whose bearing had impressed her deeply, she several times opened her mouth to speak but could not utter a word. Sedgwick turned toward her abruptly.

"Mrs. Fletcher," he said severely, "remember that you are responsible for all the poor whom you could have succoured, and I am here only to remind you and to save you. You will not be able to take your money with you everywhere."

Mrs. Fletcher, without replying, followed him to the door of the parlour. As he walked past Emily he stopped and said to her:

"Miss Fletcher, you can help me greatly by working for our poor."

"What kind of work is it?" Emily asked, unperturbed.

"You told me that you do sewing."

"Yes, I do," said Emily; and, "Yes, she sews very well," her mother said, almost in the same breath.

"If you will call at the workroom in Wilmington, they will give you some cloth and the necessary instructions. Are you willing to give us a little of your time?"

"Yes, sir."

"Wilmington is not very far," Mrs. Fletcher put in.

"You must go there once a week," Sedgwick continued. "If you work hard for an hour a day, you

will finish the assignment without any trouble. Here
is a note for you to give to the lady in charge of the
workroom."

She took the envelope which he offered her and
put it in her pocket, saying: "I will do my best."

"That is all I ask of you," Sedgwick answered,
and after bowing gravely he crossed the hallway at
a rapid stride and went out.

The whole scene had occupied only a few minutes,
but it left Mrs. Fletcher in a sort of stupor; and
when she found herself alone with her daughter again
she repeated over and over: "Well, I never expected
a call like that!" She seemed unable to express her
feelings in any other form; still violently flushed, she
paced up and down the parlour, while Emily examined her letter. Finally she came to a halt at the
window and stared at the roadway by which Sedgwick had departed from Ashley House. In a little
while she said aloud:

"He ought not to have talked to me the way he
did."

Emily raised her eyes to her mother, who stood
with her back turned. Mrs. Fletcher's words had
a constraint about them which surprised her.

"What's the matter, Mamma?" she asked from
where she sat.

"I am as good a Christian as anyone," Mrs.
Fletcher went on without turning. "Is it my fault
that the church is too far away? And as to this
money—how can I draw on my bank account?"

"You ought to have explained that," Emily said.

Silence followed, and Mrs. Fletcher stood unmoving, still looking out of the window. Finally she answered, in a tone that was low and indistinct:

"No, it would have been no use. He would have given me reasons why . . ."

"What reasons?" the girl demanded.

"Oh, reasons that I would not have seen," Mrs. Fletcher answered impatiently. "Ministers' reasons, that's all."

Suddenly she faced about and cried out, as if feelings long pent up had pushed their way out at last:

"Am I not as good as the next person? I have no desire to carry my money with me to my grave. It's not for myself I am saving it."

Shining rivulets marked the course of tears across her cheeks.

"Don't worry any more about what that man thinks," said Emily, who never could endure to see tears. "You will probably never set eyes on him again."

"That makes no difference." Mrs. Fletcher's voice quivered with wrath. "I don't wish anyone to think I am not like other people. I have feelings, like everyone else."

She began pacing up and down the room again; her steps were short, and she went from one piece of furniture to the next, touching each one mechanically and repeating this phrase that seemed to have caught her fancy: "I have feelings, like everyone else." And she added in a tone of the most assured conviction: "Heaven is my witness that I have not a cent to give him."

After a few minutes she rolled up her sleeves again and returned to the kitchen.

CHAPTER TWENTY-FOUR

* * * * * * * * * * * * * * *

WHEN MRS. ELLIOT SAW HER granddaughter again she was impatient to learn the details of this visit. Emily gave them not too willingly. Her mood was preoccupied since Sedgwick's departure; she would have preferred to sit by the fire reviewing the schemes that her mind kept manufacturing and then abandoning, and she did her best to shorten the narration. The old woman was not to be put off.

"You are going too fast," she said, fluttering her hands. "Talk to me the way you used to. A month ago you would have made me see exactly what this minister looked like."

"You are right," Emily admitted, her pride piqued by this reproach, and she proceeded to describe the Reverend Mr. Sedgwick to Mrs. Elliot's complete delight.

"What a fine man he must be!" she exclaimed when Emily had completed the portrait. "He is surely a faithful Christian soul. He belongs to the type of pastor that I remember from my mother's time. No doubt his manner is severe, but take my word for it, you must not lose touch with him; he is a friend

in need; he will be useful to you some day. Did he
say anything about coming back?"

"No."

"I want to see him. In 1850 there were some
Sedgwicks in Savannah; it might have been the same
family—though they were not Methodists."

Emily returned to her narrative of the meeting.
When she repeated the conversation between Sedgwick and her mother, on the matter of the donation,
Mrs. Elliot clapped her hands in malicious glee. "A
donation!" she burst out laughing. "So he came
to ask for money—to ask Kate for money! I would
have gotten out of bed to have heard that; I would
have gone downstairs!"

The girl was stricken with a sense of shame at the
sight of her grandmother holding her sides and rock-
ing with mirth; she remembered her mother's tearful
face and regretted that she had told her story to
such effect. Mrs. Elliot caught her sudden change
of mood and quickly sobered down.

"Well," she said bluntly, "don't you think it was
funny? You seem displeased. I guess I have a right
to make fun of that fool woman. I am mightily
pleased that you saw her in that light, do you know
it? She talked about her bank account, eh? That is
too funny. Here we are at Ashley House dying of
cold and starvation so that the bank account of Kate
Fletcher can remain untouched at Wilmington. Tell
me, doesn't that strike you as . . ."

"Let me finish my story, Grandma," Emily interrupted. "The minister went away a few minutes later. I don't think he was here more than a quarter of an hour altogether; he seemed to be in such a hurry. If you want to see him, I can write to him in your name, and the next time he comes this way he can stop at Ashley House."

"Would you like to see him, Emily?"

"Yes, Grandma, I would like to see him," Emily answered deliberately.

Mrs. Elliot looked at her inquiringly and broke into a smile.

"Why do you want to see him?"

"I have several things to ask him," Emily answered coolly.

"Why don't you ask me, instead?" Mrs. Elliot reproached her. "You promised once to confide everything in me, to take only my advice. Was that so long ago that you have forgotten it?"

"I have not forgotten," the girl replied, "but this is something particular."

"Oh, something particular," Mrs. Elliot repeated, mimicking Emily's expression of obstinacy. "You forget that I was your age once myself and had just such secrets as you have now. Well, never mind," she concluded with resentment. "You are as close-mouthed as your mother. What's the use of hoping for generosity from a heart like yours?"

Seeing Emily's frown, she continued almost at once.

"Come now," she forced a smile, "I have said too

much, as usual. Listen. You don't need to tell me a thing, since you don't want to—so much the worse for you, that's all. But we must write to him; he may very well prove useful to both of us. I have my reasons for wanting to see him, too."

She paused and glanced at Emily.

"You really don't want to tell me? I shall be wondering about it, you know, and that is going to make me cross and unhappy. All day long I have nothing to do but think. Some day I believe it will drive me crazy. Well, never mind. Write to him right away, if you want to."

The girl went over and sat down at the writing-desk.

"Do you want to dictate the letter to me now?" she asked.

"Very well." Mrs. Elliot pondered a minute, while Emily snipped at a quill pen with the scissors, anxious and impatient. Finally her grandmother began to dictate:

"Dear Sir: It is only severe illness that keeps me away from the church where I am summoned by my faith."

She repeated this sentence several times in a penetrating tone, while she hunted for what to say next. Her face betrayed arduous labour; she passed her hand across her forehead and mumbled uncertain words; it was apparent that the effort taxed her. Finally she proceeded:

"But perhaps the same Providence which condemns me to this grievous affliction will inspire my pastor to bring me the consolation of the Word."

She came to a halt again and repeated this second sentence with fumbling tongue.

"That will be plenty," Emily said in a few minutes. On her own account she had added the following postscript:

> DEAR SIR: I am writing in behalf of Mrs. Elliot, my grandmother. I am the one to whom you gave the note for the Community House at Wilmington. It seems best that I should let you know about my poor grandmother's state of health: she is very ill, and I believe you ought to come and see her as soon as possible. When you come, I want to take a moment of your time for several important questions that I have to ask you. Please excuse this hasty letter, and I beg you never to say anything to my mother about this postscript: she must not hear our conversation nor even know about it, for reasons that I will explain to you.

"That's plenty," she repeated, folding the letter. "I signed your name. Do you want me to read it over?"

"Yes, please," said Mrs. Elliot. "I think it will do."

Emily recited the letter from memory as she slipped it into the envelope.

"Isn't it a little short?" asked Mrs. Elliot. "Let me see it!"

"It's too late!" Emily laughed. "The envelope has been sealed, and it was the last one." And leaning over the back of the chair, she waved the envelope which she actually had just sealed.

"I'll send it to-morrow morning," she added, putting it into her pocket.

Unheeding the pleas of her grandmother, who hated to be left alone, she went briskly out of the room.

CHAPTER TWENTY-FIVE

* * * * * * * * * * * * * * * *

THE NEXT MORNING SHE WAS early up and made her bed before breakfast. It had turned to freezing during the night; from the window she looked out on a heavy carpet of frost over the lawn. A boreal wind stirred the branches of the pines and rattled the draught in the chimney. She wrapped herself in her shawl and went downstairs. Her mother was already in the dining room, setting the table; she started with surprise when Emily appeared.

"Why did you get up so early? It's not seven yet."

"I am going to Wilmington," Emily briefly answered.

"This morning? It's too cold out."

"Oh no."

She sat down and rubbed her bony hands together, the joints crackling with stiffness.

"Are we going to have a fire here to-day?" she asked in a moment.

Mrs. Fletcher, who was getting the spoons from the cabinet, faced about with affected incomprehension.

"What? If you feel cold, you must go and do your sewing in—"

"I know," Emily said brusquely, and she tapped the floor with her heel to set her rocker moving.

"There's not going to be any fire in here," Mrs. Fletcher went on in an aggrieved tone. "We *must* economize." And she added: "The water is almost boiling. Will you read the prayers, please?"

They knelt down one behind the other, Mrs. Fletcher leaning on the arm of a chair, Emily kneeling upright without support, her shawl wrapped tight about her shoulders. She began a Psalm while her mother buried her face in her hands, bowing deeper and deeper and uttering long-drawn sighs. They rose again as Josephine brought in the tea. Mrs. Fletcher put her arm over Emily's shoulder and brushed her cheek with a kiss.

"What a farce!" Emily thought. "Is that what she calls her spiritual life? She really despises me."

Not a word passed between them until after the meal; then Emily put on her black cloth bonnet and worsted mittens.

"Are you going right away?" her mother asked, putting on her army coat to go out on the porch. "You must wrap up good and warm."

"I have my shawl," Emily answered, tying the ribbons of her bonnet.

Mrs. Fletcher considered. "That's not enough," she said hesitantly. "You should put something else on over that."

"What do you suggest?"

Mrs. Fletcher went out in the hall and returned

with the black shawl which she had acquired at the sale.

"I make you a present of this," she said, a little flushed.

"I won't take it."

"What?" exclaimed Mrs. Fletcher, unfolding the shawl and holding it in her outstretched arms. "But why not?"

"Because it is dirty!" the girl replied, and she escaped through the door and across the hall before her mother could restrain her.

Mrs. Fletcher ran to the window just as Emily went down the porch steps. "Listen!" she called. "You will be sick. Take my coat."

She made the gesture of taking it off. Emily turned and laughed in her face when she saw her expression of concern, and her laughter quickly brought on an attack of coughing.

"You see," she called hoarsely as she moved away down the drive, "when you dress me decently perhaps I won't cough so much." Then she commenced to run and the hard ground echoed underfoot.

She soon came to their mail box, which stood at the cross-roads near Ashley House. Emily inserted the letter which she had written the day before, and went on her way in less haste.

The wind had died down and the day opened fair. The girl's road wound between two high banks of red earth topped with brush; rock-strewn fields lay out on either side of the way to the foot of the mountains, whose weathered slopes and snowy crests loomed in the distance.

Emily walked rapidly along, cheered and invigorated by the cold. She was pleased with what she had just done and thought with satisfaction of her postscript to the letter. For the first time she had taken the initiative and acted for herself; and her daring gave her a new sense of pride. It was a certainty that the week would not pass without a visit from the minister; he could hardly disregard the imperative words of the postscript. Perhaps she had exaggerated the gravity of her grandmother's illness, but she felt that Sedgwick needed some such incentive. Ashley House was so remote, so far from any town.

Besides, Mrs. Elliot's condition was bad enough to justify the fear that she was at the mercy of another attack. Perhaps she might live another year, or two years, but what assurance was there? Perhaps even to-day when she came home, Emily would find her rigid in her bed, as she had two weeks before, and this time it would probably be the end. She began to find more truth in what she had written than she herself had intended.

It seemed of vital importance to her that she should see Sedgwick at once. Since his visit to Ashley House, she did nothing but contrive new questions for him to answer. It was from him that she should ask advice. She would explain everything to him. Surely he would understand, and she would act

on his counsel. This man of whom she knew next to
nothing, who had spoken to her only to reprove or to
command, attracted her with a sudden and immense
curiosity. In her untutored heart a strange sensation which troubled and yet delighted her was working to make her dream obedience to him. If he had
been a younger man, she would probably have understood the nature of her emotion; but her conventional
dream of love could not reconcile the fifty years
which removed him from her. "If only he were my
father!" she mused. With a sort of reverent ecstasy
she repeated his name over and over, her eyes agleam,
and she cherished the hope that he might be at the
Community House when she arrived there.

Enjoying the play of her thoughts, she tramped
along without tiring. It was almost three-quarters
of an hour after leaving Ashley House before she
reached the outlying houses of Wilmington. She
went up the main street of the town, which resounded
with the voices of children sliding on the ice in the
gutters. People went up and down wrapped in
shawls and scarves, and wearing enormous overshoes
that made an odd, dull thumping on the pavement.
The stores were almost all decorated with wreaths
and garlands of green for Thanksgiving day, which
came that week.

Emily was unused to so much activity and went
on in sustained surprise. She crossed from side to
side of the street, drawn first to one window and
then to another. The passers-by chaffed her and she

stared at them in bewildered curiosity. Urchins commenced to follow her, fascinated by her odd appearance; she noticed this and took embarrassed refuge in a grocer's and asked the way.

The Community House was situated not far from the centre of town, on a wooded knoll that dominated the main street. It stood half hidden by trees, a long wooden building with a dark red roof and large windows in which wreaths were hanging. Above the door she read an inscription in Gothic letters: Community House of the Second Methodist Church.

She stopped a moment to recover her breath, assured herself that she had not lost her letter, and resolutely rang the bell. She waited for some time. From within came a muffled sound of talk and laughter which gave her a little uneasiness; she wondered why no one came to let her in, and was about to ring again when the door half opened.

"What do you want?" a voice demanded. "You can't come in . . . we are getting ready for the party."

Emily saw a woman's face staring at her mistrustfully.

"I was sent by the Reverend Mr. Sedgwick," she answered. "I want to speak to the directress."

"Oh, very well," the voice replied, and the door opened a trifle wider. Emily promptly entered, and found herself in a large bare room with grey walls. A placard tacked above the door bore a quotation from the Book of Proverbs: "She seeketh wool and flax, and worketh willingly with her hands. . . . Her candle goeth not out by night. . . . She stretch- eth out her hand to the poor." Boxes of all sizes were heaped in a corner; a fire was burning in a small tiled fireplace.

"I am the directress," said the one who had opened the door. "I am sorry that I can receive you only in this room," she added, "but we are planning a sur- prise for the Wilmington poor children, and all the rest of the building has to be decorated."

She spoke in a gruff but not disagreeable voice. The girl delivered her letter without a word.

The directress was a woman in her thirties, strongly built and tall. She was dressed in black and wore white linen collar and cuffs. Her severity of features seemed to accord with her Puritan garb; but it took only a little study to distinguish the real from the apparent in her look of discontent. Her habit of knitting her brow had scored a heavy wrin- kle in the middle of her forehead, and added to the slightly malignant look of her greenish eyes; the flatness of her forehead and thickness of lips re- moved all possibility of calling her pretty. She gave the impression, at second sight, that she was con- scious of her plainness and that her brusqueness was more to be credited to an extreme timidity than to a naturally cross disposition. If she had been pretty, she would have been sweeter of temper—this second impression counteracted the first.

"Where do you come from?" she asked after reading the note.

"From Ashley House, about an hour from here."

"Shall I read you this letter?"

"I read it."

"You read it! But it was not addressed to you."

"The Reverend Mr. Sedgwick gave it to me unsealed, and I thought I had best find out what it said so as to know what to expect."

The letter read as follows:

> *To Miss Prudence Easting.*
>
> DEAR MISS EASTING: Kindly provide Miss Fletcher, the bearer of this note, with whatever work you deem suitable. She sews, and she seems to have a great deal of free time. Give her something fairly easy to begin with, and keep me informed of how she makes out.
>
> JOHN SEDGWICK.

Prudence Easting folded the note again and tucked it into her waist.

"Well," she said after a moment's consideration, "I must carry out the Reverend Mr. Sedgwick's orders. But it will take less time than he thinks to find out how well you sew, and there is no point in giving you work that is too easy if you can do harder things. Will you follow me, please?"

They went into a small adjoining room and sat down facing each other across a long table on which workbaskets were ranged. Each basket was covered with a white cloth bearing a number embroidered in red. Miss Easting uncovered one basket, took out a shirt, and unfolded it.

"Will you finish this hem for me, please?" She gave Emily a needle and a spool of thread. The girl pulled off her mittens and puffed on her fingertips.

"Are you cold?" the directress asked. "Rub your hands a minute. While we wait, I can ask you some questions. How do you pass the time at Ashley House?"

"I sew part of the day, and I read . . ."

"What do you read?"

"That depends. One hour each day I read the Bible. I also read novels."

"Heavens! What novels?"

"Oh, we have all kinds of them. Disraeli . . ."

"I don't know him."

"The last novel I read was *The Last Days of Pompeii*."

"That's very bad. Have you read many books of that sort?"

"Many novels? Why, yes. We have a lot of them in the house. My father . . ."

"How dreadful! Do you never go to church?"

"The church is too far away."

"Too far away! But heaven is farther, my dear, and you surely hope to go there."

Emily blushed. "Certainly," she replied. "I do

my religious duties as well as I can." Then she asked suddenly: "Is it the Reverend Mr. Sedgwick who preaches at Glencoe?"

"Why, surely! Do you mean to say that you have never heard him preach? I can't believe it! He is a saint from heaven, my dear, you must hear him." The blood flew to her cheeks as she said this and she stopped abruptly. "Let's see, now," she went on in a more subdued tone. "Show me how you turn a hem."

It would undoubtedly have shocked the directress if anyone had told her that she was in love with the minister, but it is one of love's tricks to conceal itself so nicely that the heart it dwells in is often unconscious of its place there. Miss Easting would willingly say of herself that she stood in the relation of a daughter to him—just as Emily was quite ready to envisage him as a father, though she would never have dared to love him. Such are the small hypocrisies of this persuasive and much-misjudged emotion.

Emily took the shirt and began sewing without delay. Gladly she would have passed the whole day in this agreeable company—in the company of any woman who was not her mother or her grandmother, and who seemed disposed to take an interest in her. Prudence Easting watched her work and stopped her at the end of a few stitches.

"All right," she said. "I am going to give you some cut pieces that have to be sewn." She went over to a large cabinet, removing a heavy garland of greenery that festooned it. "I didn't think it would have to be opened again until the end of the week," she explained. "This room all has to be decorated as well as the others. Chains of laurel and wreaths tied with ribbon. You will have it at Ashley House too, I suppose."

"No, none at all."

"No?" The directress returned to the table laden with linen. She smiled and added: "At least you will have a turkey."

"Turkey!" exclaimed the girl, laughing outright at the idea. "No, indeed."

The directress stared as if she suspected Emily of making fun of her. She raised her eyebrows and set the shirts down before her.

"Here you are. I am entrusting you with five—one for each day of the week, excepting Sunday, of course, and to-morrow, since it is a holiday. I'll do them up in a package for you and put in a book. Have you read Fox's *Book of Martyrs?*"

Emily shook her head.

"No?" the directress exclaimed. "I'll lend it to you; but you must be careful of it. It belongs to the school library. And now," she smiled, "do you mind if I ask how old you are? It's on account of the books—they can't be loaned to girls under twenty. But of course you . . . Anyway, I have to ask you in accordance with the rule."

"Under twenty!" Emily exclaimed. "Why, I'm not sixteen yet."

"What!" The directress leaned across the table and stared at Emily speechlessly. Finally she muttered: "Why, Miss . . . my dear child, I had no idea you were so young."

"It's because I am so homely," Emily said. "I know."

Prudence Easting made a gesture of denial and sat down. She flushed slightly, and said in a kindlier tone:

"You must not think about vanities like that. The Lord has made us according to his will, and it is all for our own good." After a lingering silence she went on: "I'll do up the bundle for you. It must be brought back next week—if you come in the afternoon we can have more time to talk. Will you?"

"Yes, indeed, Miss Easting," Emily answered. She lifted her eyes to Prudence Easting's face, and there was something about the bright round cheeks and the eyes now softened with kindness that made her want to stretch out a friendly hand.

While the directress wrapped the shirts, Emily put on her mittens again and carefully fastened the pin that held her shawl. "Does the Reverend Mr. Sedgwick ever come here?" she suddenly asked.

"He comes twice a month, the first and the fifteenth. Sometimes he comes for the holidays. Do you want to talk to him?"

"Yes, Miss Easting."

"Then come on Thursday instead of Wednesday next week. Oh, you will enjoy meeting him. He is the simplest and most natural man in the world, and he understands everything." She tied up the parcel, adding: "No doubt you have something that you want to ask him—some advice . . ."

"Yes, I have."

They relapsed into silence. Finally the directress got up and handed the parcel to Emily. "There you are," she said. "Don't forget to bring back my string and wrappings. And now your book."

Again she went to the back of the room and foraged in the cabinet. After a moment she returned to Emily, her eyes intent on a book which she held in her hands.

"Since you are too young to sign a card, I am taking the responsibility myself," she explained. "Remember!"

She walked around the table and cordially took Emily by the arm. "See," she said, as they walked toward the door together, "we needed only a few minutes to become good friends." In saying this she looked Emily in the face and laughed a forced little laugh. "I can see that I am going to call you Emily. Why not begin to-day?"

"If you like," Emily answered in the habitual curt tone which she found herself unable to soften.

"You don't want me to?"

"Surely, of course I do."

At the door the directress gave a sigh and lowered

her eyes. She was a corpulent young woman and breathed hoarsely as if her clothing constricted her. Presently she looked up again and resumed the severity of mien that had met Emily at the beginning.

"Good-bye for the present, Emily."

The girl shook the flabby hand that she extended.

"I'll see you Thursday, Miss Easting."

CHAPTER TWENTY-SIX

* * * * * * * * * * * * * * * *

IT WAS NEARLY NOON WHEN EM-
ily saw the Ashley pines upon their hill. She
stopped at the letter box to make sure that the postman had taken her letter, and found one addressed
to herself. The penmanship was clumsy and suggested the laboured efforts of an unschooled writer.
She opened it and read:

> DEAR MISS FLETCHER: I am in trouble to
> which you cannot be indifferent. My wife died
> four days ago. No doubt she was not properly
> cared for, but that costs money and we haven't
> a cent in the house. It is a hard winter—there
> is nothing to sell and therefor nothing to eat.
> When I saw Mrs. Fletcher on the day of the sale
> she promised to help us as far as possible (those
> were her words). If she has forgotten, can't
> you speak to her about us? If you hear of any-
> one wanting a gardener or farmer, remember I
> am out of work. I hereby appeal to your kind
> heart.
>
> FRANK W. STEVENS.

Emily slipped the note into her book and went on.
She found her mother sewing, with the slow and

attentive care that was habitual with her. It was bitter cold in the dining room, even though the kitchen door stood open, and Mrs. Fletcher had kept on her coat with the big lapels. When Emily appeared she glanced up at her unconcernedly and said nothing.

"You know, it's even colder in here than it is outdoors," the girl said as she took off her gloves and bonnet. "You ought to take a little exercise."

Mrs. Fletcher's regular stitches went on; she made no answer.

"Here, Mamma," Emily said suddenly, putting in her lap the letter she had received. "See what Frank Stevens has written me."

"Frank Stevens!" exclaimed Mrs. Fletcher. She dropped her work and unfolded the letter. "It's about that sickle of his again, I suppose," she groaned. "I don't like that fellow; he hasn't an honest face."

She squinted at the letter, which she held in an unsteady hand.

"Oh, I can't make out this handwriting," she finally said impatiently.

Emily took the letter and began to read it aloud, but Mrs. Fletcher listened with an expression of uneasiness and insisted on her beginning it over again, saying that she went too fast for her to understand. The girl reread the entire letter, enunciating slowly and carefully, and pausing at the end of each sentence to watch its effect in her mother's face.

With her hands folded in her lap, Mrs. Fletcher sat as if chained; at the end she arose and walked up and down with heavy sighs.

"Dead!" she repeated. "Why, it was less than a week ago that he was talking to me about the poor woman, and she was alive then. How sad, how dreadfully sad!"

"What are you going to do for them?" Emily demanded, folding the letter without taking her eyes from Mrs. Fletcher. Her mother looked at her as if she failed to understand.

"Oh, let me alone!" she said in despair. "It is all so sad. There are too many unhappy people in this world." She walked a little farther and sank into an armchair. "What a blow!" she said, shaking her head.

"Yes, what a blow!" the girl echoed drily. "And what are you going to do for them?"

"What? I?" Mrs. Fletcher interrogated.

"Why, certainly," Emily insisted, raising her voice. "I suppose you are going to give them some clothes and some money."

Mrs. Fletcher about-faced. "Money!" she cried. "Are you insane? Have I got any money? Do I look as if I had money?"

She planted her hands on her breast with a theatrical gesture, as if to call attention to her wretched garments of worn-out serge.

"Surely," Emily said, "you have money in the bank."

"What about my bank account?" Mrs. Fletcher blurted. "I'm not going to touch that. What do you mean by talking to me about that, anyway?" she added, getting up. "Who told you I had a bank account?"

"Why, you did!" Emily burst out laughing. "Didn't you say to the minister that you refused to draw on your bank account?"

"That's true," Mrs. Fletcher admitted in a troubled tone; "I did say that." She sat down again, grasping the arms of her chair, and murmured: "I had to tell him something."

"You told the minister the truth," Emily answered imperturbably. "I know very well that you have money deposited at Wilmington. Why should you want to hide it?"

These words set Mrs. Fletcher trembling and she averted her head without replying; her fingers buried themselves in the upholstery of the chair as if to tear it out by the roots. Such keen distress was written in her face that anyone but her daughter would surely have pitied her.

"Do you think I am planning to rob you, Mamma?" Emily asked after a momentary silence. "Is that what you are afraid of?"

"Let me alone," Mrs. Fletcher contrived to say. She was breathing heavily and her breath seemed to tear at her throat. Suddenly she rose to her feet and shook her arm toward Emily. "Yes, let me alone," she cried. "Go to your grandmother's room."

She was visibly trembling while she spoke, and remained with her mouth half open as if to say more, but found herself inarticulate. Tears glistened in her eyes; she stamped her foot.

"She was the one who told you," she finally declared in a broken voice. "She hates me, and you do, too. O, good Lord!" And she buried her face in her hands.

Emily watched her mother with contempt; she was sitting on the sofa and had not stirred since the beginning of the scene.

"You return it in kind," she replied. It was as though she enjoyed her mother's anguish and confusion; she smiled and asked: "Why shouldn't Grandma tell me where your bank is? Is that any proof that she hates you?"

Mrs. Fletcher shrugged her shoulders and made no answer. She sat down near the window and resumed her work after wiping her eyes with a handkerchief; but her hands were trembling and she could not find her needle. There was a long silence. Emily looked at her mother with an air of triumph; folding her arms beneath her shawl, she reclined at ease on the sofa.

"You are free to do what you like with your money," she said. And she added more softly: "That is nobody's business but your own. But you must leave the house just as it was in Father's time."

She was hoping that her mother would answer, but Mrs. Fletcher appeared oblivious and remained with her eyes on her work, turning it this way and that attentively. At the end of a few minutes Emily took her parcel and left the dining room.

CHAPTER TWENTY-SEVEN

* * * * * * * * * * * * * * * *

EMILY INVESTED SO MUCH DILI-
gence in the work allotted to her that she finished it on the Saturday following her visit to Wilmington. But she did it only at the expense of some
of the little tasks which her mother each week assigned her. It seemed, however, that Mrs. Fletcher
had relaxed some of her attention, for she made no
remarks. Since her last scene with her daughter she
was more distraught and more beset with anxiety
than ever; she never spoke a word any more, nor even
looked at anyone except from the corner of her eye
when she believed herself unobserved. Wrapped in
her army coat, she sat at the window of the dining
room; all her habitual industry and self-imposed exactions gave way to hours of moody indolence, while
she sat with hands folded in her lap, head bent, an
image of exhaustion. Now and then great sighs
would well from her bosom and she would shake her
head lugubriously.

In order to keep warm she often had to march
up and down the dining room, her hands buried deep
in her sleeves. Either because of advancing years or
because the weather was more severe than usual, she
suffered from the cold far more than in other win-
ters; but she held to her determination to light no

fire downstairs and limited herself to leaving the
kitchen door open.   Nevertheless, a freezing afternoon came when she was unable to hold out.   Sewing
was impossible in the unheated room.   She had tried
the expedient of pacing rapidly from one end of
the room to the other, blowing on her fingers, but
the pains in her legs had been too much for her.
After much hesitancy, she decided to go and sit by
the kitchen stove, though her discomfort in the presence of Josephine made even the thought repugnant.

The old negress was busy cleaning the vegetables;
she looked up in astonishment at Mrs. Fletcher's in-
vasion of her domain.   Mrs. Fletcher smiled timidly
and was about to sit down, when the pervasive odour
of the sink assailed her; she struggled vainly to hide
a grimace and hurried out at once.

She returned to the dining room.   For a while she
remained in the most desperate doubt; she estimated
that a fire would cost nearly twenty cents and recoiled before such an outlay; on the other hand, the
prospect of an hour or two in her mother's room
was not alluring.   But the cold was too much for
her; her teeth were chattering.   She took her head
in both hands and deliberated.   She knew what she
could expect in Mrs. Elliot's room——taunts and even
insults; but she wondered if it might not be prefer-
able, at that, to a waste of money.   She mastered
herself with an effort of will and climbed the stairs,
whining half aloud with the cold.

Before the door she paused and asked herself

whether she should knock or go in softly, unannounced. She stood indecisive for several minutes; her heart was in her throat and she offered a silent prayer that her mother might be asleep when she went in. Then she opened the door.

Mrs. Elliot was not asleep. She lay in her bed, staring straight before her, and occupied herself with twisting a long loose strand of hair around her finger. It had been fully two months since Mrs. Fletcher had seen her, and although her immediate purpose was to sneak unobserved into a corner of the room, she halted in spite of herself beside the bed, unable to take her eyes from her mother's face. That face had not greatly altered, to be sure, but there was in it something more indefinable and more compelling even than material changes. The features carried a haggard look which gave place now and then to an expression of complete abstraction and other-worldliness; her mouth hung slightly open; her fingers moved with a continual unrest and ceaselessly plucked at her disheveled hair.

After a moment the old woman turned her eyes toward her daughter and regarded her vacantly. Mrs. Fletcher gave a start and caught her breath, but Mrs. Elliot said nothing and appeared not to see her.

Emily had arisen at the sound of the door opening and stood watching with surprised curiosity. Seeing her mother transfixed beside the bed, she involuntarily laughed, covering her mouth with her hand.

"It's all right, Mamma," she half whispered. "Don't be afraid. She won't hurt you."

Mrs. Fletcher emerged from her dream. Recovering her wits, she walked across the room to the chair which her daughter had just given up. Her eyes were wide with a sort of stupor; she muttered: "Your grandmother . . ." and stopped.

Emily folded her arms beneath her shawl.

"What's the matter?" she asked quietly.

Her mother lifted her hands. "I never saw her looking so ill."

"Well, you never come in to see her." Emily smiled maliciously.

Mrs. Fletcher settled down in the armchair and stretched her feet toward the flame; but she quickly drew them back, saying: "I hope you don't keep the fire burning like this all day."

"She is quite sick and she needs to be kept warm," Emily said, shrugging her shoulders. She sat down opposite her mother and resumed the work which she had laid aside; it was the last of the five shirts.

"How long has she been like this?" Mrs. Fletcher demanded after an interval of silence.

"She has been worse the last five or six days."

Mrs. Fletcher leaned toward her daughter and whispered: "You're sure she can't hear us, Emily?"

"She could," Emily replied, "but she is thinking

about something else; she's not paying any attention to us."

"You don't think she is going to die, do you?" Mrs. Fletcher's voice was scarcely audible.

Emily made no answer. She often contemplated her grandmother's possible death, but these words from her mother struck her unaccountably as ugly and unnatural, and filled her with a kind of horror. She bent her head over her work and continued sewing in silence.

Her mother eyed her furtively, and several times seemed on the point of speaking, but each time reconsidered. Finally she again leaned toward her, beckoning with her finger for attention.

"You take good care of her, Emily?"

The girl nodded silently; more minutes passed. Mrs. Fletcher opened her coat and leaned toward the fire a little, stretching her hands to the flame. Her forehead was clouded with deep debate, when the voice of Mrs. Elliot roused her with a start.

"Emily," the old woman called, "are you there?"

"Yes, Grandma."

"What are you doing? Why don't you come and sit by me?"

"I'm sewing. I have to sit by the window to get a better light."

Mrs. Elliot could be heard tossing and turning in bed and sighing with impatience. After a moment she said with great effort:

"I feel sick. It's too hot in here."

Mrs. Fletcher, curled in her chair, cast a look of reproach at Emily.

"Lie quietly, Grandma," Emily answered without putting down her needle. "Try to sleep a little."

"Sleep?" Mrs. Elliot repeated quaveringly, as if she failed to understand the meaning of the word. "What time is it? Will we have lunch before long?"

"It's nearly four o'clock, Grandma."

"Four o'clock! Then I must have been asleep."

"Very likely," the girl answered tonelessly.

During the long silence that followed, Mrs. Fletcher made frantic and unavailing signals to attract Emily's attention and make her understand that she was not to tell of her presence in the room; but Emily pretended not to notice this little byplay, or, when she looked up, feigned not to understand what it meant. Never had her mother appeared so absurd and contemptible in her eyes.

"Emily," asked Mrs. Elliot after a while, "did you write to the pastor?"

"Why, yes; you dictated the letter."

"When is he coming?"

"I don't know. Next week, perhaps."

"You see, I have something most important to tell him, Emily."

The girl offered no answer. Mrs. Elliot continued petulantly:

"Why don't you say anything? It's about you that I am going to talk to him. Aren't you interested at all?"

Emily appeared surprised. "You are going to talk to him about me?" she asked.

"Certainly—about you and your future. I know I am not going to live very long, Emily. The day is coming when you will have no one to protect you."

"Don't worry, Grandma," Emily answered, going on with her sewing. "I'll be able to take care of myself if anyone tries to hurt me."

Mrs. Elliot sighed deeply and repeatedly; then she asked: "Are you sure your mother was not walking about the house the other night?"

Emily met her mother's enquiring eyes.

"I didn't hear anything," she countered to her grandmother.

"You will surely be sorry if you are hiding anything from me," the old woman pursued. "Some day she will have it in for you as she has for me. How many times do I have to tell you that?"

These words brought violent alarm into Mrs. Fletcher's face. Emily glanced at her with an ironic smile and answered more softly:

"You are mistaken, Grandma. Mamma never even thought of doing you any harm."

"Will you never learn to know her?" Mrs. Elliot exclaimed in accents of impatience. "I was sleeping a little while ago, and do you know what I dreamed? I saw your mother at my bedside; she stood there looking at me asleep. It seemed as if I needed only to reach out my hand to touch the long black coat she had on. If you could have seen the look on her face! How happy she would have been to have seen me lying there dead!"

Mrs. Fletcher buried her face in her hands.

"My dreams never deceive me," Mrs. Elliot repeated, "and I know what this one means. It was sent by Heaven to put me on guard against her. She's just waiting for a chance to get me out of the way."

Emily laughed off these words as a harmless joke, but her eyes never left her mother, who sat doubled up in her chair with her knees almost touching her forehead.

Day was rapidly falling. The girl put aside her work and lighted one of the lamps on the mantelpiece; then she took up the shirt and went on with the sewing. Mrs. Elliot had stopped talking and in a few minutes she fell asleep. The rasp of her difficult breathing came audibly in the silence.

Raising her head, Mrs. Fletcher found her daughter staring at her fixedly; she turned about in her chair and closed her eyes. The blood had flown from her cheeks and her compressed lips betrayed her violent efforts to contain her wretchedness. Some time went by before she could get up and cross the room to the door; when she came to the bed where her mother lay in a restless sleep broken by confused mutterings, she turned away her eyes and departed precipitately.

On the stairs she feared that her legs would give way beneath her; she clutched the railing with her hands and descended step by step like a small child. Her head hung limp on her chest, her face half hidden by the collar of her coat; she contracted her eyebrows with all her energy, as if to wring from her eyes the tears that trembled just below the lids.

She stumbled into the dining room and sat down. Labouring under an emotion such as she had never known, her heart hammered as if it would crack, and resounded loudly in her ears; she had a strange sensation of giddiness; a single thought possessed her mind, commanding over the turmoil in her spirit: "All this must not go on." She said this over and over in an undertone.

This inner distress of hers was of short duration. She wept silently, and in a few minutes she had recovered from the surprise and horror of the encounter, but she pondered for a long time over the condition in which she had found her mother and the singular words which she had heard her utter. "They are the notions of a crazy woman," she thought, and in that thought found consolation.

Josephine, coming in to set the table, roused her from her brooding. She got up, lighted the lamp, and tried to resume her sewing until dinner should be ready; but the cold, which she had forgotten for a moment, made her fingers ineffectual for work.

When Emily came downstairs a little later she found her mother standing by the table, her hands on the globe of the lamp, and in its leaden light her face showed anxious and aged.

CHAPTER TWENTY-EIGHT

AFTER EMILY HAD FINISHED HER allotment of sewing, the days seemed interminable. She stood at the window hour after hour in the hope of seeing the minister on his way from Glencoe. Sometimes, when her grandmother was sleeping, she entertained herself by sitting at the desk and writing letters to Sedgwick—letters which she tore up immediately or tucked away in her Bible. Or she would sit by the fire and indulge in long meditation on what she would say to him when he came to Ashley House, the conversations they would have; and now that she had no more shirts to sew for Miss Easting, this game of daydreaming was her most satisfying diversion. Untiringly she rehearsed in her mind the dialogue that was to take place, adapting her opening words to the idea of a Sedgwick grave or a Sedgwick gay. She wondered if he ever let down to the level of joke or banter, or if he were always as he had appeared the day when he called on them, and she was inclined to believe that the latter was the correct conjecture. "I must talk seriously to him," she thought; "that is what he would prefer."

As Saturday dragged along, she made up her mind to go to church the next morning, in spite of the distance from Ashley House to Glencoe and the

difficulties of the road in this most inclement season.
The cold was terrific, and the frozen earth beneath
its blanket of frost gave a sense of slipping away
from underfoot. Mrs. Fletcher, who practised a
daily stroll outdoors in the cause of health, no longer
ventured in the garden without a cane, and she could
be seen making the tour of the house with a tentative
caution, her hand feeling its way along the wall.
Mrs. Elliot, for her part, whimpered and called for
her shawl whenever the window was opened even a
crack. Such a degree of cold had never been known.
Mrs. Fletcher and her daughter ate their morning
meal in the kitchen, with no question made of the
odours that sometimes lingered there. The dining-
room fireplace remained unused.

To avoid possible argument, Emily did not tell
her mother of her Sunday plan and went out without
a sound while Mrs. Fletcher was settling herself in
one of the kitchen chairs. She ran as far as the gate
and set out along the little hollow lane that she had
followed the day she went to the Stevenses. Beneath
her shawl she pressed her Bible, in default of a
prayer book. Her teeth chattered with the cold and
she felt a sort of gnawing at her ears, even though
she had fastened the flaps of her bonnet down over
her cheeks by means of a black velvet ribbon tied
under the chin. From time to time she stopped for
breath, or bent almost double with a cough and
stamped up and down while she stood with pain-
smitten face. When she passed Rockley she stopped

to lean against a tree and stare at the house as she had done when she came to see the Stevenses. A thread of black smoke rose up straight from the chimney. No matter how badly off they were, she was driven to say half aloud, at least these folks had a fire to sit by. Then she went forward again.

An hour later she came to Glencoe, and went immediately to the church. It was a wooden building, painted green, built on a terrace dominating the town. Some women who entered as she did stared at her without a greeting; one of them, who was dressed in black and carried herself imposingly, raised her eyebrows on seeing the girl and paused to watch more closely what she was doing. There might have been fifty years in her sallow, fleshy face; her black eyes seemed to search out the core of what they looked at, and her lower lip stood slightly forward in a scornful smirk. Her hat was of shiny black straw adorned with a medallion of jet, and over her shoulders she wore a kind of velvet surplice.

Emily brushed past her and chose a place at the rear of the church, from which she had a good view of the preacher without being seen by the congregation. After a silent prayer she sat in the pew, unclasped her shawl, and opened the Bible in her lap. It was comfortable in the church; not far from Emily, in the corner, was a large round stove, and she could hear the murmur of the flames and sometimes the faint sound of the burnt coals falling in the grate. When she had grown used to the darkness, she made out the white altar cloth and the enormous Bible that stood on a lectern of light-coloured wood. People came in and bent over the pews to read the names that were marked on them; the group of women who had stared at Emily at the door had taken their places just under the pulpit. Only the woman in the velvet surplice had not sat down—she stood erect and slowly scanned the congregation until she distinguished Emily. She watched her for a moment, then sat and bent to whisper in her neighbor's ear.

This personage was Eliza Hess, who, like Prudence Easting, belonged to that category of unlucky mortals who call upon love with all their souls and for whom love seems to have no use. She, too, was smitten with Sedgwick, but, being older than the directress, she understood the nature of her emotion and confessed it to herself in sorry solitude. This self-knowledge of her heart had soured her, and she was impatient with herself for loving the one man in all the parish who was practically inaccessible to love. Her chagrin brought ill temper with it, for the years had tutored without mellowing her. She hated the minister, yet she found herself powerless to depart from Glencoe, to support the thought of no longer going to the church where she was certain to see him, no longer sitting at the foot of his pulpit where her futile passion had drawn her for ten years; and in her jealousy she continued to mount guard over his person.

In short order the pews were all filled. An anæmic young man took his place next to Emily; one guessed in his half-closed eyes an inquisitive glance that took in all it could see without lifting the lids. He sat unmoving for a long time, his hands clasped in his lap, patiently studying the girl's shawl, her stockings and shoes. A confused noise made him start and look up quickly—the congregation was standing.

This was the moment which Emily had awaited with waxing emotion. When she saw the Reverend Mr. Sedgwick step forward toward the pulpit in his white gown she lifted herself on her toes and craned her neck in his direction. Many of the worshippers noticed her in this posture; her neighbour watched her curiously while he turned the pages of his book, and she discovered this and blushed a little. The service began.

After the advent hymns chanted with general zeal there followed the reading of the Nicene creed; Emily knew none of the liturgy well and was pained at her ignorance. The anæmic young man sang and read with a confident voice, pretending to keep his book closed. A woman behind Emily delivered the ritual sentences with a sharp and ear-shattering assurance. Above the voices of all the others rose the voice of the minister, firm and clear, with an accent of faith and zeal which stirred the young girl's heart. Entirely at random she opened her Bible to the

Psalms and moved her lips in time with the people about her, uttering no sound.

It was a comfort to her when Sedgwick took his place before the lectern and commenced the reading of the chapter. With his hands on the book he read along without bending his head, and from time to time he lifted his eyes to some point in the rear of the church. Emily, who watched him with rapt attention, found something strange in his look which surprised her and distracted her from what she read; it was as if he cast a spell on her. She hung on his glance and followed it wherever it was directed, as if to discover what might be in his mind. Once Sedgwick felt her eyes upon him and glanced in her direction, without interrupting the sentence which he had begun and which he completed from memory. Emily grew red and felt as though she had been suddenly plunged in a sort of trance. When Sedgwick stopped reading, at the end of the chapter, she had the painful sensation of being rudely aroused from deepest slumber.

But the congregation had risen to its feet again and was intoning a hymn; the woman in the surplice was making the rounds of the church, still singing, offering the plate to the worshippers. When she came near Emily she caught her eye and stared at her, singing a trifle louder. The girl felt beads of perspiration on her forehead and pretended to search her pocket. Her neighbour reached across her and dropped a coin in the plate, winning a nod of approval from the deaconess, but she gave no sign of returning toward the altar or continuing her way around the side aisles. On the contrary, she remained stationary at Emily's side until the end of the hymn, her eyes fastened upon her with an insolent glare, her bosom swelling with her efforts at song. Finally she moved away, disappeared a moment at the rear of the church, and returned to her place after setting the plate on a small stand not far from the altar.

Although she never removed her eyes from the preacher, Emily understood not a single word of the sermon. She had suddenly conceived the idea of going up to speak to him at the end of the service, as he was going into the vestry, and the idea held her with such force that it forbade all other thought. She turned inward and probed herself as to the real motive for her churchgoing—whether it was not more for the sake of a talk with her pastor than for purposes of devotion. She hastily phrased the things she had to say to him, compelling herself to be calm, although she felt stirred with unfamiliar emotions which robbed her of all ease. She was impatient for Sedgwick to finish his sermon, and yet she dreaded the moment when it would come to an end. A dozen times she abandoned her project and determined to leave the church as soon as possible without so much as a look in his direction. Why did she need to ask his counsel? But then, was her trip on foot from Ashley House to be all for no purpose? If her object was prayer—she could pray just as well at home. If she hoped that her piety would be warmed by contact with the piety of others—she looked around her and felt that no one else was listening, either, but that many of them were staring at her with an unfriendly curiosity; the deaconess, in particular, indefatigably turned her eyes in Emily's direction. Emily shot her a glare of contempt and promptly returned to the minister, who talked in unimpassioned tones, his arms inert at his sides, his face devoid of any sign of emotion.

He was then drawing to a conclusion. He took up the Bible and the prayer book which he had placed before him, descended from the pulpit, and retired to the altar. The congregation joined in a final hymn, while Emily hurriedly pinned her shawl and hunted for the gloves which she had dropped. At the end of the sermon her indecision had grown to agony, and she no longer had any idea what she should do. Finally, when she saw the minister leave the choir and close the door of the vestry behind him, she lost her last ounce of courage and joined the congregation filing out.

The icy air smote her in the face and she fastened down the brim of her bonnet, tying the ribbons under her chin. Men and women passed her, jostling her a little as she stood on the threshold, unable to come to the point of going down the stairs. Suddenly she discovered that she had forgotten her Bible and she turned back into the church through the emerging crowd.

She found it in the pew where she had left it and was about to slip it under her shawl when a voice behind her sharply asked:

"What are you doing, miss? Don't you know that those books are parish property?"

Emily turned her head and met the glance of the deaconess.

"Let me see what you are taking," she went on.

"Why, no, ma'am," Emily whispered. "This is my own Bible."

"I am the caretaker of this church," the woman went on, raising her voice. "I insist on your showing me what you have under your shawl there."

Suddenly reaching out, she snatched the Bible from Emily's hands under the shawl. Some women who had been drawn by the disturbance gathered around the lady of the surplice and eyed the girl mistrustfully; two of them exchanged whispered words and shook their heads in surprise.

As soon as she could recover herself, Emily went up to her accuser and said in a low voice: "I warn you I am going to make a complaint. My name is written on the first page of this Bible. I am Emily Fletcher and I live at Ashley House; the Reverend Mr. Sedgwick knows my family and I am going to speak to him about this."

"What impudence!" the woman replied excitedly. "Here's a note addressed to Mr. Sedgwick himself in the Bible. Why wouldn't you have given it to him if it were yours? You see, you are caught!"

And she looked up triumphantly at the other women, who whispered approval. Emily fell back against a pew; she had suddenly paled and no words would issue from her open mouth.

"Well, miss," her adversary proceeded, "we had better go to Mr. Sedgwick and clear this matter up." She took the Bible under her arm, heedless of Emily's protests, and walked rapidly to the door of the vestry. They went in together.

The minister sat at a table, filing the pages of his sermon in a notebook. When he saw the two women and the agitation marked in their faces he stood up in surprise. Emily he did not appear to recognize. He nodded but said nothing, waiting for an explanation.

"I am returning this Bible to you," said the deaconess. She put the Bible on the table and added, turning half toward the girl: "This young lady, who doesn't belong to the church, anyway, saw fit to go off with it."

"But it's my Bible, sir; my name is written on the first page," Emily explained with indignation.

Sedgwick took the Bible and opened it.

"You are Miss Fletcher?" he asked when he had examined the flyleaf.

"Yes, I am. You saw me at Ashley House ten days ago, and I am the one you gave some work for the Community House at Wilmington."

"Miss Hess," the minister said, addressing the deaconess, "the Bible belongs to this young lady."

"Maybe so, but this belongs to you," retorted Miss Hess. And she proffered him the letter which she had found in the Bible, one of those that the girl had written in a moment of idleness.

Emily wanted to snatch it from her fingers, but the gesture had been too quick and Sedgwick already had it in his hands.

"What am I to do?" he asked with a little smile. Holding the note still folded, he looked from one to the other. Emily recovered at once.

"You must keep it and read it," she said assuredly.

"Why not read it now?" Miss Hess demanded with growing anger. "Is there a secret about it?"

"Miss Hess," replied Sedgwick evenly, "I shall not read this letter until Miss Fletcher chooses. Furthermore, she is at liberty to take it back if she wishes, since she did not give it to me voluntarily."

There was a catch in the girl's throat.

"It was right of Miss Hess to give it to you," she said, "but please read it when you are alone."

Miss Hess flushed at these words and turned upon Sedgwick to exclaim:

"Am I to understand that my pastor has lost confidence in me? Does he wish me to resign my post as caretaker?"

"That is not in question," the minister answered severely. "Your zeal has led you to make a mistake. I am compelled to set it right, that's all."

"No one hereabouts knows this girl," Miss Hess continued warmly. "I can swear to that, and I insist on her showing proof that the Bible belongs to her."

"I know her, and that will have to satisfy you, Miss Hess."

The deaconess flung up her arms in exasperation, her surplice billowing about her shoulders.

"A stranger in the community! I say she should read aloud what she has taken the liberty of writing to the pastor of our church! Your flock has a right to the truth."

Emily laughed. "You're joking," she said. "It doesn't concern you at all."

"Joking?" repeated Miss Hess indignantly. "Don't you think I saw you in church? Yes, young lady, I am the caretaker, and I watched you all through the service. It is my duty not only to denounce you, but to demand that the pastor of this church forbid you to enter it. You are unworthy . . ."

"Take care," Sedgwick interrupted. "If you have anything to say about Miss Fletcher's conduct, say it plainly, without mixing insults with your accusations. What is it?"

Miss Hess poured a glance of contempt upon the girl and continued breathlessly:

"Her behaviour in church was unpardonable; she was continually standing on tiptoe and leaning over the shoulders of the people in front of her."

"Well?" queried Sedgwick.

"Well, it was perfectly plain that she did not follow the words in her book," Miss Hess said with gleaming eyes.

"Is that all you noticed, Miss Hess? Inattention like that is hardly a capital crime; it's not even worth bringing up." The old man looked firmly and impassively before him.

"Oh!" said Miss Hess as if she had been struck. "Can it be that you don't understand what she was doing, that . . . that . . ."

"Careful," said Sedgwick.

Miss Hess burst out with: "It's incredible! All my neighbours noticed the same thing. She didn't pay the slightest attention to the service; she had eyes only for you, Pastor."

The minister's wrath was aroused.

"You are going beyond your right in speaking like this, Miss Hess. That will do!"

"I'll resign my position if I'm not allowed to do my duty as I see it," she cried, pounding on the table.

"You must do as your conscience directs. If you withdraw your assistance, there are others I can call upon."

He took the Bible and offered it to Emily, who stood in silence beside him.

"Here is your book," he said. "I'll answer your letter, or else come to Ashley House myself."

"What is this Ashley House?" Miss Hess demanded aggressively.

"Miss Hess, your conduct is unpardonable. Kindly leave this room."

"I'm not going to leave you alone with that creature—or I'll publish it all over your parish to-morrow. I'm a power here; I have influence; I can have you run out of Glencoe if I choose." She planted herself before the minister, hands on hips; her breath came short and raspingly. Sedgwick bit his lip and turned his eyes away a moment.

"Miss Hess," he finally said, "as long as I have the confidence of my flock, I shall consider myself at home here. Whenever Providence decides that I am to go, I shall go at once. But for the present I shall see that you obey me."

Miss Hess turned her back on him in rage; her surplice floated out around her shoulders. "All right!" she shouted. "You won't be here long." She moved rapidly to the door. Suddenly she paused, as if struck with an idea. Opening the door quickly, she tried at the same time to get hold of the key, which was on the inside; but her trembling hand was unsuccessful, and the girl, who had been following with her eyes, had time to spring toward her and wrest it from her.

Emily threw the key into the middle of the room. The encounter had been so brief that Sedgwick, who was shortsighted and had not seen clearly what went on, did not understand the cause of the disturbance. He stared at the two women in surprise and remained in his place. Miss Hess appeared to hesitate a moment; then she went out.

"You see what she wanted to do!" Emily cried, pointing to the key.

"What was it?" Sedgwick asked.

"Lock us in. She's a vile woman!"

"Not vile, just mad, Miss Fletcher. There are many like her in every parish of the world."

"But why should she have anything against me? What have I done to her?"

Sedgwick shrugged his shoulders. "Don't think about it," he said, and added almost at once: "Goodbye, Miss Fletcher."

CHAPTER TWENTY-NINE

* * * * * * * * * * * * * * * * *

SINCE HER EXCURSION TO THE church at Glencoe, Emily was growing more and more self-contained, but her face was suffused with tranquillity and at times a secret happiness which made her young again. She answered her mother's questions briefly and abstractedly, and she seldom said a word in the presence of Mrs. Elliot. All day long she sat by the fire, and whether she was reading or sewing she maintained a silence that her grandmother succeeded in breaking only with difficulty. The old woman's efforts to draw her into confidences, as she had before, were vain; she had lost all dominion over this spirit which no longer had need of unburdening itself to her, and now devoted itself instead to weaving a variety of dreams which no one at Ashley House suspected.

One morning, however, coming into her grandmother's room, she broke her custom and went over to sit on the bed. She was out of breath and she raked her fingers through her wind-tossed hair.

"Well, where have you been?" her grandmother asked with curiosity, and reached out a hand to her.

"I've been running in the garden a little," the girl answered in short gasps. "It's a beautiful day."

Mrs. Elliot seemed disappointed.

"Is that all you have to tell me, child?"

Emily smiled and shrugged her shoulders.

"Why, what would I have to tell you, Grandma?"

"Of course," Mrs. Elliot said, drawing away her hand, "you never talk to me any more. You used not to treat me this way." Her face took on an aggrieved expression.

"Come now, you're always whining," the girl laughed. "Can't you cheer up?"

"Cheer up, Emily?" Mrs. Elliot asked gloomily. "What good would that do me? Would it keep me from dying?"

Emily tossed her head as if to say that the question was too much for her; then she arose and went to her chair by the fire. From under her shawl she drew a letter, which she began to read with attention. Apparently she already knew its contents, for the little seal of black wax had been broken. This is what it said:

DEAR MISS FLETCHER: It is part of my ministry to give you a reply, however difficult the task may be. I am sure you could not have considered very carefully before writing me so confused a letter; but it is not so much what you say as the way you say it that makes me uneasy and compels me to give you my time to-day.

You must understand at the outset that my words would have more meaning if you had taken the pains to be a little clearer and more explicit. We shall surely see each other again and freely discuss the matters which are troubling you and which you speak of in such obscure terms. But I do not know how soon that may be, and my duty forbids me to delay in helping you to the extent of my ability.

You are restless and unsatisfied; first you talk about wanting your life to come to an end, then about wanting it to bring you everything you ask of it without delay. That's a very unfortunate state of mind for anyone your age; and yet you seem to think that these are only minor worries, for you tell me a little farther on that your chief distress comes from "evil thoughts" that get into your mind in spite of you. I shall not dwell on this point, and you must fight it out alone according to the dictates of your conscience, but what have your mother's money troubles to do with this? You speak confusedly of things which you claim to have by natural right and which some unnamed person appears to dispute with you. What does all this mean, and how can you expect me to help you, as you ask, unless you make up your mind to tell me clearly just how I can serve you?

You make a great point of wanting to see me and talk over your troubles. Yet you had a chance to speak to me last Sunday, when we were alone in the vestry, and you did not take it. Was it because you were afraid? I must remind you that you will not succeed in anything on earth unless you exert the courage and endurance which are the great virtues of our race. It is weakness and hesitation which forfeit the world, I am sure, much more than will, no matter how misdirected it may be.

If the conditions in which Heaven has placed you seem unfavourable, you must consider whether it is more right to evade them, or to submit and grow used to them. I don't know what you want, but remember that a desire for change is almost always to be mistrusted: for it implies a spirit that is dissatisfied with the lot which Providence has assigned to it.

Have you ever thought seriously of marriage?

Although there were sentences which puzzled her, Emily was pleased with the letter and reread it tirelessly. As a matter of fact she had expected something quite different, advice of a practical nature; and instead he had written largely in generalities, which enlightened her not at all on the course she should follow in order to become mistress of Ashley House. For it was about that, no more nor less, that she had written to the minister, and the "evil thoughts" of this innocent girl were not at all the ones which the elderly Sedgwick inferred; they all arose from her impatience at seeing her mother in possession of what she coveted keenly for herself, and from an unconfessed desire for her death. Shame forbade her to mention these things except in a rather vague way, and the minister had been misled as to the direction of the words she had used to veil her moody thoughts. Nevertheless, she felt comforted and hopeful. Far from condemning her, he even talked of another meeting. What was more, he found her confidences interesting enough to call for an answer, as he said, without delay. It was this that impressed her most; the rest seemed unimportant, because she was uncertain of its meaning. The last sentence, which she disregarded at first, came to have more force and she considered it curiously; she failed to see its connection with what preceded, but something warned her that she would think more of it later. After reading the letter several times, she folded it away in her Bible.

That afternoon she wrapped up the shirts which she had hemmed, and walked to the Community House at Wilmington. At the last moment she was unwilling to trust the minister's letter to her Bible and slipped it into her dress, fearing that some unlucky accident might let it fall into her mother's or grandmother's hands.

Prudence Easting greeted her with an expression of disappointment. "He's not coming to-day," she said.

The words were a blow to Emily and also somehow comforting; she felt that so soon after reading Sedgwick's letter she could not have talked to him; but it was a disappointment, nevertheless.

"Come in," the directress continued. "It's a free day to-day, and we can chatter all we want." And she led her into the little room where they had had their first conversation, the week before. The baskets were still in their places, with their numbers stitched in red, but the wreaths and laurel had been taken down and the walls were white and bare.

While Emily removed her bonnet and mittens Prudence Easting opened the parcel which she had deposited on the table.

"Good," she said, after unfolding one of the shirts. "I see you pick it up very well. Do you want to take six more of them?"

"Surely," Emily answered, sitting down at the table. "I came on purpose to get them."

"I hope you also came to talk to me a little," said the directress. She laughed and added at once, "I am all alone to-day."

"Do you get tired of it?"

"No. I work, but I like to talk while I sew." She sat down opposite the girl and took up her needle. "Do you know that I have been thinking about you —a great deal?" she said after a moment. Emily seemed surprised. "But have you time . . . ?" Prudence Easting asked.

Emily folded her arms on the table attentively. "I have absolutely nothing to do," she said.

"Yes, I have been thinking about you . . . I was wondering if you are happy."

"Happy? Why, yes, surely." Emily had not expected the question and was unprepared to answer.

"Yes?" Prudence Easting raised her head and glanced at the girl; she appeared disappointed.

"You seemed troubled the other day," she said. "Naturally, I didn't venture to ask you, but you know it is sometimes good to confide in some one. Lots of troubles disappear if you just talk them over with people who can understand and sympathize. One never gets anywhere by hiding away inside oneself."

Several minutes passed in silence. The directress went on with her sewing, bending her head above her work; now and then a faint sigh would break the even rhythm of her breathing. A fit of shyness kept Emily from answering. She would have liked to say something friendly to this woman. Though she scarcely knew her, she felt a sort of kindred pain and unrest in her, and as she looked at her massive head with its braided bands of hair, the big red hands, the bosom swelling under a tight black dress, she felt pity for her without knowing quite why.

"Are you sorry not to have seen the Reverend Mr. Sedgwick?" the directress asked.

The reply came without hesitation: "Yes. I was counting on seeing him."

"I hoped he would come, too, especially for your sake, Emily." She raised her eyes. "I am to call you that, am I not? . . . Oh, he's a man who does a great deal of good in the world."

"You called him a saint."

"Did I?" The directress's hand stopped for a second in the act of completing a stitch. "Well, yes, it's perfectly true." Her cheeks grew a trifle pink, and she added: "You must have thought that I spoke rather warmly of him, Emily, but I owe him a great deal of gratitude."

She resumed her sewing.

"Please don't say a word about this, of course," she added after a moment. "I have had a very hard life."

Emily no longer restrained her curiosity; she, too, blushed, and said without looking at her new friend:

"Have you been unhappy?"

"Yes, Emily, for years and years; but as he explained to me, it's all for our good in the end, even our faults—nothing that happens to us is wasted. You will understand later on . . ."

"Yes? Are you happier now?"

Prudence Easting did not reply at once. She went on sewing and appeared not to have heard.

"I'm not unhappy," she said at last.

They both lapsed back into silence, busy with the thoughts that were coming to birth in their minds. Emily toyed with her mittens and felt herself suddenly downcast and disheartened.

"And what about you?" Prudence Easting demanded suddenly. "At your age one rarely has big troubles—and didn't you tell me you hadn't any?"

The girl made a motion as if to ward off the necessity of speaking more plainly; but she could not suppress a sudden rush of feeling, and said almost at once, with unwonted expansiveness:

"Yes, I have some, too. I'm not always happy. But it would take too long to explain to you," she added, seeing the directress's expectant glance.

"Why not tell me all about it?" Prudence Easting said, laying her work on the table. "I am your friend, I am older than you, and you ought to confide in me. I know a great deal about life, you see."

"And I don't know anything about it," Emily exclaimed wretchedly. "I never know what I ought to do, and my plans all go wrong."

Prudence Easting had become very serious. She planted the palm of her hand upon the table and said, with her eyes fixed on Emily: "Listen to what I say. Whatever happens, be firm. Never let yourself be discouraged by what seems like bad luck."

"That's right," Emily murmured. Her eyes grew suddenly brighter and she said, after a brief hesitation: "I'm going to confess something to you. He wrote to me—in answer to a letter I sent him."

"Who wrote to you?" The directress drew slightly away.

"Why, the Reverend Mr. Sedgwick. Weren't you talking about him just now? I asked his advice about several things that were worrying me and he sent me an answer."

The directress withdrew her hand and said in an embarrassed tone:

"He sent you an answer? What did he say?"

Emily remained mute. She seemed unable to recall a single word of the letter except for the last line, and that, just then, sounded unaccountably absurd.

"Excuse me," Prudence Easting returned. "I didn't think what I was asking."

"Here," Emily said. She failed to understand the frigidity of these words and suddenly felt the ground giving way beneath her, and she took the letter from her dress and placed it on the table under Prudence's eyes.

The blood flew to the directress's cheeks; she bent her head and stared stupidly at the letter. Finally she turned away and said dispiritedly: "It's none of my business, Miss Fletcher."

Her words cast Emily into the deepest confusion; she recovered the letter, folded it, and slipped it into her dress again, all without a word. Prudence Easting resumed her sewing.

Emily was the first to break a silence that made her acutely ill at ease. "I must go, Miss Easting," she said, putting on her mittens. "It's four o'clock."

"Just as you like, Miss Fletcher." The directress did not look up from her work. "When you come again don't forget to bring back the book you borrowed. They can be kept only two weeks or a fine has to be paid, and it's out in my name."

She pointed to a parcel on a chair.

"I wrapped the shirts for you. There are six of them."

"All right," Emily said. She got up and took the parcel, but paused at the door. "Thank you for your advice," she said, softening her voice as well as she could. "I'll see you again, Miss Easting."

"Very well. Good-bye, Miss Fletcher," the directress quietly answered. She had turned toward the window to thread a needle, which seemed to absorb her completely.

CHAPTER THIRTY

* * * * * * * * * * * * * * * *

A S SHE DREW NEAR TO ASHLEY
House, Emily made out the figure of her
mother on the porch in her army overcoat, staring
toward the gate. As soon as Mrs. Fletcher saw her
she called out and began to beckon violently to make
her hurry. Emily started to run.

"What's the matter?" she called when she saw
her mother's agonized face. Mrs. Fletcher was completely white; tears had been coursing over her face
and had left their tracks in the wrinkles. She
stretched out her hands, slightly trembling, and
stammered out: "Your grandmother . . . your
grandmother . . ."

"Well?" Emily stamped her foot. Mrs. Fletcher's
emotion terrified her and at the same time made her
impatient.

Her mother turned away without answering, as if
to hide her grief, and stumbled into the house. When
she reached the dining room she sank into a chair.
Emily snatched off her bonnet and planted herself
before her mother.

"Has something happened to Grandma?" She
shook Mrs. Fletcher by the arm. "Tell me,
Mamma."

"She is dead," said Mrs. Fletcher.

"Oh!" Emily stood quite still, with her bonnet in her hand, staring at her mother in amazement. Finally she went and sat down on the sofa.

"She can't have suffered very long," she said after a silence. "That's a blessing."

"Go look at her, child," said Mrs. Fletcher, blowing her nose. "You must give her a final kiss."

These words sent hideous shivers through the girl; she remembered the kiss of several days before and the violence which she had had to do to her impulses to make herself touch her lips to that sallow forehead. Of all the emotions now disturbing her, overwhelming revulsion was the strongest. It made her shudder to think that a dead old woman was lying up there in the room overhead.

She rose and lighted the lamp.

"Are you going upstairs?" Mrs. Fletcher asked.

"Not right away." Emily set the lamp on the table.

Mrs. Fletcher wiped her eyes with her handkerchief. "You know you must sit with her a little while. It's always done, child."

Emily sat down and folded her arms beneath her shawl.

"Well," Mrs. Fletcher insisted, "what are you going to do?"

"Leave me alone, Mamma," the girl said angrily. "I still have to get used to this idea of never seeing Grandma again."

"That's true," Mrs. Fletcher conceded. "It is terrible to learn it suddenly like this."

"What time did she begin to feel ill?"

"She called me a little before three o'clock. I was so upset that I had no idea what I ought to do. You know I had not seen her since that very cold day. She cried and screamed horribly."

Emily twisted her hands in agony. "That's enough, Mamma. Don't tell me anything more." And she went on after a few moments: "Have you done anything about the funeral?"

"Josephine has been to Glencoe. The minister has promised to take care of everything."

She looked at her daughter and said in a tone of sudden emotion: "You will sit with your grandmother, won't you, Emily?"

"I'll stay there one minute and no more."

"Oh, you are not going to leave her all alone tonight! Just think that . . ."

"Stay with her yourself," Emily exclaimed gruffly. "Don't be afraid. She won't hurt you."

She left the dining room and went into the kitchen; almost at once she returned with a candle, which she lighted. Mrs. Fletcher watched her in silence, her face wry with emotion.

Without volunteering another word, Emily went out of the room and up the stairs. Shame for her mother's cowardice incited her to display a little courage; she remembered, too, what Sedgwick had said about the necessity of being firm in all contingencies, and she quickly mounted the first few steps; but the candle threatened to go out and she had to slacken her pace. All the compelling and commonplace thoughts that attend on death came into her mind. Her grandmother would never speak to her again—this woman whom she had seen every day since childhood. The idea was impossible to grasp. She asked herself what would become of Mrs. Elliot's room and whether it would be given to her: "It belongs to me, like the rest," she thought.

At the top of the stairway she lifted the candle high above her head and looked around. A sudden nervousness seized her; she stopped short, thinking that she saw something before the door.

"It's the shadow," she said aloud, and she swept the candle in a great arc, down and up, to reassure herself. With her arm extended before her, eyes straining, she moved a few steps forward. Suddenly she gave a cry; a human figure appeared to have slipped between her and the door—a little stooping figure of a man with his back turned. Rooted with terror, she thought of her father and of the steps that Mrs. Elliot had continually heard on the stairway at night. A hoarse voice called to her from below; it was her mother, and for a moment she could not answer. But she quickly recovered herself—for a careful look assured her that she was mistaken. She could distinctly see the panels of the door and the key in the lock. The blood returned to her cheeks. She leaned over the banister and called: "It's all right, Mamma. I thought I saw a rat."

Then she went in. The silence in this room, where she had always heard the rasping breath of her grandmother, seemed stranger and more sinister than anything she could have imagined. Not until now had she felt the presence of death.

Her heart was beating fast. She had to lean against the door, and stood there a moment without stirring, her eyes on the curtains of the bed, which her mother had drawn together and fastened. Some remnants of logs were burning out on the hearth— the same logs which Emily had put on the fire before leaving—and she paused before this thought as though she would find in it a whole explanation of the mystery of death.

She began to cross the room aimlessly. Countless thoughts assailed and tormented her. What did it all mean? She had understood well enough that her grandmother was dead, yet now she seemed no longer to understand it. Everything was just as before— her chair in its place, her Bible on the table. (She blessed the foresight which had warned her not to leave Sedgwick's letter in it.) She walked around the bed, saying to herself half aloud: "No, nothing has changed at all."

Then she sat down in her chair and said out loud: "If nothing had happened I would be sitting here, anyway, by this same fire, just as I am now." This being so, it seemed incredible that her grandmother could be dead, and for several minutes she could think of nothing else.

Suddenly the reality took form in her imagination. Rousing herself, she ran to the bed and tried to unfasten the curtains. She wanted to see. What she would see was frightful, no doubt, but she must say farewell to her grandmother or later she would blame her cowardice as an irreparable fault. She had loved her once. She remembered her arrival at Ashley House, her black hair under the big black hat, her brusque manner of speaking to her, calling her "little stupid." Emily tore at the curtains and they partly opened.

The sheet that lay over the body accentuated all its heavy and graceless lines, the abdomen, the shoulders massive as a man's. The hands and several strands of hair hung out from under the sheet, betraying Mrs. Fletcher's haste to cover the corpse.

Emily recoiled, shuddering so violently that she had to set the candle on the table and steady herself against a bedpost. Her mother's words surged back into her mind: "You must give her a final kiss." It was for this that she had come; she must lift the sheet and see that hidden face. The more she considered, the less she believed herself able to carry it through. She was seized with terror such as she had known on the day when she saw her father lying in this same bed. The hideous notion that she had had a few moments before returned to torment her again. Was it not her father she had seen at the

door before she came in?   He had come in with her,
perhaps; he might be there now.   She fell to her
knees and began to recite her prayers with hysterical
haste.

The sweat streamed down her forehead and tickled
her cheeks; but little by little, under the influence
of the words that she recited, she felt her composure
returning.   At the end of five minutes she stood up
again.

She moved a small table to Mrs. Elliot's bedside,
placed her candle on it, and the big Bible, which she
opened to a chapter of Corinthians.   On all her motions she imposed the slowness and dignity of a cere-
monial rite, though now and again she was moved
with a fierce desire to rush from the room screaming
with all her lungs.

She mastered her terror and bent above the body.
No force could bring her to lift the sheet, but she
touched her lips to the contour of the forehead.
Tears of dread and disgust streamed over her face
and she tasted their acrid flavour on her lips.   Why
must it be that everything which death has touched
becomes vile to the living?   She drew away shuddering from the bedside; the blood clamoured in her
head.

She opened the door and went out.   Then she took
her handkerchief and violently wiped her lips.

CHAPTER THIRTY-ONE

* * * * * * * * * * * * * * * *

TWO DAYS LATER, ON THEIR return from the cemetery, Mrs. Elliot's room was the scene of a quarrel of major proportions, which taught the girl that in spite of her mother's saccharine tongue and tearful face, she had lost none of the ferocity which lay at the root of her nature. They had scarcely set foot in the house when the two, with a mutual impulse, turned to the dead woman's room. Emily hurried to the fireplace and threw a handful of kindling on the fire.

"What are you up to?" her mother asked, coming in behind her.

"I expect you can see!" the girl replied. She let down the screen with a jerk, scratched some matches and slipped them under the wood along with a sheet of paper.

"No, no!" Mrs. Fletcher exclaimed, gesturing violently. She hurried across the room and tried to push the girl aside, but Emily had risen to her feet and stood her ground, calmly flicking the dirt from her hands.

"I'm making a fire," she said. "What of it?"

The roar of the flames could be heard from behind the screen.

"You are burning up my money!" Mrs. Fletcher

shouted. "This room is not to be used any more. Get out of here!" She seized Emily by the arm, but the girl fiercely shook herself loose.

"Do you think I'm going to live all winter in an ice box?" the girl demanded. "Do you want *me* to die, too?"

She had said this without thinking and the effect of her words surprised her. A fearful pallor spread over her mother's features. They stood there for a moment face to face. Mrs. Fletcher breathed a little heavily under the dominion of her excitement; she stared at Emily with a look of enraged astonishment, but offered no answer.

Emily forced herself to speak more gently. "You know very well that I'm not strong. Haven't you heard me coughing?" She turned and placed two logs on the fire. "It's not such a terrible expense," she went on, arranging them with the tongs. "You can make the wood last by covering it with ashes— but there's got to be one room in the house where a person can keep warm."

Mrs. Fletcher sat down with lowered head, her crêpe veil falling over her face. She seemed borne down with an enormous weight which bent her double. Emily glanced at her furtively. She coughed, and folding her arms beneath her shawl continued quietly:

"See! Do you think I am coughing on purpose? If you knew how much it hurts . . . !"

She pounded her chest with her fist and sat down

opposite her mother. Mrs. Fletcher remained absorbed in her thoughts. Her immobility began to frighten the girl; she had never seen her mother in this attitude and did not like it. "Is she sick?" she wondered, and said aloud:

"Move your chair up. The fire is hardly warm yet."

Mrs. Fletcher seemed to waken from a trance. With a sudden gesture she brushed back her veil and stared at the flames, which were springing up faster and faster.

"You are going a little too far!" she exclaimed fiercely. "Not content with disobeying me, you dare to make fun of me!" The crêpe of her veil hung down around her shoulders and bothered her, so she snatched off her hat and let her hair fall in disorder, increasing her look of frenzy. Emily sprang to her feet.

"Is there nothing you respect any more?" her mother continued, likewise getting up. "In this room . . . in this room . . ."

Her breath suddenly failed her; she stood with her mouth half open and glared at her daughter in hatred. Emily folded her arms and stood before the fire as if to defend it.

"Here where your grandmother died," Mrs. Fletcher choked, "you defy your mother. You demon! Yes, demon!" she cried, with a stamp of her foot, and she echoed the epithet several times with a strange ferocity. A trace of foam seethed out at the corners of her mouth. All at once she strode quickly past Emily and hurried into the adjoining dressing room.

The girl grew pale. The notion that her mother might attempt suicide crossed her mind, and she was on the point of calling to her when Mrs. Fletcher reappeared, carrying something which she tried to hide with her arm. With rapid strides she hurried over to the fireplace, and before Emily could guess what she intended she threw a pitcher of water over the flames. A loud sizzling muffled Emily's cry; billows of black smoke rolled through the room and made the women recoil.

"There!" Mrs. Fletcher shouted. "There!"

She threw back her head and watched her daughter with the glint of triumph in her eyes. Her quavering hand still held the pink china pitcher which she had used; in the smoke which still enveloped them and slowly dissolved she looked like a sort of avenging deity.

"You are out of your senses," Emily cried, recovered from her first surprise. She violently drew back her chair from the fireplace and sat down in the middle of the room. "Did you do that to frighten me?" she continued scornfully. "I am as strong as you, you know. You can never bind me to live the way you want."

"You are in my house and you will obey me," Mrs. Fletcher answered, "or I'll turn you out."

Emily burst out with a laugh.

"Just try! In the first place, you haven't the right, and, anyway, you couldn't do it if you were allowed to. Don't you know me better than that? I've had enough of your treatment. I am going to write a complaint about you this very day. You know that I am sick and you deprive me of the simplest care—which is to keep the house decently warm where I have to live."

"Write, write!" Mrs. Fletcher stammered. "Write to whom?"

"To whom? Why, what difference does that make, Mamma?" Emily said in a voice restrained and ominous. "Do you think there isn't any law in the country? Do you think you will be able to kill your daughter without any interference, without being punished?"

Mrs. Fletcher leaned against the bed and let her pitcher roll on the counterpane. Her eyes were wide with a look of apprehension.

"What are you saying?" she muttered. "Why do you talk about killing all the time? Do you think I would dream . . ." And suddenly she gave a little start and declared passionately:

"I'm a good woman, a good Christian! I never did your grandmother a stroke of harm. I am a woman like any other. I never wanted you to be sick."

"You won't let me make a fire."

"Oh, that has nothing to do with it. Good Lord!" Mrs. Fletcher cried, clasping her hands.

"You are either a fool," Emily said, getting up, "or you care more about your money than you do about my getting well. Look at me. I shake and shiver all day long. I'm as thin as a post. Do you suppose I ever eat my fill?"

"And how about me?" Mrs. Fletcher said piteously.

"Oh, you—you don't need to eat as much as I do. I'm still growing. I'm not sixteen yet, and you are old. But I warn you, the dollars you save now will go to paying doctors' bills some day."

"Be still!" said Mrs. Fletcher in anguish.

"Why should I? Grandma was right: you are afraid to hear the truth. She said that the day she came here. Oh, if you had had her taken care of, she would still be with us, there in that bed where you are sitting. But oh, no! we had to economize."

Mrs. Fletcher quickly arose. These last words had scored, and she was about to retort when Emily went on:

"I'm right, I know I am. If you love your money more than your child, why did you ever bring me into the world?"

"Be still!" Mrs. Fletcher said again. She was ashen white with wrath. "It's the Evil One who makes you talk this way. Only a few hours ago my mother breathed her last in this very room, and already you are profaning it with your blasphemous words. You have forgotten God's commandment . . ."

Emily laughed fiercely.

"Your mother hated you. Didn't you hear what she said about you the day you came in here to get warm? Her dream—don't you remember?" She imitated Mrs. Elliot's cracked, hoarse voice. " 'Will you never learn to know her? . . . How happy she would be to see me dead!' "

"She never said that!" Mrs. Fletcher shouted.

"No doubt you wish she hadn't, but she did," Emily continued more quietly. "And do you know what she dreaded above everything, Mamma?"

"What?" Mrs. Fletcher was shivering.

"Why, that you would poison her. She always made me swear that I had seen you tasting the food you sent up to her."

"That's enough!" Mrs. Fletcher's throat was dry. "The devil is in you . . . But God will punish you for tormenting me so—me who brought you into the world and suffered everything for you."

"Never mind about me. I don't want anything of you," Emily retorted, shrugging her shoulders.

Mrs. Fletcher cried out at that, and shaking her fist as if to confirm her words, she called in a voice that echoed through the room:

"To my dying day, I shall never speak to you again. You will live here like a stranger, and if you dare to defy me again I shall turn you out of this house."

Emily leaped up and seized the poker that stood against the wall.

"And you, if you dare to lay hands on me, I'll defend myself. I've had enough of your tyranny. How much respect do I owe you? Do you treat me like a daughter? I'm too big a fool, anyway—I'm too patient."

She paused for breath and held her mother with burning eyes. There was a moment of silence, the two standing motionless face to face. Presently Mrs. Fletcher lifted her hands to heaven in a gesture of horror and precipitately left the room.

CHAPTER THIRTY-TWO

* * * * * * * * * * * * * * * *

EMILY CLOSED AND BOLTED the door and set herself to mopping up the hearth. The water had run as far as the first boards of the floor and still dripped from the charred and glistening logs. Several times she had to go to the window to wring out the rags she was using. Finally, when she had wiped the hearth nicely dry, she lighted some newspapers in the fireplace and put what remained of the kindling under the logs. Lowering the screen again, she lay down flat and spent several minutes blowing with all her lungs on the kindling, which alternately caught and went out and caught again. Suddenly the fire blazed up.

She stood up, happy in the success of her efforts as if it augured other successes more important. "It means something," she said, half aloud. "I'm going to win out." . . . And she clapped her hands together to shake the dust off.

She found her anger all at once appeased and her calm self-possession restored. The fire flamed high and went roaring up the chimney; she sat down and reviewed the scene that had just been enacted. It was plain that Mrs. Fletcher's violence sprang from a real weakness of character. What had she profited by her tantrums? Had she succeeded in intimidating

Emily? On the contrary, she had driven her to firm resistance and had put herself in a ridiculous light. Could she hope in the future that Emily would obey her as before? The girl wondered why she had not understood long ago how easy it was to stand up against her mother.

"From now on my life is altered," she thought. "I'll do as I like. I'll live in comfort in this house which my father left me. Would he ever have let us go through the winter without lighting the fire? Is there really any need of such privations—not enough to eat, beds without sheets? Grandma got what she wanted, and how?—merely by a little firmness."

She recalled all that Mrs. Elliot had told her about her mother, and the sound of that voice that she would never hear again came ringing to her ear. It was as if her grandmother still counselled her in spirit: "When you have real troubles you must let me know about them. . . . I know my daughter better than you ever will. . . . You must listen to what I tell you about how to treat her; otherwise she will rob you of everything."

Oh, if she could only come back for a moment, just long enough to be told about the scene of that afternoon! How the old woman would have enjoyed her daughter's posturings! "Did she really have a water pitcher in her hand? And what did she say? Doesn't she know how ridiculous she is? Can't she see herself?"

Then Emily seemed to hear her grandmother's

cracked little laugh, and it was as though she lay there again in the bed behind her. What would her advice have been? And forgetting that in all probability she would not have asked Mrs. Elliot a thing, she imagined her leaning on her elbow and talking in her rasping voice: "Listen, Emily. Don't let her fool you. Don't try to reason with her. She is too narrow to understand. Anyway, it is instinct that rules her, and instinct is stronger than reason. Her one idea is to get along without spending money and never to draw on her bank account. Don't you see how delighted she will be to get rid of me? She grumbles every time she sends up my wood or my meals. She hates me because I cost her money. She doesn't love you, either; she loves nothing but her money. Mark my word, she would like to get rid of you, too. She wants to empty the house. Perhaps she will keep Josephine, so as not to die of fright all by herself—no, not you, but Josephine, because Josephine fears and obeys her. Listen to me carefully; I know what must be done. Force is the only way of convincing her. No use shouting, no use insulting her; you've got to take her by the shoulders and throw her out."

How many times Emily had heard her grandmother offer her this counsel! During that latter part of Mrs. Elliot's life, Emily believed that illness had robbed her of her reason and made her see imaginary dangers all about her, endowing Mrs. Fletcher with secret designs and malign intentions.

But now, was it so certain that she had been altogether mistaken? Emily had been astonished at the glances her mother had cast at her during their dispute just now. Could there be so much hate in the eyes if the heart was guiltless? She wondered if there was much difference between so fierce a sentiment as this and the sentiment which prompts a criminal. "She will be after you when she is rid of me," Mrs. Elliot used to say. And why not? A sudden flood of suspicion assailed her. How had her grandmother died? In two hours' time. She remembered her mother's agitated look in telling her about it—and grief was not a sufficient explanation. She had trembled; she had been unable to speak; she had not been willing to go up to the death room. Guilt would hardly have made her act any differently—and what good evidence was there to show that she was innocent?

Emily remained in this room throughout the day; she had no appetite, and the idea of eating a meal with her mother was abhorrent to her. She stayed in her chair, reading, sewing, ruminating her sinister thoughts. Why not believe that her mother had poisoned Mrs. Elliot? All her interests had directed her to the act; and on the other hand, what was there to stay her? Ashley House was so isolated that people at Glencoe and Wilmington scarcely knew of its existence, much less how many people lived there. In that direction her immunity was sure. For an avaricious spirit like her mother's, this last consideration would have more weight than all the scruples of conscience. She preferred to hear her daughter coughing rather than give her four sticks of wood to warm the room, and where was the line between an act like that and murder pure and simple?

All day Emily deliberated about her future, shaping plans and abandoning them one after another, galloping off after all the chimeras of her fancy; and she came to believe, in her unnerving loneliness, that life was no longer safe for her at Ashley House. Late in the afternoon she lighted the lamp and walked up and down from one end of the room to the other, peering about her uneasily. Never had she felt so agitated, so wretched; and still, a few hours earlier, she had been calm and contented with the turn of events. The coming of night brought with it a strange sensation which she had never before experienced. Why was she living through these trials while others led such apparently calm existences? She answered her own question, speaking aloud to herself: "Because you are not like other people."

No sound could be heard in the house. She listened; nothing stirred. The downstairs doors were undoubtedly closed or she would have heard her mother. She was alone. The idea frightened her at first; then she took courage from it and nursed a sense of pride. Alone in this room from which she had driven her mother—just so she would later be all alone in life. She wanted no friends, she asked only one thing—Ashley House. Was it much to expect?

She would live here according to her own will, mistress of her possessions, mistress of her life. This room would be hers, and the others with it; she would have fire, and plenty to eat. . . .

Thoughts seemed to press and jostle in her brain. They dizzied her and she returned to her chair. What time was it? Had dinner been served? She went to open the window and stood there awhile with her elbows on the sill. A fine snow lightly fell, with a scarcely audible sound as it touched the pine branches. The cold air flowed into the room in great floods like a river. She breathed it deep in long delight. How good it all was, the coolness upon her skin, the silent snow beneficently falling. A vast regret possessed her. Closing the window, she knelt at the foot of the bed and the tears flowed freely. She had need of talking to some one, to confide her burden of cares, and she began to pray.

CHAPTER THIRTY-THREE

* * * * * * * * * * * * * * * *

THE FOLLOWING WEEK, EMILY went again to Wilmington with the shirts she had finished hemming. Miss Easting received her without a word; taking her hand in both of her own, she held her in a long regard. "How ashamed I have been!" she said at last, when they were settled in the workroom.

"Why?" asked Emily in surprise.

"The Reverend Mr. Sedgwick told me. He came here the day after . . ."

"He told you about my grandmother?"

Miss Easting nodded her head. "And to think that I was so cool to you the very day that this . . ."

"It doesn't matter, Miss Easting," Emily interrupted. "I never even thought of it again."

Miss Easting sighed. "Such is life, my dear. You think you are happy, and suddenly a catastrophe hits you."

"I have never been happy," Emily said.

"Why, Emily! you told me just the opposite a week ago."

"I was mistaken, I guess."

They were silent for a moment. "Yes," Miss Easting went on, "I know how it is; I understand. I've been through the same thing. In times of great mis-

270

fortune you have the impression that you never have
been happy. Your whole spirit is afflicted, and you
can't remember. You will see her again, Emily."

"What do you mean?"

"Your grandmother . . ."

"Oh, excuse me," the girl answered, flushing.
"Yes, it is a great loss. . . . Did Mr. Sedgwick talk
to you about me?"

Miss Easting stretched her hands across the table
and forced a smile. "Yes, Emily," she said. "Let's
talk about him. I will explain to you."

She seemed to gather her forces, lowering her eyes
but not relinquishing Emily's hands.

"You probably didn't understand," she said at
last, "what caused my bad humour when you confided
to me that the Reverend Mr. Sedgwick had written
to you. You see, I had no idea how well you knew
him. You must understand, to begin with, that he
confides everything to me. I am almost a daughter
to him. I owe him a great deal, Emily."

She paused a moment and gave vent to a deep
sigh.

"I know his life as no one else does. He comes here
twice a month and I report on the work of the
House; in exchange he gives me all the news of what
has happened since his last visit, all the events of the
parish . . ."

"You are very religious, aren't you, Miss
Easting?"

"Why, surely, Emily!" Miss Easting answered,

blushing violently. "I am a devout Christian, and so I am as interested in the life of the church at Glencoe as I am in the salvation of my own soul. It is my greatest cross that I can't go there on Sundays. Remember, it is a long way from here to Glencoe."

"Why don't you go and live at Glencoe?"

"And what would happen to the Community House? Nothing would be done here without me. I have to be here. So in order to make up a little, the pastor is good enough to let me know about all the little happenings of his ecclesiastical life."

"The service is very interesting," Emily put in, encouraged to talk by Miss Easting's warmth. "I also . . ."

"So you can imagine my surprise," the directress continued, ignoring Emily's attempt at conversation, "when you told me that he had written to you. But he explained it all to me. You saw him first at your house, didn't you, and your mother was there?"

"Yes, surely. He came to ask for a contribution."

"Then you next saw him on the Sunday after his call. Is that right?"

"Yes."

"And where?"

"What did you say?"

Miss Easting began to laugh. "Forgive me," she said. "I mean you saw him on Sunday when he was officiating in church."

"Yes, and again in the vestry."

A smile lighted up Miss Easting's features, and she said: "That was it. You had a letter to give him. Now we have come to what we were speaking of before. He talked to me about you quite at length. You interest him."

"Really?" Emily's start of pleasure was spontaneous.

"Yes, my child. You don't mind if I call you that? You are even younger than I supposed the first time; and I feel old beside you—like an elder sister, or even your mother, in a sense. Yes, the pastor has thought a great deal about your future. He has ideas which he naturally confided to me, and we discussed them backward and forward. This is what we have in mind for you. I wonder if I ought to tell you. It's almost a secret, Emily."

"Oh, please!" Emily said.

"Well, first of all, you must marry, my child. I told the pastor so and he thought it was an excellent idea. He undoubtedly spoke to you about it in his letter. Remember that you are going on seventeen . . ."

"Sixteen."

"Sixteen is a very good age to marry, Emily. You are well off and there must be a good match for you somewhere in the district. There's no doubt about it; you will be much happier than you are now . . ."

She talked on in this vein for several minutes with

a sort of restrained vehemence.   It was as though she were acting in her own behalf to defend a personal interest. She leaned across the table toward Emily as if to kiss her, and repeated now and again in a tone that betrayed strong emotion: "Don't you think so? Don't you think so?"

Emily listened in silence, delighted to find that her happiness could be conceived as a possibility, but troubled over the means proposed to attain it.   Ashley House was not brought into the whole discussion. "Why marry?" she thought.   "What improvement could that bring to my present life?"   This thought imposed itself so insistently that she suddenly exclaimed: "Do you think that would be a good thing, Miss Easting?   But how would I be any better off than I am now?"

"In every way, my dear," the directress replied with ardour.   "When you are married you have more freedom and more to do at the same time.   You will have a home to take care of, and perhaps a family.   Being a woman, you can arrange your time to suit yourself, but your mind is not so idle and so it will be less open to sorrow or to . . . to those bad thoughts, don't you see?   After all . . ."

"Where would I live, Miss Easting?"

"Why, at your husband's, my child!"

"But it would have to be at Ashley House.   I won't think of living anywhere else."

"Well"—Miss Easting laughed as she answered—

"tell your husband so. That won't stand in the way, I suppose."

Emily shook her head. "It's out of the question for me to leave Ashley House. The house is my own."

"It will be your own some day, surely. But think over what I have said to you. Perhaps you already have some one in mind. You must not hesitate to tell me, my child."

She moved a little nearer and rested her elbows on the table.

"Think of me as somebody to confide in—to whom you can tell everything. Don't you ever plan about your future?"

"Oh yes!" the girl replied with ardour. "I very often think about what my life will be a few years from now. It's my favourite pastime. Whenever I am bored, all I have to do is fold my hands in my lap and all sorts of thoughts come rushing through my mind. You don't know Ashley House, do you? It's a big house with twenty rooms, many of them full of things my father brought back from Europe. And it's all mine!"

"Or at least will be, you mean."

"I am the head of that whole establishment," Emily went on without heeding. "I go about doing just as I please there. Fires burning all day long in the parlour—in both parlours, for I'll open up the little one again—and in the dining room and all the bedrooms. I spend my time reading—I'm happy—it all belongs to me!—furniture, pictures, everything. I must tell you about my most beautiful picture."

She gave a warm description of "Dawn." Miss Easting, watching her, said not a word. "So you can see how impossible it would be"—Emily's eyes were glowing—"for me ever to give up Ashley House. You must come and see me there some day!"

"But there are surely other things to worry you," the directress said with a suspicious glance. "You must consider the fact that you can't live alone."

"There's only my mother . . ."

"And may Heaven keep her with you for a long time still, Emily; but later on—after that—do you imagine you can live all alone in that huge house? Haven't you thought of having anyone to keep you company? Oh, don't hide anything from me, my child. Tell me everything so that I can help you."

Emily thought a moment, then shook her head. "It wouldn't bother me at all to live alone at Ashley House. I wouldn't be afraid."

Miss Easting sighed. "That's not the point, as I think you know very well. Will you do something for me? Will you? Well, promise me to think over everything I have said. Think about this, repeat it to yourself again and again: Marriage is the solution for a great many difficulties. Surely among your mother's friends there must be some young men you like. There's nothing to be ashamed of in that . . . But I see you cling to your secrets, Emily dear."

She arose and made up a parcel of six of the shirts.

"Will you take these again? The others were very nicely done. We were complimented on them."

As they came to the word of good-bye, she drew Emily to her and kissed her.

CHAPTER THIRTY-FOUR

* * * * * * * * * * * * * *

ASHLEY HOUSE HAD BECOME as sombre as though death, not content with its one victim, had established itself as a dweller there. Emily and her mother ate together in silence, each one buried in her own thoughts, and exchanging not even a glance. Early in the morning, before her mother was up, the girl sneaked down to the kitchen for coal which she later burned in Mrs. Elliot's bedroom. She made no noise and carried it off adroitly, hiding it under the bed and bringing it out when she went to install herself in the room with a book and Miss Easting's sewing. Unluckily, the coarse coal used for the cook stove burned badly in the open grate. The wood, however, was kept in the cellar, and the key never left Mrs. Fletcher's own chain.

"What can she be thinking about?" Emily sometimes wondered, when she saw her mother staring about her at the table. Her abstraction was keenly irritating to Emily. "I don't exist at all for her—except when she notices that I am costing her a few dollars." Her anger mounted and she sat taking stock of her mother and all her detestable traits. Fat face with its sallow lobes of flesh; vacant eyes; every little motion she made—her timorous and uncertain way of picking up fork or bread or glass of water; her hypocritical mildness; her craven and high-strung spirit that betrayed itself in every glance and gesture.

For some time past Mrs. Fletcher had seemed more preoccupied than usual. Her daughter came upon her mooning over old newspapers, tirelessly reading the advertisements. She often found her at her desk in the corner of the dining room, writing with the intense concentration of a child. Letters came for her and she tucked them away in her dress. Now and then she would look up and glance about her with an empty stare, her eyes alighting now on a table, now on a chair, for no apparent reason and as though she had never in her life beheld them before. She seemed like a being detached from the physical world and uninterruptedly in pursuit of some eternal vagary of the mind. Sometimes she would happen to glance at Emily without a sign that she noticed her; then all at once a sound of some sort, or a word of Emily's to the cook, would make her start and turn away her face with a look of embarrassment. Once she forgot the convention which forbade her to speak to Emily, and volunteered some remarks, which met with no reply except a scornful glance. She was so chagrined at her blunder that tears gleamed in her eyes and she bit her lip; but this inadvertence plainly proved that her resentment was not deep-seated and that she would have welcomed a truce.

In the afternoon, when Emily had gone up to her

room, Mrs. Fletcher sat down at her desk and began to write. It was a difficult procedure which required long preparation. After sighing several times and carefully reading some letters and papers which she had arrayed on the desk, she would bring herself to the point of writing a few words, but would scratch them out almost at once. She would put down her pen and sit with her head in her hands for several minutes; or again she would get up and pace the floor, muttering to herself, her fists buried in the pockets of the heavy coat which she wore habitually. She required an endless amount of time to compose the simplest letter. When she returned to the desk she would write and rewrite a few lines five or six times, accompanying them with groans and sighs of fatigue. Her face would take on an almost tortured look from its lines of strain and concentration. If her daughter or anyone else surprised her in this pursuit, she would precipitately gather up her papers, her scribbled tags of letters, and the letter she was working on, and carefully lock her desk.

In the morning after she had swept the porch, she took her station near the window with her eye on the road to catch first sight of the postman. The moment he appeared over the little ridge she went out to meet him, waving a sealed envelope which she took from her dress. Nothing could have persuaded her to entrust it to the box before he came—it could so easily have been stolen! One morning she returned to the house reading a letter that had just come for her. Her hands trembled slightly, and she paused after each step, with the letter so close to her face that her eyes seemed riveted to it. Coming up the steps to the porch, she discovered Emily watching her from behind the window curtains; she reluctantly folded the letter away in her pocket.

During the following days she seemed obsessed with a frenzy of impatience. She ate less and less at meal times and kept her eyes continually on the window, with a look of uneasiness that drove Emily frantic. There was no more letter writing, but she read over and over the last one to arrive and also the newspaper clippings that she had folded up with it in her pocket. She had lately acquired the habit of biting her nails, and this completed her fall to contempt in her daughter's eyes.

Emily continued to work at the shirts for Miss Easting. Any leisure that might remain she passed in reading the old-fashioned novels from her father's library—the same that she used to carry up to her grandmother, with the titles that had so offended the directress of the Community House. She had sampled the *Book of Martyrs*, but she found nothing in it which touched her sympathies, and preferred the translations of foreign romances, which agreeably piqued her curiosity. "I'm sure those people would have understood me," she thought, closing her book. "We have so much in common." And she reflected harshly on the lot which committed her to live with a woman devoid of all sensitive sympathy, of all the qualities of mind and heart which she discovered in herself. What most embittered her was the absence from her life of everything romantic—the fact that all her troubles were commonplace and uninteresting. What novelist would ever have made a story out of the unpleasant fumes that rose from her fireplace? There was something ignoble about it.

Constantly preoccupied with herself, the lonely girl had fits of depression which caused her cruel pain. They made her disgusted with all the schemes and projects that she had nursed through many months, and tearfully she told herself that hope was vain and that she must be resigned to live as she always had lived. Sometimes she read over the letter that the minister had written her, searching it for comfort in her present trouble; but his vague and embarrassed phrases showed clearly enough that he had not understood what she wanted to say. Still, how could she complain to an outsider about her mother's harsh treatment of her? He should have understood her half hints. Why had he talked about marriage? She recalled what Miss Easting, too, had said, and was surprised at so much insistence on the subject. What could they both be thinking of? Marriage she thought of as something for other people, not for herself: in her mind this notion acquired the weight of an indisputable truth and it never occurred to her to examine it. In pondering on the advice she had received, she only asked herself: "What good will it do me? Will it make me any

happier? Why should it?" And none of the answers which she could summon were convincing to
her.

In less than four days she had finished her work;
she was held in her room by the cold and had nothing
but books to keep her occupied. After a few hours
she tired of these and was at her wits' end for amusement. Her solitary life, without a soul to talk to,
without the slightest exercise, had made her increas-
ingly nervous, and she burst into tears at the mildest
provocation. She would pace up and down the room
from end to end, pausing before the pictures on the
walls or examining the collection of stones with indifferent attention. She often looked at her father's
portrait. He seemed to smile at her, sad and sardonic at once, and to speak to her in a voiceless
language which she interpreted according to the moment's mood. At other times she would hum to herself and trail her eyes about the room in a sort of
uneasiness; then suddenly she would drop limply into
an armchair, her eyes streaming tears, or fling herself
on her grandmother's bed with little cries and bursts
of hysterical laughter, and bury her head in the pillow—though she ordinarily never touched it except
with repugnance and a sense of gross uncleanness.

CHAPTER THIRTY-FIVE

* * * * * * * * * * * * * * * *

THE LONGED-FOR DAY OF HER visit to Wilmington brought the only distraction of her strange existence. But after counting the hours impatiently, she found when the afternoon arrived that she no longer had any desire to go. This is a fatality common to such delays. Though she had been a prisoner in the room for a week, she would gladly have stayed at home, and she set off in ill humour. When she opened the front door to leave the house, she found her mother on the veranda in her army coat, one hand on the banister, the other shading her eyes as she scanned the near horizon. At the sound of Emily's step she suddenly turned and seemed about to say something, but thought better of it. Her face was almost radiant with an unexplained satisfaction, and she walked off, rubbing her hands.

It seemed as though the girl's bad humour had infected Miss Easting. She welcomed Emily coldly, took the shirts and examined them without a word, merely approving them with a nod of the head. There was the same expression of annoyance on her pudgy face that Emily had encountered on her first visit; in the dim light she could recognize lines of irritation which met at the corners of the mouth and rayed out across her childishly plump and rosy cheeks. Emily made the mental note that the frown added ten years to her age.

"What's the matter?" Miss Easting asked, uneasy under Emily's searching eyes. The girl only shrugged her shoulders. She took the *Book of Martyrs* from under her shawl and laid it on the table. Miss Easting quickly took it up. "Books are not supposed to be kept out so long," she said. "Remember that others are waiting for them and need them." Her voice was so harsh and piercing that she was surprised at herself. "You must excuse me if I don't keep you to-day," she added, a little more mildly. "I'm not feeling well." Almost at once she handed Emily her new parcel of shirts and led her back to the door.

Though the days were the shortest of the year, it was still broad daylight when Emily returned to the house. She was somewhat weary and walked along at an easy gait, thinking agreeable thoughts of her comfortable chair by the fire. Now and then she stopped for a rest and set her parcel on the turf while she folded her arms beneath her shawl and looked about her. She could already make out the tall Ashley pines, their tops lightly tossing in the chill wind. She seemed to lapse into reverie for a moment, then shook her head, sighed a little, and took up her parcel to go on.

The moment she entered the house she met with a

shock. Her mother's voice, unheard for many days, echoed from the stairway, calling to the cook, and at the same moment she heard other footsteps moving about upstairs. This puzzled her so that she stood rooted, as if she dared not stir. "Is that you, Josephine?" Mrs. Fletcher called again, still leaning over the banister. The girl was about to reply when she heard another voice, a stranger's, coming from one of the bedrooms. "Never mind, Mrs. Fletcher. I can manage nicely by myself."

Emily leaned against a chair. Surprise and a vague premonition restrained her from going upstairs. In a very few seconds she had imagined every sort of explanation for the presence of a stranger in the house: a visit from a friend of her mother's; an accident to some one on the Ashley road. A name flashed up from her memory: Grace MacLellan, and she repeated it dully under her breath.

Suddenly she called out: "Mamma, what has happened?"

"Oh, it's you!" Mrs. Fletcher muttered, and Emily heard her move away and close a door behind her. She dropped her parcel and hurried up to the first landing. It was from her room that the sounds were coming. She opened the door precipitately and stopped dumfounded.

A wood fire replaced the blocks of coal that she had left burning in the grate—it was this that she noticed first. Next her eyes moved to a large black trunk that stood open in the middle of the room. Small articles from it were strewn about on the rug and the chairs: books, a cane, an umbrella with cord and tassels on its handle—a detail which fascinated her and held her eyes as if the clue to the whole mystery were hidden there. But the sound of talking reached her from the dressing room. Listening, she heard her mother's voice, low and deferential, mumbling confused replies to another voice, shrill and garrulous. There was a humming in Emily's ears and she suddenly ceased to understand; but a sentence that came more articulately than the rest assured her at a stroke of what she had feared to learn.

"Very well, Mrs. Fletcher," the strange voice said. "I'll get along with whatever you give me. But the room must be heated, and I agree to pay the extra amount required."

"What does this mean?" the girl called out without moving.

She was trembling so violently that she had to sit down. Mrs. Fletcher appeared framed in the doorway and raised her arm in anger. "Get out of this room!" she commanded in a whisper. Emily shook her head in refusal, but lacked the strength to reply.

"Miss Gay," Mrs. Fletcher went on in a friendly tone, turning again to the dressing room, "if you will come in I should like to present my daughter." And she moved aside to let Miss Gay pass by. She entered with a firm and energetic tread; her figure was diminutive, but strong, and she wore a wide cape of black satin which floated out about her and billowed like a veil. The flaps of her tulle bonnet were fastened down on her cheeks with a broad mauve ribbon, firmly knotted below the chin. She was a red-faced, loose-tongued individual; her mouth stood open ready to talk and her eyes seemed perpetually busy hunting for something. With a toss of her head that seemed like a nervous spasm she uncovered a fleshy neck bound round with thin gold chains. She saw Emily and moved toward her, only to draw back in embarrassment under the sullen and silent fixity of her glance. Mrs. Fletcher briskly stepped between them and said in a businesslike tone:

"This is my daughter Emily, Miss Gay. . . . Go and call the cook for me," she went on, turning to Emily; but as sometimes happened to her in moments of stress, her tongue became twisted and what she said was something like: "Go and call me—and call me, the cook." The girl smiled at her. "Go on!" Mrs. Fletcher shouted, suddenly furious; and she flushed violently.

"Oh, Mrs. Fletcher," Miss Gay put in, moving toward her with a sweep of her little cotton-gloved hands, "perhaps Miss Emily would like to stay and get acquainted with me. She could help me put away my clothes, if she liked."

Since Emily continued to stand there, she placed a hand on her arm.

"We are going to be good friends," Miss Gay continued. She had the voice of a mediator who wants

to restore peace by drawing attention away from the
object of the quarrel. "That picture on the wall is
very much like you, Emily." She motioned respectfully toward the photograph of Stephen Fletcher,
who surveyed this scene from his post on the wall with
bitter irony. Mrs. Fletcher moved off to the end of
the room, ostensibly to arrange the books and clothes
there, but really because she felt constrained by her
daughter's presence and Miss Gay's conversation.
"I suppose it's your father," Miss Gay suggested.

"Yes, it is," Emily answered, swallowing her
words.

"Oh, and . . . and what does he do? Will I see
him?" Miss Gay went on tentatively, as if she regretted the question almost before it was out. "Oh,
forgive me!" she exclaimed, when Emily made no answer; and she turned to Mrs. Fletcher to say hastily:
"You are very lucky to have a grown-up daughter
to help you, Mrs. Fletcher. She must be very energetic and industrious." Mrs. Fletcher glanced at
Emily from under her lashes, without replying.

Miss Gay began to sense that her words were in-
creasingly ill-chosen. "Well," she said, "I must put
my room in order. Girl, are you going to lend me
a hand?"

Emily suddenly stood erect and folded her arms
beneath her shawl, as if these words at last had
roused her from the daze into which she had fallen.

"No, Miss Gay," she answered peremptorily.

Miss Gay was flustered. Her smile disappeared and her blue eyes became suddenly hard.

"Oh, I see," she murmured. She turned to Mrs. Fletcher, who was making desperate gestures toward her daughter. "I think I can manage very well by myself. I thank you." Deliberately and with affected calm, she undid the pin that held her cape and laid the garment on the bed. Her hands trembled slightly and she looked straight before her, with her head held high. Her black satin shirtwaist modelled in glossy surfaces the vigorous contour of her shoulders and back; it was cut so close as to make breathing difficult, and her breath had the sound of an angered animal's. She sat down in the armchair and crossed her ankles, lifting the soles of her feet to the heat of the flame, and ignoring both the outraged face of Mrs. Fletcher and the impassive one of her daughter. There was a long silence. Mrs. Fletcher also sat down and seemed about to speak, but Emily took her stand before Miss Gay and demanded belligerently:

"Do I understand that you wish to rent this room, ma'am?"

Miss Gay clutched the arms of her chair and leaned toward Mrs. Fletcher. The mother's face was aghast.

"Is there some . . . er . . . misunderstanding, Mrs. Fletcher? Doesn't this house belong to you?"

"Certainly it does," Mrs. Fletcher replied in a low tone. The eyes that she lifted to her daughter

were transformed and discoloured with the flame of
hatred.

Emily watched her a moment. A violent drumming seemed to fill the air and drown out all sounds
about her. Never before had she felt within herself,
as she did now, this surging and frantic violence of
wrath. She struggled to restrain herself from physically attacking these two women as they sat there
mutely watching her. Her long black locks were
quivering over her forehead: she brushed them back
again and again with a convulsive gesture. There
was a knife in her heart. She leaned against a bedpost and seemed to be feeling her next step. Suddenly she turned away and walked rapidly toward
the door, which she opened and slammed behind her.
Miss Gay's sharp voice followed her through it, saying:

"Do you want me to help you break her, Mrs.
Fletcher? You have to be merciless with types like
that. Take my young brother, for example. At
thirteen . . ."

She listened for a few minutes longer, but the voice
was suddenly lowered for emphasis, and the girl could
no longer separate the words from the incoherent
murmur. She moved away from the door.

Following her usual course in perplexity, she went
to her bedroom and seated herself at the table. Only
there did she feel entirely free, only there did she
have no fear of her mother's hostile intrusion; for in
all the house the girl's room was the only one which

Mrs. Fletcher would not enter—a sort of instinctive reticence kept her out.

Emily's first impulse was to write to the minister, and she embarked upon a letter in which she struggled to explain her problems; but she shrank from complaining against her mother before an outside judge, and in any case she had not scribbled four lines before she recognized their futility. All that they tried to say was too obscure and involved for any use. Sedgwick would never understand them, and even if he did, what could he do about it? He would advise her to marry, she supposed—and in spite of her troubled mood she laughed at this notion. Tearing up the letter, she began to pace the room to warm herself. The wind was whining in the hall and rattling the draught in the fireplace. These falling afternoons in the big bare house were gloomy beyond all measure. She pressed her forehead to the windowpane and stared at the wintry sky; a melancholy red already showed on the horizon and the day was beginning to darken.

She coughed, and clasped her arms about her chest as if to check its retching; then, as it passed, she leaned against the wall, breathless and exhausted, with a tiny beading of sweat at the roots of her hair. Her legs grew weak beneath her and she sat down; drawing her shawl more closely about her shoulders, she lowered her head and surrendered herself to thought.

CHAPTER THIRTY-SIX

* * * * * * * * * * * * * * *

HALF AN HOUR LATER EMILY went downstairs. As she passed the room where her grandmother had died, she heard her mother and Miss Gay chattering merrily. A flickering light wavered below the door, and Emily judged that they were keeping up the fire and had not yet lighted the lamp.

The girl went on down, and out to the veranda. The sky had suddenly darkened and the wind blew fiercely; but the air was much less cold, and heavy raindrops buffeted the walls of the house. Emily walked a short way under the trees, then changed her mind and abruptly returned indoors.

In two or three minutes she reappeared in a small velvet hat, wearing gloves and carrying an umbrella which she opened as she went down the stairs again. She knew intimately every path in the grounds and very quickly reached the gate, in spite of the opaque darkness and the wind which forced her to bend her head. The swaying limbs of the pines made a curious whir and brushed her as she passed, and she could hear great branches creaking in the gusty wind. She was terrified and at the same time stimulated by all this tumultuous motion; it was a relief to come out in the open country where the noises lost their force.

She walked along rapidly, hunched under her umbrella and holding it with both hands. The soft dirt of the roadway was already turning to mud, with little puddles standing on its surface.

She clutched her shawl close about her and began to run. The road lay between high banks whose outlines were indistinguishable against the blackened sky, and she found her way along by following the large white stones that lay scattered over the ground. She was trembling and exhausted. Again and again she thought she could go no farther; but an imperious urge compelled her on and she came to the point of exhaustion where she no longer felt the weariness of her limbs. When a light finally appeared at a bend in the road, she was surprised to have arrived so quickly. She leaned against a tree to catch her breath, and tucked away under her hat the strands of hair clinging damply to her face. The wind had spent itself, but the rain fell with a precipitate patter that sounded like the footfalls of an invisible throng.

A few minutes later Emily knocked at the Stevenses' door. The old spaniel, asleep on the porch, awoke and sniffed at her boots, barking huskily. Some one came to the window and peered through the rain and darkness, trying to make out who the visitor might be. Presently the door was opened.

The glare of light made Emily turn away and close her eyes, but she entered quickly, followed by the dog, who settled himself at the end of the room near a feeble wood fire.

Up to this point Emily had been able to maintain a resolute composure, but once she had crossed the threshold her strength seemed to flow out of her in a flood. She sank down on a bench against the wall. There was an acrid odour in the air, the smell of smoke which she recalled so well and which reminded her at once of old Stevens with his fleshless and sinister face. He was there in the room now, she discovered; he came over and stood before her in his soiled and shabby clothes, craning his neck as if to see her better, with his corncob pipe pushed out in front of him. There was a chilling stare in his eyes that repelled her and she turned away.

"Let us alone," Frank said brusquely, coming up to his father and taking him by the shoulder. The old man moved off grumbling and went to his place in the chimney corner.

"Don't mind him, miss," Frank added in a softer tone. "He's an old man. Come and get warm by the fire."

Emily signified that she preferred to stay where she was. At length she said in a voice that betrayed the effort behind her words:

"We must be alone a minute. I have something to say to you."

He looked at her without appearing to understand. His hands hung awkwardly at his sides and his face wore a look of blank surprise, like a small boy being catechised. His open shirt exposed the tanned skin of his chest; he noticed this and quickly fastened his collar.

"Don't you hear?" The girl was recovering her assurance in the face of his greater timidity. "It's something important."

"Yes, miss."

He turned to his father, who was bending over the fire with his hands to the flame, and called out: "Pa, go on upstairs. I'll call you when supper's ready."

The old man looked up, but stayed where he was.

"Go along!" Frank ordered. He went over to him and shook him by the arm.

"Lemme alone," the old man grumbled. "Shame on you"—he put on a pathetic face and looked over to Emily—"to treat me this way before the young lady!"

"Be quiet!" Frank answered, forcing him up. "You've treated me badly enough in your time. You can't complain now." And he led him to a door at the end of the room, like a naughty child being sent to bed. There was something so grotesque and so gross in this procedure that Emily blushed in spite of herself.

When old Stevens was out of the way, Frank set a chair in front of the fire and offered it to Emily. She sat down without a word, and mechanically stroked the ears of the spaniel asleep at her feet. Her eyes roved restlessly over the objects assembled about the fireplace, almost as if she were counting them: hoes, spades, a brush broom and a trowel. After all, she had come and she must say something. Anyway, this was only a country fellow, not much more than a farmer boy.

She lifted her eyes to Frank, who was sitting on a bench, waiting for her to speak. From the same impulse that had led him to fasten his collar, he had now rolled down his sleeves and buttoned the cuffs, and he sat with his hands clasped, elbows on his knees. The firelight struck across his face in profile and gilded the tanned cheeks sharply etched by their three days' growth of beard. In a man so robust and vigorous, the sly and shifty glint of his blue eyes was disconcerting. Emily watched him suspiciously.

"I hope my being here does not displease your father too much," she said presently.

"Think of it!" the young man laughed. "He grumbled because I drove him away from the fire. But he forgets what he made me go through when I was younger. When he was in the house he never allowed me to come anywhere near the fire."

"Really?" said Emily.

"He would have kicked me out if I had put up a fuss. And it went on like that for years, until I realized I was as strong as he and decided to stand up against him."

Emily's cheeks warmed with colour. She was strangely moved at the young man's words and wondered if he could have had the same difficulties with his father that she was having with her mother.

"So you stood up against him?" she said.

"Yes. I was eighteen then—it was one winter night like this and I was sitting right there where you are when he came in. Seven years ago he was huskier than he is now and he had such a voice that everyone was afraid of him. Now he's a harmless old cripple. Anyway, when he saw me he tried to kick me to make me get up, but before he could touch me I was on my feet."

"What did you say to him?"

"First I rolled up my sleeves. Even then I had as husky an arm as I have now, and you see . . ." He modestly presented an enormous fist. "Do you know what he said? Not a single word. He just looked at me a minute, as if he would like to kill me, and then he turned his back on me. He knew I couldn't be treated like a small boy any longer."

He stopped and lowered his eyes, fearful of having said too much, and idly began to rub his hands together. The minutes passed.

"I also have something to say about myself," Emily said at last. Her voice was calm, but not without the stress of authority that it often bore. She seemed to consider for a moment, and then went on: "I didn't forget about that letter you sent me last month. If I could have helped you just then, I surely would have done so."

"Oh, Miss Fletcher, won't you help us now?"

"We are going to talk about that," the girl replied. She arose and took a few steps toward the window. Her face betrayed a lively agitation and her cheeks were crimson; she clasped her hands so vigorously that the joints creaked and crackled. There was a little mirror hanging on the wall, and she furtively glanced at herself in passing and said half aloud:

"Good Lord, but you're homely!"

It was true. With her prominent nose and thin, hard lips, the sudden flush that glowed in her cheeks had a mockery about it, like rouge on a wrinkled old woman. She jerked off her bonnet and tossed it on the bench where she had been sitting; then she returned briskly to the fire. The young man had likewise risen and stood contemplating her in silence, with the obvious fear of having given offence.

"You told me you were poor," she suddenly said, fixing him with her black eyes.

"You can see for yourself . . ." Frank swept his hand over the room where they were. Emily folded her arms beneath her shawl.

"And you need a lot of money?"

"I have a baby girl to raise, you see."

"A baby girl? Where is she?"

"She's out at nurse in Glencoe. It was on that account that I wrote you, when my wife . . ."

"I know," the girl interrupted. She returned to her place by the fire and played with the poker. "Well," she said after a moment, "if I should offer you some help . . ."

"Oh, Miss Fletcher!" Frank exclaimed.

"Awhile ago you spoke about working at Ashley

House, the way you did before," she went on evenly.
"Now I have come to propose not only that you
come and work there, but . . ."

She faltered and turned away.

" . . . not only that you come and work there,"
she said with an effort; "but that you come and live
there."

"Live there?"

"Don't you understand?" Emily suddenly lost patience. "Yes, come and live there for good." Her
face went scarlet, and she added: "Ashley House is
as good as Rockley, isn't it?"

"Of course it is," Frank exclaimed. "I'll do whatever you wish. All I ask is a job . . ."

The girl controlled her confusion as well as she
could.

"Now listen," she said. "You told me about the
troubles you have had, and I am going to tell you
about mine. But whatever we agree upon to-night,
I want your word of honour that you will never repeat anything I tell you."

"I give you my word."

"You may be sure I would not say anything about
this if I weren't compelled to," she continued with
a quiver in her voice. "I do it because I can't help
it." She paused to draw herself together. "Well,
perhaps you know that Ashley House will be mine
some day, the house and everything in it. I consider
that it is mine already, or at least that no one has
a right to do anything with it unless I agree—to

sell the furniture, for instance, or any other part of my legacy."

Her voice rose little by little; she pounded the arm of her chair with her gloved hand, exclaiming violently:

"It all belongs to me! What my father left when he died ought to come to me intact. If the silver and furniture are sold off piece by piece, and outsiders come to live there as if they owned the place, why, by the time I am twenty, or when my mother dies—whenever that will be—there won't be a thing left for me. And God knows what I'll do then!"

She realized that she had been carried away by her own words and that Frank no longer followed her. She proceeded to explain the situation that her mother's insane avarice had created, giving vent to her grievances in a great flood of bitter words that she had harboured for weeks. Never had she let herself go in such a tirade of rancour, and certainly never had she confided in anyone as she confided now in this stranger. An amazing ardour drove the blood to her cheeks and flashed from her gleaming eyes. For the first time perhaps in her life, this heart that had fed on bitterness and defeat was finding relief in uncontrolled abandon.

"You yourself have suffered from your father's tyranny," she said. "No doubt he treated you brutally; perhaps he beat you: but you have no idea what it is to live with a creature like my mother. You have seen her—she looks meek and mild enough;

there are even people who call her 'good Mrs.
Fletcher.' But I'd rather be beaten black and blue
every evening than live out my life in the same house
with her. I owe all the misery of my life to her alone.
I'm cold day in and day out; there's no heat in my
room, not enough covers for my bed. I cough all the
time, I'm sick, and it's her fault. I'm wretched and
homely—yes, homely—and it's all her fault. Whenever I see her and have to speak to her, there's something inside me that makes me want to attack her,
insult her, beat her; my hands begin to tremble and
I feel all fierce and feverish. You call it anger, but
that doesn't mean anything. If you are digging in
the garden and your spade gets bent on a stone, you
throw it away in anger; or if your horse balks it
makes you angry and you whip it. But tell me why
it is that the mere sight of my mother makes me want
to kill her, before she says a single word or even looks
at me. Once when she was away I saw her hat on a
chair, and I picked it up and pummelled it the way
you would treat a mortal enemy; I stamped up and
down on it! Of course it's ridiculous, but I'm telling
you everything. Remember that I hate her instinc-
tively—have hated her ever since I was tiny—and
add to that all the things she has done to make me
miserable. She secretly carries away everything my
father left us. I don't know how or when, but she
sells all the most precious things we own. The silverware, for instance—we haven't any left. I found
a list of the things she was planning to get rid of

—everything that's not an absolute bare necessity has to be sacrificed to what she calls economy. She even talks of selling the house itself . . . !"

"Selling Ashley House?" Frank exclaimed, wide-eyed.

"Yes," Emily answered. She grew silent and lowered her eyes. Presently she continued in a calmer tone: "I came here to ask your help."

"My help? How can I help you?" he asked. His face became uneasy as he spoke, as if he suddenly feared to embark on a venture that might turn out unluckily.

Emily sat erect in her chair and resolutely said:

"Let me explain to you. You live here all alone with your father—not very happily, do you? You don't know from day to day how you are going to get along, nor where the money is coming from. On the other hand, here am I with a big house that will some day be mine entirely, perhaps fairly soon—in fact immediately, if I stand up for my rights. Because if I wait until I come of age, my mother may very well have sold off everything we own, and where would I live then? Can you think of a way out? Since she's determined not to listen to reason—just try to reason with her!—I'm going to use force!"

Her hands quivered in her lap. She took her handkerchief from a pocket in her skirt and blew her nose.

"Do you understand what I want?" she asked in

a voice prophetic of tears. "I must have your help; I must get control of Ashley House. Yesterday she brought a woman to the house—a total stranger—and rented a room to her. It was the room where my father died, where my grandmother died just last month. And she did it in the name of her hateful economy! Do you suppose she is poor? She's rich! She's a miser like the ones you read about in stories. She has money in the bank at Wilmington—all the money my father left us, and he was a rich man. When he was alive we had servants in the house, and fires in all the rooms as soon as cold weather came, and plenty of good food to eat. I want it all to be that way again, the way it was in his day. It will be easy enough, I know how to manage it, but I must have some one to help me—some one strong who will make my mother afraid—a man. First of all, this Miss Gay has got to be thrown out. . . ."

She stamped her foot at the thought of her. Frank looked on uneasily, torn with his effort to understand what the girl was driving at, and particularly anxious not to displease her.

"You must come with me," she went on. "All we have to do is threaten my mother and she will turn over everything to me. You have no idea what a coward she is. She sometimes does a little shouting, but that's when she's most afraid."

"But I . . . I can't . . ." he stammered.

"You can't what?" she said cuttingly. "And why not, please?"

"But I haven't anything to say about Ashley House!"

"What!" Emily shouted. "Nothing to say about it if you are my husband?"

Frank stared at her as if she had lost her mind. "Your husband? You didn't say . . ."

"Of course I did!" she cried. "But you prefer to go on living here, I suppose, in your dirty Rockley—while Ashley House . . . Ashley House . . ."

She echoed the name in a changed and choking voice. Suddenly she wilted in the chair and a deathly pallor overcame her. She drew off her gloves and lifted her hands to her face.

"I beg your pardon," Frank said. "I didn't understand." He apologized elaborately.

For several minutes, dumb and bewildered, he sat there, not daring to give credence to what she had said. The rain beating on the panes filled the silence with a monotone of sound, and the damp wood sizzled quietly in the fireplace. Night was coming on. Frank arose from his bench to light a lamp and set it on the table. He moved languidly, like a man absorbed in thought and propelled by mechanical effort.

"All right, Miss Fletcher," he said at last. "We'll go up to Ashley House whenever you say. Rockley I can sell."

She glanced up to give her reply:

"Why sell it? I don't want your father at my house. There are enough old people at Ashley House already."

He laughed quietly and shrugged his shoulders. "Just as you like," he said.

CHAPTER THIRTY-SEVEN

* * * * * * * * * * * * * * * *

EMILY STAYED AT ROCKLEY overnight. She did not sleep, but sat without stirring in the armchair, powerless to move, plunged in a reverie that gave her face a bitter fixity.

Frank tried in vain to make her talk; his questions earned no other reply than a lifting of her eyebrows. With equal obstinacy she declined the dinner which he urged her to share with him. Her attitude surprised and troubled him; he wondered if she already repented of her proposal. In any case, he judged it the part of wisdom not to be insistent. He called his father, and they sat and ate the vegetable soup and corn pone that made up their supper.

The two men ate at a leisured pace and eyed the girl surreptitiously; she appeared not even to see them, although she was facing in their direction and they sat in her line of vision. She seemed to be sunk in a dream from which nothing could recall her; but once in a while she would let her head drop lax on the back of the chair and sigh with an almost inaudible little murmur. She opened her shawl; the fever she was in made her blood flow fast and warmed her through all her limbs, though the fire had left them chill. A dull pain gripped continually at her head. She closed her eyes and dozed off unawares.

When she awoke the room was empty. The dog lay asleep at her feet, stretched near the embers with his head on the stones of the hearth. A doleful, indefinite glimmer of light fell through the slats of the shutters, and with its help she rediscovered where she was. She shuddered a little at the thought of what she had done, and felt a repugnance already growing for the task she had taken in hand. A cold perspiration slowly oozed from her forehead, tickling her skin. She pinned up her shawl across her breast and tried to revive the fire from its lingering sparks, but she only succeeded in disturbing the dog, who yawned and noisily began to lick his paws.

It was no longer raining. Only the plaintive wail of the owls disturbed the silence. Emily grew frightened at their almost human voices; she quickly arose and fumbled about in the dark until she found the lamp, and lighted it hurriedly. Comforted by the light, she knelt by her chair and prayed.

CHAPTER THIRTY-EIGHT

* * * * * * * * * * * * * * *

MRS. FLETCHER, MEANWHILE, was not in the least concerned at her daughter's absence. She imagined her in her room, brooding the way she had so often found her, and she was glad to be rid of her so that she could dine in peace with her new boarder.

She liked Miss Gay; her talk and opinions of people and things had a wit and good humour about them that delighted her. After Emily left the room, the two women warmed to a conversation that quickly made them intimate, the girl's chilling manner having left them both in a mood to thaw in one another's sympathy. Maria Gay declared that the sad state of affairs at Ashley House had been clear to her from the beginning, and she offered Mrs. Fletcher the full weight of her support as though to a proven friend.

Her words found their way to Mrs. Fletcher's heart, and she wiped her eyes as she thanked her. They went downstairs to the dining room arm in arm, chatting with a rejuvenating freedom. Never had Mrs. Fletcher known the joys of so good an audience for her misfortunes. She recited her trials since her husband's death as though she had been the victim of a harsh and unrewarding sense of duty, constantly warring against a spendthrift daughter to whom she had devoted herself untiringly.

Miss Gay attended on every word and helped her to finish out her thoughts when she fell into her habit of stammering in the midst of a sentence. She too had her cross to bear—and she catalogued her griefs with the hurried eagerness of a little girl fearful of forgetting her lesson before she comes to the end.

"We shall get along beautifully," she said again and again; and Mrs. Fletcher, tearful with sudden emotion, sighed and silently clasped her new friend's hand. To all appearance they had known each other since childhood and were meeting again to-day after long separation.

"All my life," Miss Gay murmured, "I've suffered from having no one to confide in."

She explained that she had been brought up in a family without sympathy or understanding for her ideas of life, who seemed to delight in crossing her desires. The result was that she had decided desperately to leave her mother and her three sisters and live alone so that she could live in peace. For four years she had been wandering about from place to place, all over the state of Virginia, hunting for a hotel or boarding house in which she could feel at home. But everywhere she went she found the people so disagreeable that she had to move on again. Finally she had seen the advertisement in the *Wilmington Star*. Ashley House! She had said the name over and over to herself. A sort of second sight had assured her that she would be happy at this unknown Mrs. Fletcher's (and she squeezed the unknown's arm).

"Let me call you Kate. May I?" she exclaimed with friendly abruptness, and she beamed at Mrs. Fletcher through her rounded spectacles.

She bustled about continually, eager to see the house and learn its history. Everything at Ashley House, from the arrangement of the rooms to the choice of furnishings, had her approval. She stood with clasped hands under each of the pictures in turn, and she begged Mrs. Fletcher to recite the origin of all the little curios in the parlour.

"My husband brought that back from a trip abroad," was Mrs. Fletcher's invariable reply, and Miss Gay would clamour excited admiration.

"Ashley House is beautifully situated!" she declared, when they went out on the veranda. "Oh, I want to live here! I want to get to know this wonderful landscape as well as you do, Kate!"

"That's easy enough," Mrs. Fletcher remarked. "It's always the same."

"But it's so magnificent, Kate—so majestic!"

"Do you think so?" The enthusiasm was a little wearing.

It was cold in the dining room, even with the kitchen door left open, and they went upstairs to the bedroom again directly after dinner. Once more the talk turned to Emily.

"I see exactly the kind of daughter you have,"

Miss Gay said, crossing her ankles. She wriggled
her feet and turned the soles to the flame. "She's
wilful and impertinent, exactly like my brother when
he was thirteen. The only thing to tame these little
rebels is firmness, Kate. If she sulks and pouts, just
let her alone. Shut her up in her room for a day,
without any meals, and don't be afraid to smack
her."

In this vein she continued for some time, beaming
with satisfaction and red-faced from her inner di-
gestive efforts. She sat with her head resting against
the back of the chair and rolled her eyes from side
to side about the room. Mrs. Fletcher from her
place hung on her words respectfully and never
moved her eyes from Maria's face except when she
turned to the fire to throw ashes over the flame if
she thought it was burning too fast. "Yes, you're
quite right," she sighed, and tossed her head at each
new mention of Emily.

Before going to bed the two women kissed an affectionate good night.

The morning opened fair and clear, the sky a
deep hard blue that heralded freezing weather. Miss
Gay proposed a tour of the garden; she put on her
pearl-grey silk gloves and buttoned them carefully.

When she found that her new friend was preparing to go without even a shawl, she gave a little cry
of astonishment. "Go put something on immediately," she commanded. Mrs. Fletcher mildly protested; in the end she flung her army coat over her

shoulders, indulging in the affectation of not using the sleeves.

"It's a travelling coat," she explained when she found Miss Gay squinting at it. They crossed the broad lawn until they came to the rocks, and rested there for a moment to enjoy the view unfolded from that point.

"Oh, and oh, and oh!" Miss Gay repeated, in a crescendo of admiration. When her original enthusiasm had waned, she raised her umbrella and pointed toward the east.

"See how much I can recognize," she said. "That must be Manassas over there. What memories it brings back, Kate!" The blood flooded into her cheeks as she launched upon the hideous war that had torn the country twenty years before.

"We could have won! We could have won if the ammunition had held out! You know our generals were better than theirs."

"Yes, yes; of course." Mrs. Fletcher folded her arms and stared at a tuft of grass at her feet.

"Who did they have on the other side?" Miss Gay went on, leaning on her umbrella like a sabre. She cocked her head to one side, her eyes aflame. "Who was Grant? Only an old tippler, a boor that people avoided on the streets of his own home town; he owed money to everybody, and he never hesitated to borrow a few cents more to go to the bar and smoke and drink with a lot of worthless riff-raff. As for Sherman . . . !"

Her clamouring voice grew harsh; she clutched Kate's arm and shook her.

"Sherman! He was the devil incarnate! He started fires wherever he went; his line of march was marked in footprints of blood. Oh, I can't bear to hear his name! He tore the rings off our fingers with his own hands, and he ordered his men to pollute and destroy our food if they couldn't carry it with them. The fiends!"

She raised her umbrella and flaunted it against heaven. Mrs. Fletcher said nothing, but this vehemence stirred old memories and old grievances within her. She shook her head and sighed. Miss Gay was mopping her eyes.

Now they turned back to the house. Going up the stairs, Miss Gay used her handkerchief vigorously; then she turned to Mrs. Fletcher and clasped her in an affectionate embrace.

CHAPTER THIRTY-NINE

* * * * * * * * * * * * * * *

JUST THEN THEY HEARD THE sound of carriage wheels on the road that led from Ashley House to the Wilmington highway. A shadow of uneasiness drifted over Mrs. Fletcher's face, and she leaned on the stair rail, listening.

"What's that?" Miss Gay demanded.

"Why, I can't imagine!" Mrs. Fletcher murmured. "Nobody ever comes this way, ordinarily, and I haven't any friends in this neighbourhood . . . It can't be anyone except Stevens or the parson," she added half aloud, and went indoors without waiting.

"Come on in," Mrs. Fletcher called from the hall. "Don't stay there or you'll be seen."

"Why shouldn't I be seen?" Miss Gay leaned over the banister for a better view.

"I don't want anyone to know that I am at home," Mrs. Fletcher choked. "Come in, do."

"Oh, let me be!" Miss Gay threw back without turning.

The door closed with a slam. Mrs. Fletcher was furious. At almost the same moment a buggy appeared in the driveway and stopped at a modest distance away from the house. Miss Gay threw up her hands and rushed across the porch to the door. She opened it, calling at the top of her voice:

"Kate! Kate! Where are you? It's your daughter!"

Mrs. Fletcher emerged from the dining room. She was pale with a sudden dread and leaned against the wall for support. "My daughter?" she repeated in a scarcely audible voice. She made a motion to go on, but suddenly changed her mind and hurried back into the dining room.

Maria Gay followed her. "Don't you hear?" she called excitedly. "Emily, your daughter, is out there in front of the house. She is coming up to the porch with some one—a man!"

She darted over to Mrs. Fletcher and clutched her by the arm. "How romantic this is, Kate! Just think! Maybe she has eloped with her sweetheart and is bringing him back with her! You may be sure she has a sweetheart—at her age!"

She shook Mrs. Fletcher's arm, and suddenly deserting her, went racing to the door. Her cape billowed behind her in great gusts as she hurried out.

Mrs. Fletcher seemed stunned with bewilderment. She was standing fascinated at the door through which Miss Gay had just vanished when she heard the sound of voices on the porch which made her tremble. Gathering up her coat, which had slipped to her feet, she scurried into the kitchen.

"Miss Emily . . ." she stammered to the negress, "did . . . did she . . . Where did she eat supper last night?"

"Miss Emily?" the cook repeated with concern.

"That's what I said," Mrs. Fletcher snapped. "Look here," she added suddenly, "there's a call. Go see who it is."

Josephine began to untie her gingham apron, but Mrs. Fletcher pushed her hastily out.

"Don't wait. Go as you are—and say that I have gone out." She closed the door vigorously behind the cook and sat down, breathing heavily. Her heart was going at a terrific pace; she could hear its dull, accelerated thuds through the heavy folds of her army coat. Several minutes went by; then she heard footsteps in the dining room and her daughter's harsh voice talking to Josephine. Mrs. Fletcher was borne down under a heavy lethargy; she dropped her forehead to the rim of the kitchen sink and wearily closed her eyes. These words in her daughter's voice came through to her ear:

"Where is she? I know she has not gone out, Josephine."

In a moment Emily entered the kitchen. Her eyes were flashing.

"What are you doing there, Mamma?" she asked in the greatest surprise. "Come out of here."

Taking her by the arm, she conducted her into the dining room. There were three people in it, but to Mrs. Fletcher it seemed crowded. Miss Gay was sitting in one of the chairs by the table, looking very much as though she were in the audience at the theatre, waiting for the curtain to rise; she kept her hands folded in her lap and peered about her with the liveliest interest; and every now and then, with the hardihood that old maids grant themselves—as if their age excused them—she fastened her eyes on Frank with open curiosity and smiled at him discreetly. The young man, troubled by this attention, remained a little aside; he wore a brown suit with large leather buttons over a coarse linen shirt, and his hand held a long willow whip, which he had thought best to bring in with him—for fear, no doubt, that some one might go off with it. In spite of this intimidating weapon, his bearing had no assurance, and he hung his head with awkward timidity. He might have been a small boy whose greatest fear is that some one will notice him and speak to him.

Emily conducted her mother on through the dining room into the small parlour, and closed and locked the door behind her. Mrs. Fletcher was too much agitated to offer any resistance; she seemed to have suddenly lost the power of speech. She had recognized young Stevens, whom she held suspect, and had no desire for any conversation with him. On this account she was only too happy to let herself be led into the parlour. After taking the linen cover off a chair, she sat down.

"I have some news for you, Mamma," the girl began in her curt way.

"What, Emily?"

Mrs. Fletcher sat watching her without another word. For the last few minutes she had seemed to be wrapped in a fog through which nothing could penetrate to her mind. Presently she muttered:

"What do you mean?"

"I'm going to be married."

"You . . . married?"

Emily threw back a look of contempt.

"Is there anything so very strange about that?" Emily's eyes flashed. "I'll be sixteen years old in a few months. Girls often marry younger than that."

"But why? Why should you?" Mrs. Fletcher leaned toward her. Her forehead creased and she pounded her fists on the chair arms, purple with rage. Suddenly she burst out laughing—but she promptly recovered her seriousness.

"What is it you said?" she asked. Her eyes were haggard.

"Are you deaf?" Emily shouted. "I'm going to be married, that's what I said. Do you think I'm going to go on living the way you try to make me, perishing with cold and hunger, and watching all the things my father owned disappear one after the other—everything that my father left us—*us*, I say, —in his will? You know very well that this house is as much mine as it is yours."

"That's not so!" Mrs. Fletcher shouted, jumping up. "I won't stand this!"

Her voice was strangled in her throat and she cried these words over and over gutturally.

"Won't stand it?" Emily said. "Just wait and

see, Mamma. I'll have some one to defend me now. My husband is . . ."

She also laughed aloud, and waved her arms like a madman.

"How happy I'm going to be, Mamma! How happy I'm going to be!"

A sudden frenzy possessed her and she clutched her mother's hand and tugged at it as though she wanted her to join a dance. Mrs. Fletcher fiercely shook herself loose.

"You're hurting me!" she exclaimed in an outraged tone. "You're a fiend, a regular fiend! You're lying to me. You don't want to get married. Who is there would take you, anyway—homely as you are?"

"Homely? Well, somebody married you! Do you know who I'm going to marry? It's Stevens—young Stevens who used to work for you. He's in the other room. Do you want him to come in here? He'll tell you just what I have, if you don't believe me."

Mrs. Fletcher stood and leaned against the wall.

"What have you done?" she muttered. "You're out of your mind."

"No, I'm not out of my mind. But now you're frightened, I see. Stevens asked me to marry him, and I accepted him."

"Asked you to . . ." echoed Mrs. Fletcher. "When?"

"Yesterday."

"You're telling a lie. You were here all day yesterday."

"I spent the night at Rockley."

"Oh, that can't be true!" Mrs. Fletcher gripped her daughter by the wrist and shook her fiercely. "You little wretch, you fiend! You've lost your honour!"

"What are you talking about?" Emily exclaimed. "Why so? What do you mean? If you don't believe me, I'll have him come in . . ."

"No, don't!" Mrs. Fletcher planted herself before the door. Perspiration was trickling down her cheeks. "He told you . . ." she went on after a moment, and gasped for breath.

"Why, yes, Mamma. Can't you understand?"

"What did he tell you?" Suddenly transfigured by her fear, she rushed at her daughter and seized her by both arms.

"Tell me what he told you," she repeated imperatively.

"He told me he would marry me whenever I chose."

"When did he tell you that?"

"Last night, at his house."

Mrs. Fletcher dropped her daughter's arms and collapsed on her knees. "Oh, I can't bear it!" she groaned.

"Don't you think your sins deserve some punishment?" Emily asked.

CHAPTER FORTY

* * * * * * * * * * * * * * * *

THEY WERE MARRIED THE NEXT morning, in the same room where Emily, so shortly before, had had her scene with her mother. Mrs. Fletcher was absent. After sending Josephine for the Reverend Mr. Sedgwick, she confessed herself beaten and went disconsolately to bed, telling Maria Gay that she wished to be left alone in her room for the next few days. Nevertheless, responding to one of those sentimental impulses that are so difficult to account for, she called Emily to her bedside on the morning of the ceremony and said:

"Do you realize that you haven't even a veil to wear on your wretched head? I am going to give you mine. Get it out of the wardrobe. God grant that it brings you better luck than it brought your mother. . . . Kiss me," she added, when Emily had found it. But the girl shook her head.

"I don't love you," she said; and she left the room.

When she went down to the dining room, dressed in white, with the veil covering her hair, she found Prudence Easting there. The directress came to meet her with arms outstretched and tears in her eyes.

"I came with the minister," she said. "I happened

to be at the parsonage going over the monthly record when your cook arrived. My dear, you have done just as I advised you!" And she kissed her warmly.

Sedgwick in turn came forward to congratulate her.

"This was a very sudden resolution—but let us pray that Heaven will bless your decision."

For these remarks Emily offered no reply, and when Maria Gay likewise made a move to embrace her, she brusquely evaded her effusions.

"How lovely!" Maria Gay kept repeating. "And how lucky that I arrived just in time!" And she asked the minister if he had known of many other marriages arranged in such romantic circumstances.

Frank stood somewhat withdrawn from the little group, and he looked out of the window whenever they turned their eyes in his direction. Hardly a word had he spoken since coming to Ashley House. He had spent the night fully clothed on a couch in the parlour, going out at five to walk in the garden.

"He's all choked up with emotion," Prudence Easting whispered.

"Handsome fellow," added Miss Gay peremptorily, and the two old maids exchanged a smile.

"Don't you think so?" Miss Gay aimed her question at Emily, and when Emily shook her head in denial the two women said, "Naturally!" and burst out laughing.

"Have you known each other for a long time?"

Miss Gay continued her inquisition.   But Emily still said nothing.   In the silence that followed, Miss Gay sought Prudence Easting's eye; but the directress was busy with her glove and kept her face averted.

The ceremony was performed a few minutes later.

CHAPTER FORTY-ONE

* * * * * * * * * * * * * * * *

IT WAS ASTONISHING HOW FEW changes Emily's marriage wrought in the life at Ashley House. Frank in his shirt sleeves was hard at work all day long out of doors. He went over the garden and prowled around the house, drearily whistling "In the Gloaming." Emily watched him from the dining-room windows, walking up and down the paths which he once had tended and which now were invaded by grass; and sometimes she would see him stop and look about him eagerly, as if measuring the land with his eye, while he absently tapped his worn-down heel with a willow switch he carried.

He was scarcely ever to be seen indoors except at meal times, and then he ate quickly and in silence. He invariably left the dining room before Emily and Miss Gay had finished eating, and he never failed to offer his little excuse:

"The open air for me, you know."

He would follow it with a curt little laugh and disappear until supper time.

Emily spent her days by the fireplace in the dining room, where she had lighted a fire the very day of her wedding. Logs were burning there continually now, and it was Emily's chief delight to poke at them, arranging and rearranging, adding new kindling and faggots under the logs, doing everything possible to insure a constant flame. As she bent above it, her grave and sinister face inflamed by the heat, she inevitably suggested the sorceress of legend, forever preoccupied with the fate of her burning brands. Now and then she would pick up a book and read a few pages until the crack of a breaking stick of wood recalled her and she tossed aside her book to take up shovel and tongs.

Except for good morning and good night, words rarely passed between Emily and Miss Gay. Not that the spinster had no desire to talk; but all her questions fell without an answer. So she reconciled herself to sit silently knitting, on the opposite side of the hearth, going up to see Mrs. Fletcher when this state palled too heavily.

She would find Mrs. Fletcher buried in covers to her chin, for she refused to let a fire be lighted in her room. It was a question whether she was really sick. She never said so, but since she did not get up it was permissible to suppose so. Her complaint seemed to lie in the liver: her skin was yellow and her eyelids heavy, and there was something puffy and unhealthy about her whole appearance. Her morning began with a visit from Josephine, who came to exact the money required for the day. Mrs. Fletcher would count out a few coins from under her pillow and entrust them to the cook, instructing her endlessly on how to spend them.

Later on, and at intervals throughout the day, Miss Gay would come in to keep her company; but the old maid's chatter wore on her now as much as it had entertained her originally, and she was not too successful at hiding her impatience.

"Don't you feel cold in this room?" she would ask her visitor, despairing of getting rid of her. "Wouldn't you be more comfortable by the fire?"

"Why not let me make one here?" Maria Gay would exclaim. But Mrs. Fletcher closed her eyes and shook her head back and forth on the pillow.

Once or twice Maria Gay attempted to bring up the subject of Emily. She dropped it quickly, however, when she saw how offensive it was to Mrs. Fletcher. But she did not abandon it altogether.

The cold would finally drive her out and she would return downstairs. Emily, hearing her step approaching, made a point of turning away.

Maria Gays are common enough in America. Kind-hearted, but odious at the same time, they want nothing so much as to be of service, yet they get no farther than to irritate the people who come in contact with them. "I have a mission in life," Miss Gay would repeat to Mrs. Fletcher as she lay tossing and groaning in bed. "I know it very well. So even if my personal interests directed me to leave Ashley House, I would not go, because I know I can be helpful here. Do you think I don't understand the difficult situation you are in? I have taken it upon myself to win back your daughter for you. She

needn't talk to me unless she wants to—I am thinking about her and praying for her all the time while
I work. I can do her good just by being near her."

Her being near, in reality, had quite the opposite
effect. Emily had never felt any kindness toward
her, and now that there were hours each day when
she could not raise her eyes without encountering
that complacent smile, she hated her from the bot-
tom of her heart. One night she found a little tract
on her pillow—a religious article on the Second Commandment, placed there by the spinster's well-inten-
tioned hand. She tore the paper up and threw it
into the fire, only to find it miraculously restored in
her napkin at breakfast the next morning. These
importunities enraged her out of measure.

As Emily was alone with Frank in the dining room
one day, she suddenly interrupted a prolonged
silence:

"We must get rid of this Gay woman."

Frank was busy with his knife trimming down a
stick of wood; he broke off in his work to glance at
his wife, who sat staring into the fire.

"Must we? Why?" he asked quietly.

Emily did not answer.

"Don't you think she pays for her board and
keep?" he asked.

"I'm sick of her," Emily said, pounding the hearth
with her poker. "Anyway, this is not a boarding
house. It's my own home."

Frank returned to his task without a word.

The next morning early, Emily knocked at the door of Miss Gay's bedroom. The spinster had just finished dressing and was preparing to go down. She came to meet her with arms outstretched in welcome.

"What a surprise!" she said. "You're not so bearish to-day."

"I am sorry to have to give you some bad news," she said cuttingly, "but you will have to leave us."

"What's this?" Miss Gay demanded, backing away a few steps.

"We are going to need this room," Emily went on. "My husband is to have it."

"Good Lord, Emily!" the old maid exclaimed, "you don't realize what you are saying! Your mother rented this room to me and we made all the arrangements between us, she and I. Besides, it simply can't be done. Where do you expect me to go?"

"Write . . . do anything you like. My mother made the arrangement without consulting me; and this house belongs to me as much as to her. I don't want any boarders here."

"It's treacherous and unfair, that's all," Miss Gay retorted, throwing up her hands. "You can't turn me out like that. I won't be treated this way!"

"I guess my husband is stronger than you are," Emily replied imperturbably, and she left the room.

Maria Gay rushed to Mrs. Fletcher and commenced the recital of this scene with a vehemence that made her stammer.

"Have you no authority in your own house?" she demanded. Mrs. Fletcher did not stir; she contented herself with closing her eyes and frowning deeply.

"Will you let her turn me out like this?"

But the sound of her shrill and excited voice was a torment to Mrs. Fletcher, and the only response she could command were groans and heavy sighs. Her protests availing her nothing, she worked herself into a frenzy of religious zeal and fell to her knees in the middle of the room to pray aloud for the souls at Ashley House.

Letter writing occupied her for the rest of the day; her cheeks were feverish and her pen hand trembled. Soon after dinner she stood before Emily at the fireplace and said in a level tone:

"I am going to-morrow, Emily." She accompanied the words with a sorry smile, and added: "I have been praying for you."

"I never asked you to," Emily answered without looking up.

"I shall continue to do it every day."

"You're positively insulting." Emily faced her squarely. "I forbid you to pray for me."

The old maid offered no answer. Taking up her wool, she went on knitting until dinner time. Her face was placid now; there was no sound beyond her light breathing and the click of the long needles meeting in the wool.

When she had eaten her dinner she went up to take leave of Mrs. Fletcher. Emily did not see her again. Early the next morning she heard the carriage drive up to the porch, and for a final time the hated voice penetrated to her ears as Miss Gay said something to Frank. At length the trunks were loaded in and the carriage rolled away.

CHAPTER FORTY-TWO

* * * * * * * * * * * * * * *

THAT SAME AFTERNOON MRS. Fletcher was on her feet again. Her complexion had cleared; but she still lacked strength and walked with an old cane of her husband's, cautiously as a cripple. She stopped in the doorway on entering the dining room and looked at the fire, which threw its warm flare across the entire room.

"Five logs on at once!" she muttered. "Heaven preserve us!" Going to a chair, she sat down opposite her daughter. Emily stubbornly stared into the flames and ignored her presence. Several minutes went by.

"Emily . . ." Mrs. Fletcher began.

There was no answer. Mrs. Fletcher sighed noisily and complained in a weary voice:

"Emily, Emily, think what you have done."

Emily sat in silence, her cheek upon her fist. Just then Frank passed by the window, whistling.

"He's the one . . ." Mrs. Fletcher said half aloud.

Thenceforward her life became extremely trying. She feared her son-in-law as much as she hated him; and she never ventured to address a word to him. For a while she seemed like a woman bemused by fear and despair. She went about with a crest-

fallen air and ate almost nothing at all. The afternoons she spent in her chair in the corner of the
dining room, deep in thought, or walked up and
down the veranda falteringly, stumbling along as
though her legs would not support her. If she met
her son-in-law, she would suddenly stop and lower
her eyes to wait for him to pass before she continued
her walk.

Frank, however, became adapted to Ashley House
and seemed to like it, at least as far as one could
judge from his rare words. Sometimes when rainy
weather kept him indoors he would wander through
the downstairs rooms, questioning Emily about each
of the nicknacks and trinkets in the cases and on the
mantels—where they came from, what they meant.
Emily's brief replies were attended with the admoni-
tory phrase one would give to a child—"Don't
touch!"—and he would look at her with a smile that
was almost sarcastic and return the object to its
place.

In the beginning his bedroom was a little room set
apart from the rest of the house. It had served
Stephen Fletcher as a sort of den or smoking room;
its walls were stained with blotches of damp, and
almost all the furniture had been sold off by Mrs.
Fletcher, so that it was now quite cheerless and uncomfortable. They had put up a cot in it for him.
When Mrs. Elliot's room became vacant, on Maria
Gay's departure, he was transferred to that immediately. He had accepted his first room without com-

ment, and he installed himself in the new one just as mutely.

Every morning soon after five, Emily heard his heavy foot on the stairway echoing through the house. Her ear could follow him from room to room, moving about methodically as if on a round of inspection, until he went out of the house a quarter of an hour later and walked about in the garden whistling his "In the Gloaming."

For the last few days, she had noticed, he seemed even more reserved than usual; he rarely spoke a word to her or even looked at her. Something seemed completely to absorb him. From their behaviour no one would ever have guessed that they were man and wife. Not that he was ever discourteous. He carefully raised his hat to her or her mother whenever he encountered them in his walks about the house. In contrast to his physical robustness, there was something even a little grotesque in his manner, his unnatural humility. He suggested nothing so little as the master of Ashley House.

Nevertheless, the presence of this man was a deep vexation of spirit to Mrs. Fletcher. She seemed to age perceptibly from day to day. Since her illness she stood continually less erect; her shoulders drooped in an arch; her eyes sank into their sockets and were ringed with yellowish circles. And beyond the alteration of the flesh, her ailments seemed to colour her spirit also. Her character took on a new tinge and the dreamy side of her nature grew more pronounced. She would sit long hours in her army coat, her hands lying out in her lap, engrossed in endless reveries, and her face bore the haggard lines that are marked by long and bitter thought.

More often than not she would sit and read her Bible, at her usual post in the corner of the dining room. She would look up only with a far-away stare, impossible to describe, which took in the fire burning constantly on the hearth and Emily's masculine face persistently bending over it. Whenever Frank came in, Mrs. Fletcher would turn the other way and go out soon afterward with her Bible tucked under arm. It was as if she had a superstitious dread of letting him cross her with his glance. Driven from the dining room, she sought the kitchen, and sat there without speaking, but watching every motion that Josephine made. She never talked to anyone any more, and when she was obliged to say a word or two, her voice sounded harsh and guttural.

There were days, however, when a glimmer of pleasure flickered in her face. These were when Frank announced an errand in town—"business," as he said—that would keep him away until evening. She would drape herself in her greatcoat, a shawl about her head, and tramp up and down on the veranda, impatient for his departure, watching him through the window while he finished his cornmeal mush in front of the fire. Finally he would go off and she would return indoors, less troubled in spirit than usual.

Only a few words passed between herself and Emily, and those were concerned with small domestic matters, as when Emily demanded the keys for the wood cellar so that Josephine could go down for more firewood, or when she remarked that there had not been enough to eat for dinner and that Mrs. Fletcher must give the cook more money for marketing. Mrs. Fletcher always pretended not to hear, but she scarcely believed herself in the efficacy of that ruse, and a little insistence on her daughter's part was sufficient to make her accede—remove the key from her chain or dig into her pocket for money and count it out piece by piece.

No one could know what thoughts were at work in that closed mind. That her distress was very deep seemed hardly likely. She had been cut off at a stroke from the wellspring of her contentment; Ashley House had been lost to her since the day Frank Stevens set foot there. But the pain of the loss was nothing compared with what she would have endured if she had had to go through a slow process of relinquishment—if she had had to feel her authority slipping day by day, losing day by day some fraction of her powers, giving up her keys, her purse, her little rights of domestic management. Instead, she lost all in a single moment. It was a cruel blow, but simple and absolute, and perhaps she understood.

But still she guarded as her own this much that no one could despoil her of—her money in the bank.

The knowledge that here she was invincible probably gave her courage to bear up under some of her other afflictions. Who could force her to sign a check unless she chose? It was her only weapon against her daughter and this man she had married, but it was a weapon to be relied on.

A fortnight after her illness she had the opportunity to try its mettle. She and Emily were sitting alone when Emily suddenly asked:

"Why didn't you give the cook enough money for the marketing this morning? She had to charge it."

There was a glint of joy in Mrs. Fletcher's eye. So here was the long-awaited moment! She mildly shrugged her shoulders and said, with the shadow of a smile:

"I have no more money."

"Very well, then"—Emily tapped on the hearth with the poker—"there's nothing to stop you from signing a check."

But Mrs. Fletcher only lowered her eyes to her Bible and went on reading.

CHAPTER FORTY-THREE

* * * * * * * * * * * * * * * *

THUS THE LIFE AT ASHLEY House continued for some time. Christmas had come and gone unobserved except by Mrs. Fletcher, who celebrated it in the solitude of her chill room, singing an old English carol in her doleful and cracked contralto. There was a relic of the Puritan in her which was stirred to life by adversity, and she seemed to find solace in it instead of despair.

Emily, for her part, was living now almost as she had planned and dreamed since childhood, yet she grew more nervous and sullen from day to day. She repeatedly made an effort to open hostilities with Frank, but the young man had learned from his earlier marriage that everything is to be gained by avoiding a dispute and that the one who knows how to hold his peace is always stronger than the one who does not. The result was that Emily, like her mother before her, butted her head against an obstinate silence. Since she had gained her mastery of Ashley House, time had hung on her woefully. She watched through the window impatiently for the first signs of good weather, when she could go for her walks again in the open; but winter lingered and spring was still far away.

And now for the first time in her life she learned

338

the meaning of "financial embarrassment" and realized the ironic connotation of that ambiguous phrase. All of her purchases had to be made on credit, and the tradesmen lifted their eyebrows at this new change in the Ashley tradition. She wondered how long they would permit things to go on this way, and how she would ever pay them if Mrs. Fletcher persisted in refusing to sign checks.

These troubles were great enough, but they were not all. For the last few days she had begun to see what she had hitherto sternly refused to recognize. Thinking of Frank, she saw that she had grown to despise him. Why was it? She failed to understand how a human being could become so utterly odious without changing in the least from what he had always been. And assuredly Frank had not changed. He continued as placid as ever, as indifferent in his manners, as circumspect—or more so—in his words. Emily analysed her feelings toward him and discovered that a sort of challenge, a sense of defiance, lay at the root of her hatred—an obscure sentiment that she could not explain. It was something like what her mother had felt, no doubt—and she recalled Mrs. Fletcher's much-repeated comment: "I don't like the look in his eyes." Emily liked it now no better than her mother did, nor his sinister mask of a face, nor his habit of going off all day or prowling about the house like a malefactor.

About her money troubles she could not bring herself to speak to him. It seemed somehow undignified,

for she still regarded Frank as nothing more than
an outsider. Yet she would gladly have used him,
if she could, to intimidate her mother into signing
the needed check. She went to Mrs. Fletcher's room
one day and abruptly said:

"I want to talk to you about money. You will
have to do something about it."

Mrs. Fletcher stared at her in silence.

"I warn you," Emily threatened with upraised
hand, "I'm going to speak to my husband about it."
But Mrs. Fletcher only put her hands together pray-
erfully and lifted her eyes to heaven in silent disregard. Emily interpreted this to mean that she would
sooner die than yield. Her courage failed her, and
she hurried out of the room to hide the tears of frustration that quivered on her eyelids.

Two or three days later she received a letter from
Prudence Easting, conveying an offer of the post of
deaconess at Sedgwick's church in Glencoe. Miss
Hess had finally departed, as the sequel to a shocking
scandal. She had actually tried to make people believe that the Reverend . . . But Miss Easting
found it unspeakable.

"I had to wait until you were married before offering you the post," the directress wrote, "on account
of your being under age. You may be sure you will
have every reason to be congratulated if you accept.
You will be a deaconess and take up the collection,
which means that you will be accepted in the best
circles of Glencoe. They will ask you to be a patron-

ess at the monthly charity bazaars, and a member of the Daughters of the Confederacy. . . ."

She mentioned additional posts and honours and ended with all good wishes.

The letter touched Emily on the raw. Fine things to tell her in her present wretchedness! Convinced that Prudence Easting was mocking her, she sent her this for an answer:

"You need never write to me again, Miss Easting. I have already had enough punishment from following your bad advice, and I want no more than the Lord sees fit to inflict."

After writing this sentence she paused to hunt for a major grievance. Then she continued in her girlish scrawl:

"I have been married for two whole months and I haven't a single baby."

The children that might some day be hers were often in her mind, and she regarded it as strange and even humiliating that Heaven had not yet sent her any. Her desire for motherhood, however, had nothing more behind it than a sort of vanity. She had no love for children; she never thought of asking after Frank's little girl, even when he spoke of her. But a day came when some words of his struck terror to her heart and at the same time profoundly surprised her. He had been talking of how expensive it was to keep the child out at nurse, and saying that only the rich can afford to have children—a common-

place which he had lately been fond of repeating—
and he unexpectedly added:

". . . as if it wasn't enough that Laura cost her
mother her life."

Emily trembled and looked up in astonishment.
Her eyes met his, but she found herself speechless,
and the questions that urged her tongue were buried
down, along with the terrifying thoughts that his
words had summoned. Thenceforward the little girl
was constantly in her mind; she dreamed of her at
night, and when she was alone in the daytime her
image pursued her. Emily's imagination conjured
her up in every possible form, from the horrible to
the absurd. She saw her as a sort of monster whom
nature had chosen to endow with the most repulsive
deformities: claws for hands, glassy green eyes like
a little ogress, stooped and spying about with a
ghastly leer. These imaginings held Emily's mind
unhealthily in prey; she sat by the fire for hours
gruesomely contemplating them, and at night they
haunted her even more imperiously. Little by little
she grew used to them and presently put them aside,
but each time that her husband spoke of his daughter
they returned to torment her—and he spoke of her
often now, even though he talked so little of other
things.

One afternoon in January he harnessed his buggy
and drove off toward Glencoe. Two hours later
Emily heard the buggy return, and when it stopped

she heard the crying of a baby and her husband's step on the porch stair.

She hurriedly rose from her chair by the fire and hastened out to the kitchen. All colour had left her face and she muttered breathlessly to herself: "It's she—it's his little girl!" And it cost her a struggle of will to return to the dining room.

It was, in fact, Laura; not the Laura that Emily had imagined, but a sickly underfed infant, blue-eyed and continually crying. Emily stood in mingled surprise and terror and failed to understand what Frank was saying as he held out the child for her to see. Even when she discovered that it was not so different from any other baby of its age, her revulsion was still so violent that she could not bring herself to touch its little clenched hands and tear-dampened cheeks.

She presently learned that Frank had decided to have his Laura brought up at Ashley House. This verdict overwhelmed her. When she recovered herself sufficiently to talk, she demanded an explanation. Frank looked at her unflinchingly and said shortly:

"Better to keep her here than pay for a nurse."

"But I'm not her mother." Emily's voice whitened with wrath. Frank ignored her.

"What's more, I won't have hide nor hair of her in my house!" His silence exasperated her until she shouted: "You must take her back to Glencoe."

"Will you pay for her nursing?"

"Why should I?"

"Somebody certainly has to do it," he answered. "You have the money, and I haven't a cent. In the meantime she can stay here."

"Here at Ashley House? In my home? You idiot—do you think I married you so you could come and enjoy yourself in this house, and bring your little girl here? This isn't your place, remember. I can turn you out if I want to." She commenced a shrill-voiced tirade, which ended in a naïve threat to complain to Sedgwick.

"I'll have you thrown out of here," she repeated with obstinate fury. "We'll soon see who is master here!"

The young man gave no sign even of listening; he sat by the fire with the poker in his hand, tapping the hearth with little tentative strokes. Emily took up her stand before him.

"What will you say if I call the authorities in?" she asked. "Don't you know that there's a law to make you respect other people's property?"

At last he raised his eyes from the poker.

"The joke's on you, Emily. I'm your husband now, and that gives me certain rights in this house— the law says that I have them."

Emily blanched.

"That's a lie! We agreed between us . . ."

"We agreed to nothing in writing," Frank reminded her. "And now go and read what your prayer book says about marriage. It will tell you that you must obey me. No matter what the law says, those words would be enough to give me the best of it."

Emily's heart was stifled at these words. Existence seemed to recede from her and she found herself powerless to answer. The full enormity of her mistake suddenly rose to her mind. They had made no written agreements and she had been taken in. Could she ever have suspected that Frank would act as he did? He had such a meek and timid look! Yet her mother had put her on guard against him with her continual remarks about his treacherous eyes. . . . Emily's ears began to drum and whir, and with the sudden sensation that a black fog was oozing from the floor and walls to encompass her, she collapsed unconscious.

Several days went by, and Emily wrote to Sedgwick. She asked him if Frank had not lied to her, if she truly had only a limited claim to the house now—if she truly had been such an utter fool as to give her beloved Ashley House away to an outsider whom she despised. His answer drew a cry of anguish from her throat. For the remainder of her days she was sentenced to live under this man's authority; her only possible escape lay through a divorce which might deprive her of Ashley House entirely.

A black despair invaded her whole spirit. She spent an entire day wandering from room to room, effortless and dispirited, laying her hands on the furniture that she knew so well and that now seemed suddenly altered. It was not the same house any more. She wondered if she was losing her mind. She sat in the parlour, hollow-eyed, staring about her and scarcely seeing the things that her glance alighted on; and she talked aloud to herself in the monotone of an old woman who is frightened at being alone and seeks comfort in long soliloquies.

CHAPTER FORTY-FOUR

* * * * * * * * * * * * * * *

IN ACTUAL FACT THE LITTLE girl brought very few changes to the way of life at Ashley House. She fell to Josephine's charge, and when Josephine was out a niece of hers came in and tended the child in return for a meal or two. The baby spent the day in a room on the second floor, and nobody ever saw it; but Emily would sometimes hear it crying and listen with a sort of savage attention.

Frank and Mrs. Fletcher continued to pass their time just as before, and life dragged along in a monotony emphasized by wintry weather. Mrs. Fletcher looked at the infant just once and promptly appeared to forget that it existed. Her chief preoccupation was her Bible, and when she was not in its pages she walked about in the downstairs rooms at a slow and unsteady pace, or sat in her armchair in the dining room, absorbed in long meditations. Even Frank never went to see the child. From morning till night he spent the time out of doors, sometimes walking in the garden, sometimes driving off in his buggy to one of the neighbouring towns. Punctually at meal time he would return and take his place at the table, where his formal greeting to Mrs. Fletcher went unanswered and Emily also turned away from him. He ate slowly, keeping his eyes on his food, and drank only water; and he never rose to leave the table without a mumbled word or two which could be taken for an excuse.

Except for the fact that the women were homely of face and he much less so, he might have been taken for the son and brother. His manner was always gentle and deferential, and no one who saw the three of them at the table would have guessed that he was the cause of the sorrow and despair that seamed their faces. He was healthy and rosy-cheeked, un-talkative but contented, and he met all his tasks with the quiet ease of a man untroubled with a single care. The moment he was alone he would begin to whistle. Toward evening his cheerfulness tended to relax. Sometimes he went directly to bed after dinner; sometimes he walked in the garden alone and silent, and came in shortly afterward to bed. Then he would carefully bolt the door and leave the women sitting by the fireside.

Frank returned from Glencoe one evening with a letter which he handed to his wife. She opened it and glanced through it with a frown, then folded it away in her dress. As soon as the two women were alone, she passed it on to her mother.

"Read it," she said. "It's your business."

But Mrs. Fletcher returned it almost at once. "Not my business any more," she answered.

It was a tradesman's bill with a demand for remit-tance. Emily shrugged her shoulders and put it on the mantelpiece, and nothing more was said of it for a week.

Finally Frank, as he sat down to breakfast one morning, pulled the bill from his trousers pocket and asked Emily if she had paid any attention to it. She nodded.

"It's time it was paid," said Frank. "They won't give us any more credit."

Mother and daughter, for the first time in years, exchanged a glance that contained something other than scorn. But neither spoke.

That evening Frank approached his wife again on the subject.

"This money question can't go on. The tradesmen at Glencoe won't give us any more credit. It strikes me I've already told you that."

"What do you expect me to do?" Emily asked drearily, and the face she raised to his was weary and bitter. "Are you asking for money from me? I have none, you know very well."

"Your mother has," he said, and turned to Mrs. Fletcher.

"But not for you." Mrs. Fletcher did not break off in her reading.

"All right. You want to die of starvation, I suppose."

"I won't die of starvation." Her tone was gentle. "I have enough to keep me alive."

For a moment Frank paced up and down the room; then he halted in front of the fire again.

"Listen to what I have to say," he said. Mrs. Fletcher sat watching him with her hands clasped over her Bible. "Listen carefully. We can't go on living without any money. And I haven't any. You'll have to help us."

Mrs. Fletcher shut her eyes and pivoted her head in firm refusal.

"Very well," Frank went on evenly. "You can take your choice. Either you sign a check or get out of this house."

Emily sprang to her feet. "You're out of your mind!" she exclaimed. "You haven't the right . . ."

"It doesn't matter," Mrs. Fletcher interrupted. "I have made up my mind already. I am going to leave the house—I prefer to. You can take me to Glencoe to-morrow," she added, turning to Frank.

She seemed to consider for a moment; then she closed her Bible with a sigh and went out of the dining room, without a glance at her daughter or her son-in-law.

CHAPTER FORTY-FIVE

* * * * * * * * * * * * * * * *

EARLY THE FOLLOWING MORN-
ing she departed, before Emily had gone downstairs. The girl heard her mother call good-bye to
her from the stairway, but she gave her no answer.
It was not yet daylight.

All through the morning Emily was restless and
agitated. She went from one room to another and
sometimes stood awhile at the fireside; but nothing
could keep her still and she soon resumed her aim-
less excursions through the downstairs rooms. The
slightest sound made her nervously peer about, and
her glances and motions had a tension in them that
suggested an animal frightened and on the alert.
She tried to read; she toyed with the fire in her
habitual way, but nowhere could she fix her mind
even on the simplest occupations, and she threw aside
the book or the tongs with impatient annoyance.
Her forehead became lined with wrinkles, and seams
appeared in her sallow cheeks with their prominent
masses of bone. She would sigh deeply, and fold her
arms, and return to her slow march up and down
the room.

At about eleven she heard the sound of wheels in
the drive and knew that Frank was returning from
Glencoe. She ran to the window to see; then,

prompted by a sudden hysterical impulse, she dashed to the front door while he mounted the steps and flung herself against it. She pushed with all her vigour, her shoulder to the door and her hands gripping the moulding, and Frank's hand vainly struggled with the knob. He called out; then, after a moment or two, he gave a violent push with his shoulder and the door yielded.

"Why did you want to keep me out?" he asked.

She drew away from him, her hair dishevelled and her eyes flashing. He followed her into the dining room.

"Things are getting worse and worse," he said as he sat down. "This is not exactly the life you promised me."

Emily stood erect before the fire and watched him, her arms beneath her shawl.

"Do you think I intend to let myself die of starvation?" he went on. "And my little girl, too? You seem to have forgotten her."

He laughed briefly, and a certain cruelty crept into his face.

"I want her to grow up big and strong," he said, "and I want her to be happy and good-looking." He laughed again, and added: "And I want her to marry."

Emily looked away. He arose and poured himself a glass of water.

"I'm thirsty," he said. "I actually feel warm.

Look at the sun: it's fine out to-day." He drank a long swallow and went to the kitchen door.

"Josephine!" he called.

No one answered; he turned to his wife interrogatively.

"Where is she?"

Emily seemed to ignore him. He thumped his foot on the floor and his tone suddenly changed.

"Where is she?"

He flushed with anger. Just then Josephine appeared.

"I was up with the little girl, sah," she explained abjectly.

"I want to see her," Frank said. "It's too cold in that room where you keep her. From now on she is to stay in here. You can put down a blanket for her in front of the fire. Go and get her now."

With his eyes still fixed on his wife, he sat down and unbuttoned his vest. Emily stood a few steps away, silent and unmoving. She had grown pale and trembled slightly.

Presently Josephine returned, carrying the little girl, and put her into Frank's arms.

"It's a long time now since I saw you," he murmured affectionately, tickling the baby under the chin. He began to talk to her gently, holding her tiny face up close to his own.

"Do you like this pretty fire? It's baby's fire."

He hugged her close and went on:

"Do you like your daddy's fine house?"

"You imbecile!" Emily shouted. Her voice was raucous with anger. "You imbecile!" She repeated it with a sort of gathering fury.

He looked up at her without a word; then he went on talking to the baby. The anger had now all vanished from his face.

"All this belongs to us," he said to Laura. "You and I are going to live here together all our lives, here in this house with all these fine things." And he cast a proprietary glance about the room, as if to point out to her each separate object. "Unless"— he glanced significantly at Emily—"unless we sell them to buy food."

Emily started toward him; he sat and watched her in silence. She passed her hand across her face to brush back the stray hairs, and stood with her eyes askance, in the attitude of one who hears a far-off sound. A strange expression of agony and malice wrote itself in her features; with her arms inert at her sides, she waited a moment unmoving.

Suddenly she looked down and her eye fell on the child in her husband's lap. Her expression changed. Before he could move to prevent her, she had plunged at the baby and clutched it by the throat. Almost instantly he threw her to the floor and she relaxed her grasp, howling with pain under the frantic blows he rained upon her, while Josephine fondled the choking child in her arms and tried to revive it with water.

Emily, terrified at her husband's ferocity, fled

from the room and ran headlong up the stairs, with Frank shouting at her heels. She barely gained her room and double barred the door; then she collapsed on the floor. Confusedly the sound of Frank's footsteps came to her. He was quivering with fury. When he reached the door he hammered on the panels with his fists and strove to break in; but the door held fast.

"Look out! I warn you!" he shouted shrilly. "I'll turn you over to the law. You wanted to kill your mother. You have killed my baby. They'll hang you at Glencoe; they'll hang you; they'll hang you, I tell you!"

After a while he went downstairs again.

CHAPTER FORTY-SIX

* * * * * * * * * * * * * * * * * *

THE CHILD RECOVERED. ALL afternoon the negro woman held it in her lap and nursed it with the instinctive devotion of her kind. Frank watched her from his post before the fire, stern and mistrustful, standing like a sentinel.

In the evening, after Josephine had tucked the baby in bed, she went up secretly to her young mistress's room and tried to make her open the door. But her questions whispered through the keyhole failed even to get a response. This silence frightened her. She thought of informing Frank, but hesitated, and finally decided to wait until morning and then go to Glencoe to tell Mrs. Fletcher what had been happening at Ashley House.

Frank remained by the fire until late that evening. A little after eleven he opened the dining-room door to go up to bed. As he stepped into the hall a dull crackling sound met his ear, and at the same time stifling fumes made him draw suddenly back. He ran to the door leading on to the porch and hurried out into the garden.

A cry of horror burst from his throat. Ashley House was burning. From Emily's room black clouds of smoke rolled over the front of the building, shot through with gigantic tongues of flame that flickered up to the roof. He called out with all his lungs, dazed, crazed, running over the garden like a madman. He leaped suddenly up on the porch and started back into the hall; but he was forced to stop at the threshold. A tremendous volume of smoke moved heavily down, lighted with flames that growled insistently.

He put his hands to his mouth and shouted again; but he felt that his voice could not pierce the tawny blanket of smoke descending upon him. At the same time he heard a terrific crash, followed by another more prolonged, and the whole lower flight of the stairway collapsed with a deafening roar. A chasm appeared in the ceiling; long flames lapped through it in a kind of fiendish rivalry.

Then he rushed out to the garden again, howling incessantly like an animal driven to slaughter. His cries were answered from within, and he thought he saw a window opened, but a dense curtain of smoke shrouded the front of the house. It looked now like nothing more than a child's silhouette house, cut out of cardboard and lighted from behind. All the windows on the second floor stood out stark in flaming red. At length the roof began to crumble under the advancing flames, which shot up through this new outlet and climbed the branches of the near-by pines. A few minutes later the front wall wavered; but enough of the roof remained to hold it together and it continued to stand, a sheet of flame behind the trees that crowned Ashley hill.

The house burned on until daylight.

THE END

Distinguished Fiction

GIANTS IN THE EARTH   *By* O. E. ROLVAAG

A magnificent and powerful novel of the great Northwest that
deals with man's terrible struggle to conquer the wilderness.
Giants in the Earth bids fair to be one of the few books on
American pioneer life which will endure.

PRESSURE   *By* MARGARET BANNING

The driving force of business and the struggle for success experienced by a young married couple are the theme of this
appealing novel. Against the background of a thriving city
in the Middle-West, the story moves with a vigorous swing.
Mrs. Banning reveals her sympathy and understanding as a
novelist in the very human and moving portrayal of her
characters.

FROM MAN TO MAN   *By* OLIVE SCHREINER

"It conveys a sense of greatness undeniable and unforgettable.
I mean literally unforgettable."—*Gerald Gould in the Daily
News.* "Close akin to Shakespeare."—*The Nation, London.*
"Nothing short of greatness."—*New Statesman.*

ROMAN SUMMER   *By* LUDWIG LEWISOHN

An engrossing story of a Middle-Western boy who desires to
break with the Middle-West, and goes to Rome. Then comes
the great adventure of his life—his love for Esther Azancot.

HARPER & BROTHERS

Publishers Since 1817   NEW YORK

Five Great Mystery Stories

THE ASTOUNDING CRIME ON TORRINGTON ROAD
By WILLIAM GILLETTE

The murder of Michael Haworth, just after he has sold the rights in an invention to a shady company is a mystery that will puzzle the most seasoned reader of detective thrillers.

THE STARVEL HOLLOW TRAGEDY
By FREEMAN WILLS CROFTS

The real mystery-story addict, who is willing to do some work on the case, always hails the appearance of a Crofts' novel with enthusiasm and the assurance there will be an honest unravelling of an unusual and baffling crime.

THE SECRET OF FATHER BROWN
By G. K. CHESTERTON

A new series of adventures and mysteries solved by the skill and quick wits of Father Brown makes as puzzling and thrilling a book as the mystery-story could wish for.

THE KINK
By LYNN BROCK

Readers of detective stories who demand plausibility as well as action in their search for thrills need no introduction to Colonel Gore. Post-war England of the smart, fast set is the background against which the scene is laid.

BEHIND THE FOG
By H. H. BASHFORD

When two young Englishmen hear in the distance through the dense sea fog the S.O.S. sounded on a motor horn, to the dramatic and unexpected climax, the book is constantly exciting.

HARPER & BROTHERS
Publishers

T-c66